D0309925

Cath St
and crea
shortlisted for the CWA Best First Novel award. She was joint winner of the CWA Short Story Dagger in 2012. *Letters To My Daughter's Killer* was selected for the Specsavers Crime Thriller Book Club on ITV3 in 2014. Cath also writes the Scott & Bailey books based on the popular ITV series. She lives with her family in Manchester.

Also by Cath Staincliffe

The Sal Kilkenny Mysteries
Looking for Trouble
Go Not Gently
Dead Wrong
Stone Cold Red Hot
Towers of Silence

The Kindest Thing
Witness
Split Second
Blink of an Eye
Letters to My Daughter's Killer
Half the World Away
The Silence Between Breaths
The Girl in the Green Dress
Fear of Falling
Quiet Acts of Violence

CATH STAINCLIFFE

RUNNING OUT OF ROAD

CONSTABLE

CONSTABLE

First published in hardback in Great Britain in 2021 by Constable
This paperback edition published in 2022 by Constable

Copyright © Cath Staincliffe, 2021

1 3 5 7 9 10 8 6 4 2

The moral right of the author has been asserted.

All characters and events in this publication, other than those clearly in the public domain, are fictitious and any resemblance to real persons, living or dead, is purely coincidental.

All rights reserved.
No part of this publication may be reproduced, stored in a retrieval system, or transmitted, in any form, or by any means, without the prior permission in writing of the publisher, nor be otherwise circulated in any form of binding or cover other than that in which it is published and without a similar condition including this condition being imposed on the subsequent purchaser.

A CIP catalogue record for this book is available from the British Library.

ISBN: 978-1-47213-215-4

Typeset in Times New Roman by Initial Typesetting Services, Edinburgh
Printed and bound in Great Britain by Clays Ltd, Elcograf S.p.A.

Papers used by Constable are from well-managed forests and other responsible sources.

Constable
An imprint of
Little, Brown Book Group
Carmelite House
50 Victoria Embankment
London EC4Y 0DZ

An Hachette UK Company
www.hachette.co.uk

www.littlebrown.co.uk

In loving memory of my mum and dad, Margaret and David,
who instilled in me a love of walking the hills.

Apology

I have taken outrageous liberties with the geography of the Peak District, inventing places for the sake of my story, but I have tried my best to capture the beauty of the landscape which brings me such pleasure and solace.

Chapter 1

Scarlett was fizzing with excitement. Lemonade bubbles popping in her belly, tickling her skin. But mixed with that was a shadow, a cold fear that something terrible would happen. She'd forget her steps, or not be able to hold the handstand long enough. She'd drop Faye when Faye was relying on her for the shoulder lift. Or Scarlett's costume would rip and the whole school and their mums and dads and carers and all the teachers would see and point fingers and laugh. Her cheeks grew hot at the thought.

They got to the school crossing and Faye linked her arm. 'It will be *so* good,' Faye said. 'My auntie's coming with my mum. And my granny.'

Scarlett had one person coming to the talent show: Nana, whom she lived with.

'Come on.' Scarlett tugged Faye and they ran to overtake the group of littlies with their bags and buggies and mums walking, like, slower than a snail. A really tired snail.

'I can't believe they're making us do lessons tomorrow,' Scarlett said. 'We should get the morning off, yeah? Like to prepare.'

Faye put on a funny voice, like a bossy grown-up. 'They don't get time off on *Strictly*,' she said. 'They work really, really hard, for hours and hours, then go and do the day job if they have one.'

A gust of wind rattled the trees along the edge of the pavement, blowing dust into Scarlett's eyes. She stopped to blink it away.

‘I think Adam Doyle might win,’ Scarlett said, linking with Faye again. Adam was singing ‘Stand By Me’. No backing track or anything, performing all on his own with his eyes closed, and it was amazing.

In the dress rehearsal that afternoon Mrs Sullivan had practically been in tears when he’d finished. She’d wiped her eyes and said, ‘That’s just lovely, Adam.’

‘He should do *The Voice*,’ Faye said.

Spits of rain tapped Scarlett’s face and she pulled her hood up.

‘There’s a weather warning,’ Faye said. ‘Storm Dennis.’ Her dad worked for Green Flag, rescuing people whose cars had broken down. When the weather was bad he was really busy.

‘There’s always a weather warning,’ Scarlett said. ‘It’s the climate.’

Another thing that gave her a flip-flop feeling inside. Because the whole world was burning and drowning and still hardly anyone was doing anything. Or not the people in charge of stuff.

‘Will you braid your hair?’ Faye said.

‘No time now,’ Scarlett said. ‘It’ll be all right in a bun.’

‘An up-do,’ Faye said.

‘A puff.’

It took like a million hours and it really hurt to have her braids done. And Nana had to pay for it as well, so mostly Scarlett had an Afro style and it was just long enough to scrape back with a bobble.

‘I’ll have a French plait.’ Faye had really long blonde hair. She could do loads of different styles with it.

There was a clattering noise and Scarlett saw Jason on his skateboard coming along the pavement behind them. He slowed as he got closer and did a kickflip, spinning the board over and landing on top.

Faye cheered.

‘Have a go?’ Scarlett said.

Jason gave a nod. He flicked the board up and stood it at his side.

She slid off her backpack and rested it by the wall, checking for dog mess first.

Scarlett could do an ollie, popping the tail of the board, dragging the nose and pulling it into the air with her as she jumped. And she could nearly do a nollie, popping the nose instead of the tail.

She tried that now and it worked. *It worked!*

'Cool,' Jason said. He took back his board and skated off ahead.

'He likes you,' Faye said.

Scarlett squirmed but she felt a kick of pleasure too.

'Do you like him?' Faye said.

'Maybe.' Jason was really quiet. He didn't mess about like some of the other boys, who acted really stupid. He was shy, Scarlett thought. But he had this really nice smile, long brown hair and brown eyes. He was brilliant at drawing, as well as skateboarding. When they'd had to write a piece in literacy about what they wanted to be when they grew up, Jason said a graffiti artist. Like Banksy. Or the one who did the poster of Obama that Nana had. It said 'HOPE'.

'I could tell him?' Faye said.

'Don't!' Scarlett said.

Faye was smiling, lips pressed close together, wagging her head, like she was trying to decide.

'Swear,' Scarlett said. 'Go on, swear.' She held out her little finger.

'OK, swear.' Faye hooked her little finger round Scarlett's and shook.

'It doesn't matter if we don't win,' Faye said, as Scarlett picked up her bag. 'We'll still get money for the garden.'

The PTA were raising money to grow vegetables, plant apple trees and dig a pond. Scarlett wanted them to get a beehive too. When she'd suggested it lots of the other kids were, 'Eww, bees.' And then Mrs Sullivan said Charity in year three had bee allergies so it was a health and safety issue.

Scarlett was really disappointed because if all the bees died it would be a disaster for the planet. Another.

They reached Faye's house and Scarlett shucked off her bag again.

The rain was heavier now. Less like drizzle and more like proper drops.

Scarlett raised her hands to Faye's.

They'd made up the hand-jive sequence to start their piece. It was like they were these two friends, just meeting up, shaking hands, doing this big complicated greeting and then it changed into all the different dance sequences until near the end when Faye was up on Scarlett's shoulders and jumped down and Scarlett did a run, a back-flip and a dive over Faye. They finished with the hand jive again and walked off in different directions as though they hadn't just done this amazing dance sequence.

'Nonchalant,' Nana called it, when Scarlett described it to her. 'Cool, casual, laid-back,' Nana explained.

Scarlett and Faye went into the hand jive now. There were thirty different moves from fist bumps and high-fives to hitch-hiking and under-leg hand claps. At the start they did it speeding up so it was almost a blur. And at the end they had to start fast and slow it down, like in reverse. That was what they were doing now. The goodbye version.

And when they did it tomorrow they'd have to hide how out of breath they were or it would look stupid.

They ended with a little handshake.

'See you tomorrow.' Faye picked up her bag and swung open her gate.

'See you tomorrow,' Scarlett said, and walked on.

Scarlett saw a red blob in the hedge opposite Jason's house. A ladybird. Jason was still out on the pavement practising his tricks. Scarlett thought it might seem weird if she stopped to look at the insect after what Faye had said. But then she thought that changing what she would usually do would be weird too. Maybe even weirder, like she was putting on a show. So she did stop.

Nana loved ladybirds because she said they ate the greenflies on her plants. This was a seven-spot one. But ladybirds hibernate. Scarlett worried it had woken up too soon, only February: it wouldn't have anything to eat.

'Ow!' Jason shouted. He'd fallen. Scarlett saw him land and roll onto his side by the kerb.

'You all right?' she called, as he got up. He was peering at his hand.

'Yeah.' He jumped back on the board and began to bounce it round, seesawing in a circle.

When Scarlett looked back, the ladybird had gone.

She carried on up the hill, making a list in her head of all the things she needed for the talent show. The back of her calves started to burn. It didn't matter how much exercise she did, dancing or football or gym, every time she walked up the steep hill home her legs ached.

The wind snatched at her hood and she yanked it forward as quick as she could. Her hair went beyond frizzy in the rain.

A car pulled in beside her and stopped a few paces ahead. A 4x4 with those dark windows. Nana snorted whenever she saw one. 'Who needs a tank like that to do the school run and the shopping? Status symbol, that's all it is. And they're churning out air pollution. We all have to breathe the same air.'

The driver's door opened and a man got out. *Grandpa?*

Every bit of her went cold.

Grey hair, beard. But Grandpa was dead.

Scarlett froze. Eyes down on the pavement. It couldn't be Grandpa, unless it was a ghost. Or he never really died, truly died, but then—

'Hello, Scarlett,' the man said. 'It's me. Dad.'

Scarlett wet herself.

No. No. No.

He opened the back door of the car. 'In you pop. We're going for a little drive.'

Scarlet couldn't move. She couldn't breathe. Her feet were rooted to the ground.

'Come on,' he said.

Scarlett tried to shake her head, to say no. But she couldn't. She wanted to race up the rest of the hill to her house, run inside, bolt the door.

Nana would know what to do.

He came up to her.

She twisted away, rose up on the toes of her feet to run and he grabbed her wrist. Dragged her close. 'Here we go.' He slid the bag off her shoulder, lifted her, easy as anything, and put her in the back seat.

'Buckle up,' he said, fastening her seatbelt and sounding all jolly like this was what they did every day. Like there was nothing wrong. Then he slammed the door and got in the front, turned the key and smiled into the mirror.

*

Dylan's phone chirped again. He'd only just sat down, was about to order a pizza, his stomach gnawing with hunger. If Col was here maybe Col would have done the run but Col was off buying trainers. There was a shopping village on the outskirts of the town where he'd gone to get them. Pizza would have to wait. Dylan checked the text. One brown rock, one white. Daisy, the buyer's name.

Dylan stuck his head into the living room. Petey was glued to the screen. Something on YouTube. 'Don't answer the door,' Dylan said.

Petey whipped round and nodded quickly. Fear on his face. That look made Dylan want to hit him. It got under his skin, a burning irritation, Dylan itching to grab him, shake him. Tell him to stop being such a loser. Same as when Petey got into his begging mode,

'Please can I have a bump, Dylan. I need a bump, just to take the edge off. It's my nerves, like.' Or when he started whining, 'It's my house, Dylan. It's my house. I never asked you to move in.'

Course Petey never went so far as to ask them to leave. Maybe he didn't dare but also cos he was getting drugs on tap with Dylan and Col under his roof. And what junkie's going to turn their back on a ready-made supply like that? That was the way it worked when they set up a trap house to deal from: always pick on someone who's too needy, too weak to resist.

Petey should be grateful. More than grateful.

Dylan surveyed the room. The pizza boxes and drinks cans, takeaway cartons. The scraps of foil and twisted clingfilm, cigarette papers. Mugs and plates. A chocolate muffin that had grown a fur of white mould. Thin and pale and fluffy. Like Petey's hair, what he had left.

Dylan hoped he wouldn't go that way, balding. He'd have to shave his head if that happened. Was it a genetics thing? He'd no idea what his dad had been like in the hair department. Never knew who he was. *You don't need to know, Dylan. He's nothing.*

For now Dylan wore his hair undercut, longer on top, shaved round the sides. He'd had the tips bleached, and with his darker roots he reckoned it looked good. Like he had some sense of style.

At thirty-four, Petey was exactly twice Dylan's age, but he was wrinkled like an old grandpa. Watery blue eyes. He had the shakes too. A loser. At thirty-four Dylan planned to be a long, long way from this place. He'd have moved up the food chain, be running his own deal lines. Could even move abroad. Do it from there. It was all going online now, anyway.

He'd get a house, a big house, not like this shithole. With a pool and a games room and a gym. He was making three hundred a week now, but any gang leader, like Lloyd, they'd be clearing ten grand, even more.

Petey was on the sick, Employment and Support Allowance, on account of his mental health, and he was getting his rent paid through housing benefit.

All he did was sit on his arse, surf the web and get off his bonce.

'This place is a shit-heap,' Dylan said to him.

Petey looked about, fumbled with the cushion at his side.

'Needs a clean.'

'I didn't do it,' Petey said, all riled.

'Who cares? You know we got mice?' Dylan had seen the droppings in the kitchen cupboard, so many that at first he thought it was a spill, grains of some weird fancy rice or something. 'I've got work. You do it, you sort it.'

'But I—'

'Now!'

'Can I just have . . .' Petey started.

Dylan waved the baggie of crack. 'When it's done, eh?'

He went out, slamming the door. Why did Petey have to argue? Or why didn't he argue more? Stand up for himself properly, just for once.

Dylan felt the bitterness, sour inside him.

Just tired, he thought, as he left the house and walked along to the side-street. And starving. And you need a drink. A few bevvies and some hot food and you'll be more like yourself.

Petey's wasn't as bad as the last place they'd been sent. Grantham. The woman there was turning tricks. She was off her head too, scars up and down her arms to prove it. Men coming day and night, and the sound of them at it was enough to put anyone off their scran. Not that Dylan was a prude about sex – he'd seen plenty of porn and the rest – but this was just . . . squalid. That was the word. Dirty. And not in a good way.

He went down the side-street and into the alley. There was a girl there, hoodie up.

‘Daisy?’

‘Yeah. Ta.’

He checked the cash she gave him and handed over the rocks.

‘Cheers.’ She headed off, head down against the rain.

Dylan turned to go and his phone chirped again. Another sale. *Shit.* Was he ever going to get five minutes’ peace?

I want to go home. A pain in his chest. *Daft. What home?* And he didn’t actually miss Leeds – well, maybe a couple of people, mates he knew here and there. No family now. Not since his mam was living in Málaga with Irvin. Dylan hadn’t had an invite.

‘I think we need to see how the pair of us settle. I can’t really ask him to take on a teenager, can I, Dyl? Anyway, at least you got a social worker, a decent foster place. In the system, yeah? We just need a bit of time. All of us. You sort yourself out and then we’ll see, eh?’

He’d been in the pupil-referral unit then. That was where he’d met Col and the others. They were hanging around outside at the end of the day. They were friendly with him, made him feel good. Generous too. Soon he was spending all his time with them. Learning the business, making some money. At last there was a point to things, a way out. And he’d felt great then, part of something. He belonged. They had a laugh. They looked out for him. There was everything to play for.

But this, standing in the rain, never getting enough sleep, or enough to eat, living in a dump, wasn’t how he’d imagined it. The threats of violence. People screaming in your face. Lloyd always wanting more from you, undivided loyalty, unquestioning obedience. A knife to your throat if you stepped out of line, if you messed it up. Anyone wanting out, rocking the boat, then their family’s at risk. Fires set, bricks and bottles. Death threats.

At the end of the day you were stuck, really, cos even if you did decide you wanted out, where would you go? They’d hunt you down and kill you. A lesson. An example. And what would you do even if you could hide? Sign on like Petey and wait for your life to tick by, counting the pennies, on your tod and bored senseless.

No, thanks.

You'd just got to hang on and wait for your chance to move up. Things'd come good in the end. It wouldn't always be like this.

Chapter 2

Ron led the horses back into the stable-yard and let them drink from the trough before he took the saddle and bridle off Patti, the chestnut mare, the head collar and leading rein from Polly, the black. He'd taken them out along the path at the back of the house as far as Dolly Falls where the water tumbled down over the rocks and the steep-sided valley rose up to the escarpment and Lovers Leap. Three miles in all. There'd be a longer ride tomorrow for Patti, depending on the weather.

Ron was a bit heavy for the smaller horse. He weighed fourteen and a half stone so he only rode her modest distances, short hacks on the lanes and bridleways close by. Or led her behind Patti, like he had today.

He'd like to get a walk in for himself too, go over and climb Axe Edge Moor, but another storm was forecast so he might leave that until the worst had passed. The ground was sodden already. Waterfalls in full spate and floods in some of the fields. Some areas were still suffering after the floods last November, then Storm Ciara had hit them at the beginning of this month. Debates about flood defences and land management rumbling on.

Patti nickered, keen for food. 'Not so fast,' Ron told her, picking out her hoofs. When he'd groomed both animals, he settled them back in their stalls. Filled their feed.

Graybridge was the only one of his house-sits where they had horses. He'd been house-and-pet sitting for a good five years before he'd decided to expand his skills and taken a course in equine care at a stables in West Brom. Added that to his CV. Most places he'd have dogs or cats to mind as well as the property. One home had a pair of alpacas, odd-looking animals, like badly designed stuffed toys. All fuzzy heads and shaggy legs like the proportions were off, some mix-up of centimetres and inches in the blueprint.

This was his third stint at Graybridge. The owners liked to travel in the winter months. The husband had family in Florida and they combined a few weeks there with other jaunts. The husband had made money investing in property, mainly in Ireland, and she'd been something in tech, which she'd once explained to Ron but he'd not really understood.

The house was built to their own design on the ruins of an old coaching inn. It was beautifully done, dressed limestone walls, oak beams. Carbon conscious with solar panels supplying electricity, triple-glazed windows, a log-burner and composting toilets. Remote and isolated in the depths of the White Peak, more or less in the middle of a triangle formed by the towns of Buxton to the north, Leek to the south-west and Matlock over to the south-east.

Ron closed up the stables, then walked round to the chicken run next to the vegetable garden. Gardening was not in his skillset. Not beyond mowing the grass. But the Graybridges, as he dubbed them, were happy to let it tick over while they were away. He was welcome to help himself to any winter crops, cabbage and turnips, parsnips and broccoli. He was a practical man, could turn his hand to most other odd jobs, and that was enough.

And they loved that he'd been a firefighter. Everyone loved that. He had once. Before it all turned into a horror show. These days when he thought of it, even mentioned it, he felt his skin contract and his pulse speed up. If people wanted to talk about it he tried to move the conversation on. He had toyed with the idea of dropping it from his résumé altogether. So the years 2000 until 2010 he'd claim to have been a health and safety adviser or something, but he knew that when people read 'Fire Brigade' it gave him an edge. All those images of bravery and capability. Heroism. *Hah!*

And, of course, if you're choosing someone to look after your home, care for your pets, safeguard all your precious things, then a candidate like Ron would know exactly what to do, God forbid, in a fire.

Ron collected four fresh eggs then shooed the hens into the coop and bolted the door. A quick check told him that the wire fence around the run was sound. The foxes had a go on a regular basis, digging at the earth around the base, tearing at the wire with their teeth. They'd never broken in when he was here, but the Graybridges had lost chickens several times.

In the house Mungo, the black Lab, was waiting for his afternoon walk. Ron greeted him, rubbing the back of his ears vigorously. He drank a cup of tea to quench his thirst before setting out again.

They headed up the other side of the house away from the gorge. Mungo didn't need a lead: there were no sheep on the land above the house, and no public access. The farmers who owned it had come to know the Graybridges and were happy for them to use it.

The hedges that marked the boundary of this side of the Graybridge land were still bare, the hawthorn and blackthorn all prickles. The meadow beyond was littered with molehills, piles of thick, dark brown loam.

As he was climbing the hillside, a plaintive cry echoed through the air. Ron scanned the sky and spotted a buzzard circling high overhead. He watched the huge raptor for several moments and was rewarded when it fell, like a stone, to its prey.

Panting a little, he reached the brow of the hill. From there he looked out across a countryside dappled by the shadows of the clouds passing over. The hillsides were a grassy green where the sun caught them, netted in a tracery of dry-stone walls of the same pale grey as the limestone ridges that edged the tops. The wilder land on the summits was straw-coloured, daubed with rust from the dead grass and bracken.

Here and there he could see a farm, or a lone barn or sheepfold. The pinprick glimmer of headlights from traffic on the road heading west up the valley came in and out of view as the road skirted the bulk of the peak beyond. The air was fresh and cold and carried a slight bitter scent.

Mungo barked and Ron spotted a dab of white, saw the rabbit dart into the lee of the hedge as the dog barrelled after it.

'Too slow, pal,' he murmured.

There was a whippet he looked after at a place near Hull. She could catch anything that moved: squirrels, birds, cats. Hunting instinct so strong, but she never ate the kill.

Ron hadn't spoken to a soul since last Saturday, when the postie had called with a magazine for Mrs Graybridge, and that suited Ron just fine. But Mungo had an appointment at the vet's at five. So Ron would have to venture out into civilisation today, though not for very long.

And after that his evening was his own. He'd a beef stew in the slow cooker and was halfway through Muhammad Ali's autobiography. He'd sink a few bottles of Wild Bear, which they brewed in Derby. Then bed.

*

DS Laura O'Neil was not exactly watching the clock. She was simply willing the next two hours to pass quickly so she could go home.

She was exhausted, a horrible, hollow speedy feeling inside and an aching back after yet another broken night. Why did teething have to last so long? Months on end. As if she wasn't tired enough already, after the first year of night feeds and nappy changes. And Mateo hadn't even started with the molars yet.

There'd been a brief window when Mateo was seventeen months and slept through every night for a week. She and Hector thought they'd cracked it, come out the other side. That things would only get better. Suckers.

As she took a large bite of chocolate muffin, her phone started ringing. She gulped a mouthful of coffee to wash down the cake before answering.

When she heard the name, when they said the name, everything seemed to slow to a freeze-frame. Then the shock of it hit, like someone had thrown a bucket of iced water over her. All the hairs on her scalp lifted.

'How old is she now?' Laura said.

'Eleven.'

Christ. Laura stood, shutting down her computer, eyes sweeping over her desk, assessing what she needed to bring.

'I'm on my way,' she said. A glance, regretful, at her mug still half full. She should be used to that by now as a new parent – never finishing a hot drink. 'The original investigation,' she said, scooping up her bag, notebook, grabbing her coat. 'Was that Keith Craven?'

'Yes, retired now.'

'No worries.' She made for the stairs. 'Send me through the files, anything you can find. And the address. It's the grandmother?'

'That's right.'

As she left the building a fierce wind, peppered with rain, whipped her hair into her eyes.

She hurried to the car, her mind racing, all tiredness overtaken by the crisis, the urgent need to move as quickly as possible, to find this child and bring her home.

*

Dylan felt chilled through. He fancied a long, hot shower but the shower wasn't working. It only ran cold. *Sick of it.*

At least Petey had cleaned up a bit. Shoved some stuff into a black sack in the hall. Keen to show it to Dylan as soon as Dylan came back in. 'What about the rest?' Dylan said, in the living room, nodding at the mess still left: the manky cupcake and the pop bottles and the ashtray. 'And that bag wants putting outside in the bin.'

'It's raining,' Petey said.

'I know it's fucking raining,' Dylan said. 'Look at the state of me. I was out in it for long enough.'

'You need an umbrella,' Petey muttered.

'Yeah, right.' Dylan could see it now. A big brolly with a slogan on, like businesses use for advertising, *The Real Deal* or *Drugs To Go. Enjoy the Crack.*

'Just give us a hit,' Petey said, lips pulled down, all sulky. 'I'll do the rest after, I swear. Please, Dylan? You promised.'

Dylan shook his head. 'You'd better.' He gave Petey the baggie. Left him to it in the living room.

Going back into the kitchen, Dylan tapped his foot on the threshold to scare any mice away. He wasn't frightened of mice, not as such, just didn't like them darting about. Seeing the blur of movement out of the corner of his eye gave him a nasty shock.

He rang and ordered a pizza, Sicilian meatballs, extra cheese.

He'd got two four-packs of cider in from the minimarket at the roundabout and he popped a tin now. Had a few swallows.

He shivered. The house was like a fridge. Colder inside than out. The gas on a meter. He'd have to send Petey to get the card topped up.

Upstairs he put the money from the deals with the rest in the plastic zip wallet. They'd nearly sold up. He'd talk to Col about making the trip back to Leeds, stocking up on supplies. Dylan would drive. He was a clean skin, no criminal record and a clean driving licence. Lloyd had sorted him out with money for lessons and to take the test as soon as he was legal. Even bought him the car, taxed and insured and everything. OK, the car was a bit of a joke, an old Astra. Col said that was deliberate: no one would look at it twice. Not like the Beemers and Audis that Lloyd and the other top dogs drove.

Flashing the cash, Dylan thought. Same with the trainers Col was after. Someone like Petey could never afford slides like that. Col neither, not until he'd been delivering the merchandise for a while.

Dylan drank some more of his can. Strong and sweet.

A crashing sound and a great thump brought him to his feet. His first thought was that someone had bricked the window. Then that Petey was trashing the place, instead of nodding off on his trip. *Pillock.*

Dylan ran down to the living room.

The door was stuck. Something blocking it. What was Petey up to? Barricading himself in? Maybe he'd got paranoid. Sometimes people just lost it. Got the heebie-jeebies. Ticket to Lalaland.

Dylan shouldered the door, put all his weight into edging it open. Calling, 'Petey, open the door. Let us in, you tosser.'

No response from inside. Dylan kept pushing, grunting with the effort. He used his foot against the bottom edge. 'What are you playing at?'

At last he'd a big enough gap to edge himself in sideways – the latch scratched his back as he did.

Shit!

Petey was on the floor, on his back, body twitching, one leg pressed up against the door. Blood pouring out of his mouth, all over his neck and chest. Eyes rolled back in his head.

Shit. Fuck. Shit.

Panic scorched through Dylan.

What the fuck's happened?

The twitching stopped. Was it a haemorrhage? People had blood coming out of their mouths in the movies when they were shot. Dylan had never really got why that happened.

Shit.

'Petey?' Dylan knelt, shook his shoulder, careful not to touch the blood on Petey's T-shirt.

He wasn't moving, or not as far as Dylan could see, but it was hard to tell when his heart was thumping so hard that his whole body shook.

He couldn't give him the kiss of life, not with all that blood, even if he did know how to do it. Which he didn't.

Fuck. Now they were really shafted.

Go. Run. You have to. It was the only thing to do.

He squeezed out of the room and leapt upstairs. Threw the few clothes he had into his holdall along with their money.

Quick, quick, quick.

Back downstairs he pulled on his jacket, car keys and phone in his pocket. Hood up.

He opened the front door to a blast of wind and rain.

Maybe you should—

He ducked back inside. Dialled 999.

Fuck's sake, Petey. What've you done? You daft bastard.

'Ambulance,' Dylan shouted. 'Ambulance. Sixteen Coopers Gate. Now!' He hung up and ran out, leaving the door open for them.

It was probably too late. But if it was him, lying there drowning in his own blood, he'd at least want someone to give him a chance. They could do all sorts, these days, couldn't they? You only had to watch *24 Hours in A&E* to see that.

Shit!

Dylan jumped into the car and threw his bag onto the passenger seat.

The engine turned over, coughed and died. *No, please.* No, no, he prayed. Acid squirting in his guts.

He turned the key again and the engine roared into life, a belch of black smoke rising, visible in the rear-view mirror.

He shoved it into first, swung the steering wheel sharp right and released the brake. He hit the accelerator hard and the car squealed away from the kerb. Dylan crashed up through the gears, one thought in his head. To get as far away from there as fast as fucking possible.

*

Scarlett didn't know why she was there. Where they were going. Why *he* was there. When she tried to guess she got frightened, her stomach dipping, a shudder across her back. Flashes in her head, the pictures that came in her dreams sometimes.

Her bum and legs were cold and itchy from wetting herself. And she was thirsty, too. By now she'd usually be having a hot chocolate and a crumpet. Telling Nana about her day.

Her eyes prickled.

He was talking. He kept talking about how the place had changed and how there was no future here, really. He just kept talking. And when she looked up she saw his eyes in the mirror, all bright. But none of what he said meant anything to her or told her anything about what was happening.

He said something about better opportunities and laughed. He had a nice laugh, deep and rumbling. The sort of laugh that should make you smile and feel warm, but Scarlett felt cold as stone.

Scarlett had a rush of memory. Him chasing her. Crawling round on the floor. Tigers, they'd called it. Tickling her until she screamed. They'd played tigers and growled and chased. And she'd do it back until he called for mercy.

Just thinking of that made her feel dirty, guilty. Because he'd loved her and she'd loved him and she'd trusted him. Then six years ago it had all been torn away. Like ripping off a mask, or tearing up a picture.

There were traffic lights ahead and the lights were changing to red.

Scarlett tried to swallow but she had no spit and it just made her throat hurt.

As carefully as she could she slid her left hand, so he wouldn't see, down to where the seatbelt fastened. And she lifted her other hand to reach the door handle.

When the car stopped, she snapped open the seatbelt and yanked at the handle. Her heart drumming.

The door was locked.

She banged on the window, shouting, 'Help! Help me!' But there was no one to see. No one to hear.

'Don't be stupid,' he said, turning round.

Scarlett jabbed at the button for the window and it started to wind down and she kept shouting but he did something with the controls to make it close and lock.

'Stop it!' he said coldly. His eyes looked hard at her. He wasn't smiling any more. 'Put your seatbelt back on, now.'

Scarlett's eyes filled with tears. 'I want to go home,' she said.

'Put it back on.'

A tear trickled down her cheek, dropped off her chin and she wiped it with her hands.

'Now,' he said.

Scarlett did as she was told.

The lights turned to green. She looked out at the passing houses and the shops and people and dogs that were passing, all blurry and happy, and she was screaming inside. *Help me help me please please somebody help me.*

Chapter 3

'I've explained all this!' The grandmother, Beatrice, rounded on Laura, banging her fists on the table and getting to her feet. 'You're the police. You say you're in charge of finding her so why aren't you out there now?'

Laura waited a moment. 'I'm so sorry,' she said. 'I know it must be really frustrating. But I have to make sure we have everything exactly right. You called Faye's house at four o'clock?' She was making quick notes.

'Yes. Scarlett was usually back by then. I thought she might have gone in to play with Faye.' Beatrice took a couple of paces towards the bay window. A large yucca plant in a copper pot stood at one side. A broad window-seat with open shelving below filled the bay. Like every other surface in the room it was awash with all sorts of craft materials: piles of paper and card, paints and stickers, felt pens, brushes, rags and scissors.

Beatrice sifted through them as she spoke.

'As soon as I heard she wasn't there, I just knew—'

'And that was when you rang us?' Laura said.

'Yes.'

'Have you spoken to anyone else, other friends, family? In case—'

Beatrice looked sharply across at her. She turned to face Laura square on. 'There is no other family. Scarlett was coming home.'

She was a beautiful woman, Laura thought. Tall. Taller than

Laura, but then most people were. Dark brown skin, high cheekbones. Shapely, too. Her hair was covered with a colourful wrap, a few curls of grey visible at her temples. She wore a velour leisure suit patterned with turquoise and brown leaf shapes. Looking at her style and her surroundings (the heap of fabric at one end of the table, the sewing-machine and wicker sewing-basket, the strips of coloured cloth along with laundry drying on the ceiling rack above), Laura would have pegged her for an artist if she hadn't already established that Beatrice was a nurse, in the high-dependency unit at Chesterfield Royal Hospital.

In any other case involving the absence of a child, Laura might have pressed harder, ensuring the police didn't launch a full-scale search-and-rescue when the child might simply be round at her pal's, but this wasn't a case like any other. Not given the family history.

'He took her,' Beatrice said. 'You know what he's capable of.' She was quivering. Laura couldn't tell whether it was with anger or fear. Both, probably.

'And we'll make every effort to find them,' Laura said. 'What was Scarlett wearing?'

'Navy trousers and jumper, black shoes, purple coat.'

'Plain purple?' Laura was still making notes.

'Yes. Padded,' Beatrice said.

'With a hood?'

'Yes.'

'Does Scarlett have a phone?'

'No. She's eleven.' A note of disapproval.

Well, half of them do. What would Laura's policy be when Mateo reached that age?

Beatrice closed her eyes, rubbed her forehead.

'Neither you nor Scarlett has had any contact with Gregory Martin since 2014?'

Beatrice looked at her, steely-eyed. *Are you insane?*

'I have to ask,' Laura said.

'No,' Beatrice said. 'If he touches a—' She raised her hand, fingers stretched, trembling. Her eyes shone with pain.

Laura gave a nod. 'Beatrice, I need a photograph of Scarlett, please, as recent as possible. And how tall is she?'

Beatrice made a sound, a swallowed moan. She pointed to the doorjamb leading into the kitchen at the back of the house. Laura saw the marks, the scribbled numbers. *Ah, Jesus.* She moved to read the chart. The top line, black ink etched in the wood. The figures: '4' 5"' and '24/12/19'.

Laura remembered clamouring for her own mother to do the same, praying that she would have grown another inch when all her friends at high school towered above her.

Beatrice had picked up her phone and was scrolling through. Laura glimpsed her gallery. Dozens of shots, mostly of the little girl.

'Here.' Beatrice held out the phone.

'Yes,' Laura said. 'That one's good. Can you email it to me?' The photograph was well lit, an outdoor shot, uncluttered and in focus, trees in the background. Scarlett was staring slightly to the right of centre, as though something had caught her attention, a half-smile. She was lighter-skinned than her grandmother; her father was white and her mother had been black. But Scarlett's African heritage was clearly reflected in her features and her hairstyle.

'Is there anything else we should know about Scarlett? Any health issues, medication?' Laura said.

'No,' Beatrice said.

'And you were living here back then, in 2014?' Laura said, hoping to establish how Gregory Martin had known where his daughter lived.

'Yes.'

'Scarlett was living with her mother but her parents had separated. Gregory had moved out?'

'A month earlier. He wanted custody but— Has he been here all along?' Beatrice demanded. 'Waiting? And why now? Why?' She shook her head vigorously.

'I don't know. All I can tell you is that in the past six years he hasn't used any bank or any government agency. He hasn't appeared in any local-authority records and we have no record of him crossing the border. His name is still on the watch list and nothing has been flagged.'

'So he must be using another name, a new identity?' Beatrice said, quick to join the dots.

'Most likely,' Laura said. In all the time Martin had been on their most wanted list there'd never been any credible alert. The few sightings that had been investigated had led nowhere. 'Now whether or not it was her father who abducted her . . .'

Another scathing look.

Laura held up her hands, agreeing. '. . . we work on that assumption. Our priority is tracing his current location. So we need to know how he's travelling. You didn't notice any unfamiliar vehicles in the street over the last few days?'

'No,' Beatrice said.

'Any callers? Anyone hanging around?'

'No.'

'And today?'

'I was in the kitchen most of the time after I got back from work.'

'OK. Thank you. We'll be going house to house very soon. We want to establish if there are any witnesses who can tell us what vehicle he was driving.' He must have transport – how else could he abduct the child? 'Just before I leave, can I look at Scarlett's room?'

A flash of impatience crossed Beatrice's face.

'A couple of minutes,' Laura said. Not choosing to explain or justify her request. Just knowing, as a detective, that it helped. Enabled her to build a rounder picture of the child and her circumstances. And, of course, sometimes there were clues, anomalies, discrepancies to be found. Information that could help direct the angle of the search.

The bedroom at the back of the house was clean and obviously well lived-in, clothes and books scattered on the floor. A pair of gym rings was suspended from one corner. The walls were covered with posters. Many pictured wildlife, a tiger, raccoons, a brown bear. Others quoted Greta Thunberg and Michelle Obama. There was one of the England women's football team, the Lionesses, from last year's World Cup.

Smaller pictures were cut out from magazines or printed off. Images of dancers and gymnasts in gravity-defying positions.

A corkboard held a clutch of photographs. Laura peered closer and found one of a younger Scarlett with her mother, Jeanette. Jeanette was crouching down, hand open, a tiny crab on her palm. Scarlett, in a polka-dot swimsuit, was leaning in, her face intent.

A second photograph looked like a Christmas scene, Scarlett on Jeanette's lap, paper hats on. Jeanette smiling, a lovely warm smile, and Scarlett, her head thrown back, mouth wide open laughing, a front tooth missing.

A recent snap showed Scarlett doing a handstand in the room downstairs.

Laura was moved, thinking of the unimaginable trauma the girl had been through. And the fact that she had been able to thrive since. She didn't doubt much of that was down to Beatrice's love and care.

And now it appeared that Gregory Martin, having already wreaked such carnage and caused such grief, had crashed back into their lives. Prepared to destroy what had been so carefully nurtured.

She tried to imagine how the child would be coping with the situation.

Downstairs Laura asked Beatrice, 'Scarlett herself, how would you describe her as a character?'

Beatrice opened her mouth to speak, then her face swam with sorrow, lines creased her brow. She took a shaky breath, in and out.

Laura felt a swell of sympathy. She swallowed and waited for Beatrice to compose herself.

Beatrice pushed her fists against her thighs as if forcing herself to talk. She opened her eyes. 'She's bright, clever. Sociable.'

'She'd know to try and ask for help?' Laura said.

Beatrice nodded. 'But she'll be scared. She'll be terrified.'

Laura checked again whether Beatrice wanted anyone to come to be with her. She didn't.

At the doorway Beatrice simply said, 'Bring her back.' Tears glittering in her eyes.

Ah, Jesus, I hope so, Laura thought. I hope so. But I can't make any promises.

*

Ahmed knew straight off that something was wrong.

He was on his way back to the police station after attending a callout about fighting at Bet You in Wirksworth, which turned out to be a waste of police resources because by the time he got there the men involved had fled the scene. Some scrap about proxy betting and money owed. No one to press charges, or even give him the full story, just the bookie's clerk saying, 'I thought they'd kill each other. But I'll tell you something for nothing, they're barred now. One of them was barred already. That's where the trouble started.'

So driving back from that, as Ahmed turned into Coopers Gate to avoid the lane closure on the high street, this figure ran out from one of the houses, like the devil was at his heels, threw a bag into an old Vauxhall Astra and jumped in after it. Ahmed just had time to make out the last letters of the reg, D and Q, before the car tore away in a cloud of exhaust fumes.

Ahmed might have dismissed it but the lad (he thought it was a lad but it might have been a girl – back to him and hoodie up) had left the house door wide open, the hall light spilling out onto the street, the building open to the rain.

Ahmed called Control, told them he was going to check out an unsecured property, and pulled his patrol car into the space vacated by the silver Astra. He called as he entered the house, 'Hello? Anyone here? This is the police.'

He could hear a murmur from the front room. Like a TV. No sign of movement from upstairs. He listened, head crooked, for long enough. The place felt empty.

'Hello?' he called again.

Nothing.

Why leave the front door open? Had he witnessed a burglary? The person who legged it had carried a bag.

Judging by the state of the hallway, scuffed paintwork, peeling wallpaper, flecked carpet worn thin and shiny and splashed with stains, it wasn't going to be stuffed with luxury items but you never knew. Besides, the most desperate burglars, those trying to make enough for the next hit, would take anything that wasn't nailed down and might net them a tenner.

The door into the front room was partly open. Ahmed pushed it but it didn't give.

He peered round into the room.

And his guts dissolved.

Bloody hell! It was a bloodbath. A man on his back, gallons of the stuff everywhere. Ahmed stepped inside.

First aid, he told himself. The list that spelt out DIRECT-CPR.

D for Detect.

Interrogate. 'Hello, can you hear me. Hello?' Ahmed crouched beside the man.

Respiration. Scanning him for any signs of life. His chest was still.

Ahmed's mouth went dry. Like he'd sucked a lemon.

Emergency. He rang for an ambulance and soon found himself speaking to the call handler. Ahmed felt like he couldn't form his words properly.

'He's not breathing—'

'Do you know the patient's name?'

'No idea.'

The smell of blood was thick in the room, like rust. It caught at the back of Ahmed's throat, making him want to retch.

'Can you give me any idea how old he is?'

'Thirties, forties?' No shoes. Darth Vader picture on his socks.

'Is there a heartbeat?'

'There's blood all over. I can't see any movement,' Ahmed said.

'Where is the blood?'

'Round his mouth, all over his chest and neck.' He glanced at the man's hands. 'On his hands too. I think he's dead,' Ahmed said. *I think he's been killed.*

He glanced around, saw a crack pipe on the table, a twist of plastic wrap, foil and a lighter. *Drug user.*

'Is the patient warm to touch?'

Ahmed found a place on the man's arm that wasn't drenched red and put his fingers on it. 'Yes.'

'That's good. The ambulance has been alerted and is on its way. I want you to stay on the line and I'm going to talk you through performing CPR. Do you have sterile gloves and a pocket mask or mouth shield with you?'

Ahmed's stomach turned over at the thought of touching the man's mouth. *Wimp. Just do your bloody job.* 'In the car,' he said.

Loud knocking from the front door made his heart jump. 'In here,' he shouted, relief flooding through him that the paramedics were here already, so soon after he'd raised the alarm.

Footsteps.

Ahmed looked up, expecting green uniforms. A man there, small, dark-skinned, a grin dying on his face. 'Pizza?' he said.

'What?'

'Sicilian meatballs?' His words faltered.

'Outside,' Ahmed shouted, pointing. 'Go.' Then, realising it might be prudent to get some details, he shouted, 'Which takeaway?'

'Are you there, caller?' the handler said.

'Sizzle 'n' Chill.' From the hall.

'What's your name?' Ahmed called.

'Yusef.'

'Can you hear me, caller?'

'OK,' Ahmed said. 'I'll be in touch.'

'I get help?' Yusef said.

'On its way, ta,' Ahmed said.

You can do this. He straightened up. 'I'll get my mask,' he said, to the call handler.

He heard a siren whooping closer and closer. As he reached the door the sound choked off and the ambulance, flashing its blue lights, came to a halt in the middle of the road.

'The ambulance is here,' Ahmed said and hung up, trying to steady his breath.

The paramedics, two women, came to meet him at the front door. 'He's in the front room,' Ahmed said. 'You were quick.'

'Twelve minutes,' the taller woman said, which didn't make sense: no way had it been that long.

'He's unresponsive,' Ahmed said.

The taller woman went through.

'You tried anything?' the smaller one said.

'No.'

'Any information you can give us about the situation here?'

He liked meatball pizza. Ahmed was mortified to have that thought.

'No. Well, signs of drug use, class As. And I saw someone leaving in a rush. I think they might have been involved. I'm considering it as suspicious so if I can . . .' He pointed to the door.

'Sure. We've got your details?'

'Yes. There's a lot of blood,' Ahmed added.

The paramedic raised an eyebrow. *You don't say.* Gave a nod.

Back in the car, Ahmed braced his hands on the steering wheel and took a couple of breaths. He felt unsteady, dizzy. That'd be the adrenalin from dealing with the fatality. He was pretty sure it was a fatality. Ahmed couldn't see the paramedics reviving the man.

He heard his mother's voice in his head. 'You can do this, Ahmed. You can do whatever you set your mind to.' And his father would always agree, nodding sagely. 'Failure is not an option.'

The car had driven north. That way led across the hills. Ahmed would go after him. Or her.

He imagined his parents' faces when he succeeded. When he'd caught the killer and brought him in, seen him charged, then convicted. That would go some way to answering their reservations about his job, the risks it posed, the perilous situation of being Asian in a cop's uniform.

Or maybe the paramedics *would* bring the man round. And Ahmed could add that to the list: saving a life *and* apprehending a violent criminal. *LOCAL HERO PC AHMED ALI.*

'Just doing my duty,' Ahmed would say. 'Anyone would do the same.'

A warm feeling filled his chest as he put on his seatbelt. Whoever had killed that man, or left him to die, they'd face justice. This was Ahmed's patch, his world, and he was going to uphold the law and protect the public. The rule of law was the only thing standing between a civilised society and anarchy.

Ahmed checked his rear-view mirror, signalled and manoeuvred smoothly out into the road. He pressed the accelerator, soon exceeding the speed limit. Rules were there for a reason but this was an emergency. The suspect had a head start and Ahmed needed to close that gap if he was to have a chance of catching them.

Chapter 4

Dylan drove away from town. He wanted to get off the main drag, out of sight.

Once the ambulance got to Petey the feds wouldn't be far behind. He didn't know the area, not beyond the town centre, and all he knew then was the route along the A-road to join the M1. So he woke his phone and launched the map. It showed him there was a turn to the right about a mile away, a piddly little road that went over the hills, far as he could tell. That'd do for now.

You ought to warn Col, though.

He messaged with one hand, eyes flicking to the road and back again. The houses were tiny here, with small windows. They all looked crooked, leaning on each other, sliding down the hill. Some had baskets and troughs outside with flowers, splashes of colour, yellow and white and purple. Red. He didn't like the red.

Don't go back to the house. He hit send.

His phone chirped, a reply from Col: *?*

He couldn't explain, not easily, not quickly.

He put the phone on the passenger seat, kept driving.

Another message. *Where's the takings?*

What should he do? Tell Col they were safe, admit he had the money? Or let him think it was still in the house? That he'd left it there.

What was he going to do anyway? Drive back to Leeds on his own? Give Lloyd the money and hope that'd be the end of it? *Yeah, right.* They'd blame you for the mess, for the dead man, for the feds crawling all over, for losing the trap house.

OK, the line was always moving. That was the beauty of it. Find another town out in the sticks, run off any local dealers and grow the business. The whole country was ripe for the taking. Losing the odd place wasn't the end of it. Shit happens. The feds were always trying to disrupt the lines.

But the way this had gone down, a dead man an' all, could cause way more than headaches for everyone involved. Petey might not be dead, he cautioned himself, but it was still a shit storm.

Dylan couldn't see any way he was going to come out of this good.

His phone rang. *Col calling.* He let it ring.

He followed the road as it wound round the edge of a hill, switching back and forth. Out there grass and stone, sheep and rain.

Then another message. *U R dead.* Skull emoji. Knife emoji.

Fuck!

Dylan reached the turning, an old black-and-white signpost pointing the way to Birchwell and Langfield. Places he'd never heard of.

He made the turn.

Col would tell Lloyd. Lloyd would send Col to bring back the money. With or without hurting Dylan? Hard to call. Dylan, the others like him, they were expendable. He knew that. Collateral damage. Like Petey.

It didn't feel like that on the surface, definitely not in the beginning when everybody's your best buddy and they're taking you to parties and giving you booze and the latest hoodie and kecks, a new phone even. Giving you nicknames. Dyl the Pill, Gherkin (something to do with dill the herb, Col said).

And then the money. You run a couple of errands, make a few deals, help out bagging up the gear and you've a wodge of twenties in your hand.

But you know that when the wheels come off, there's hundreds more kids ready to step up and take your place. An endless supply.

Dylan could be pretty certain that mistakes like this wouldn't be tolerated.

At least Dylan's mam was well away so they'd no hold over him on that score. No one else that mattered.

Where would Col expect him to go? The motorway? The station – dump the car and take a train? London? Birmingham?

What would you do if it was the other way round? If Col was on the lam?

Ah, fuck! Dylan hit the brake before checking if there was any traffic behind him. Struck lucky. *Phone tracker. Find Your Friends.* The thought had him breaking out in sweat, stinging like nettle rash.

No one about. No houses or shit. He wound the window down and hurled his phone across the road. It landed by the hedge.

Track that, pal.

Dylan felt a twinge of regret. He'd liked that phone. But he could buy another easy enough. And hanging on to it would be mental, like driving with a live grenade in his hand. A big flashing yellow arrow pointing to him. Target here.

Of course now he didn't have any GPS, no way of knowing where he was. That was OK for a bit. He needed to be lost. To disappear.

A car appeared behind, down the hill. Dylan pulled out. He'd just see where this road took him. Lie low, sort his head out and figure out what the wise move would be.

*

There'd been a ford at the bottom of the hill. A crossing point where the coach road, which circled the peak, had bridged the stream. The lane that had replaced it was unsuitable for heavy traffic.

With significant rainfall the road still flooded, the ford reappearing, just south of the Graybridge driveway. It was always one of the first roads in the area to become impassable. So Ron would have to go in the other direction to get to the vet's in Leek. That route was about four miles longer.

Mungo sat on the floor in the back of the camper van, at ease. The dog was no trouble, well trained, biddable. Ron had told him they were going to the vet to get his eyes seen to. It looked like conjunctivitis to Ron, the redness, the yellow discharge. Mungo had had a bout before, the very first time Ron had looked after him.

Ron had cleared most of the stuff out of his van to store in one of the spare rooms when he'd begun his stint here. Between jobs, home was his camper van. He'd park up on a campsite and move on after a few weeks. Though these days the work bookings came thick and fast.

He wasn't officially allowed to be living in his camper van. It didn't give him a legal place of residence, so he used his mum's address in Birmingham. They spoke on the phone every week and every couple of months he visited to spend some time with her, stay a few nights and pick up any mail.

She'd only the one bedroom and he'd have been happy to kip in the van outside but she insisted he sleep on the sofa. 'Not in the camper van,' she'd pleaded. No doubt thinking it'd lower the tone of the street. So Ron obliged her and that meant managing with his knees bent up or his feet dangling over the end of the couch.

She'd been gutted when he left the service. When he broke up with Josh. And she'd never reconciled herself to this new life of his, hopping from job to job, no roots, no attachments. And he knew she wasn't keen on the beard that he'd finally been able to grow when he didn't have to observe Fire Brigade regulations. But mostly she kept her feelings to herself.

'Ooh, a camper van!' Lance's voice slithered into his head. 'Couldn't get much camper. Suits you, sir!' The rest of Green Watch laughing. Ron trying to smile, playing along. Not let it get to him. Like always.

Why now? Ron groaned, raised his head to stretch his neck.

He ejected the cassette tape from the player and turned it over, slid it in and pressed play. Sleaford Mods. There'd been a stretch of time when cassettes were obsolete, everyone moving on to CDs, then mp3s and streaming, but now tapes were making a comeback, like vinyl had, and Sleaford Mods were one of the bands that had been savvy enough to do limited-edition cassettes of a couple of their albums. He liked their abrasive style, punk energy, savage rants about modern life in left-behind places.

Ron changed gear as the road banked steeply, veering to the right. Below, the dale fell away. No barrier. He spotted a pair of lambs skitter away, tails shivering, back to their ewe, butting at her for milk. First he'd seen this year.

The road twisted and turned. Across the tops cloud had moved in. Slate grey, thick enough to make you think it was twilight already.

At the next bend Ron saw a trio of cyclists ahead in yellow and purple strips. Once he had a clear run he moved out to overtake.

The ache in his bladder was growing stronger, insistent.

Like an old man, he thought. These days he was up twice in the night to the bog. Surely that wasn't meant to happen yet. Only forty-nine.

Then again, forty-nine sounded ancient. Ron was still nineteen inside. Nineteen and giddy with it all. Maybe this was his prostate. Did that make you pee more? It didn't hurt. Not like an infection, or kidney stones, or anything. Just an urge.

He kept an eye open for somewhere to pull in before he reached civilisation.

Should he see the GP? He was still registered in Birmingham. He could make an appointment for sometime in May when this job was over. Would Dr Gannon still be there? It must be nine years since Ron had last seen her. And she'd been in late middle age then. His mother would know. Her doctor was at the same practice. Dr Gannon had written the letters supporting his resignation on grounds of ill-health. Prescribed a short course of anti-depressants.

On the long descent winding down the valley into Leek, the road narrowed and he met a DHL delivery van coming uphill. Ron had to back up to a passing place.

The courier raised a finger by way of thanks. Ron echoed him.

He drove on and spied a field gate a few hundred yards ahead, a wide verge beside it. No buildings visible.

He pulled in and parked.

Mungo barked.

'You've been already,' Ron said.

He walked round to the passenger side of the van to shield himself from view and had a piss. The hedgerow round the field was alive with sparrows and finches, flitting and darting among the weave of shrubs. He spotted holly and hawthorn. And hazel, was it, with the fluffy catkins?

On his way back to the car Ron heard a buzzing sound, nothing to do with the chittering of the birds, and something flashed in the grass.

A phone?

Ron picked it up.

An iPhone. Not cheap.

It wasn't damaged.

Odd place to lose a phone. Maybe someone had stopped for the same reason he had. He rubbed his thumb across the screen to wake it but it was locked. Password protected. Someone must be missing it.

He put it in the glove compartment. He could drop it at a police station in the next day or so. Check where the nearest one was that was still open.

Good deed for the day, he thought. Pleased with himself, he gave a nod and started the engine.

*

Scarlett couldn't stop shivering. Her head was hot but the rest of her was frozen. She felt sick. And hungry as well, her stomach cramping. How could she be both at the same time?

The car heater was whirring away and the windscreen wipers were on but slow, so the rain speckled the glass until everything was hazy. Then the wipers swished it clear.

She could smell plastic and thought she could smell wee too.

Did he know she'd wet herself? He wasn't talking any more. He had the sat nav on and Scarlett could see the map. The blue arrow moving along the road was their car. Where were they going?

Out of the windows were green hills, some with little woods, but mostly it was just grass. She spotted a flock of sheep, and far away, down below, a farm, but there weren't any other houses anywhere that she could see.

Should she just ask him where they were going and see what he said? But he probably wouldn't tell her. He'd ignored everything she'd said so far, like how she wanted to go home. He didn't care what she wanted.

Tears burnt at the top of her nose but she sniffed them back. She wouldn't cry.

Scarlett wondered what Nana was doing. Had she realised that Scarlett was in trouble? She must have, by now.

He put the radio on, pushed the buttons one after another. A snatch of sound, a blare of noise, like a punch in Scarlett's heart each time.

He left it on a channel playing classical music. Scarlett recognised it from *Swan Lake*.

Nana had taken her and Faye to see the ballet at the Pomegranate Theatre. A man in the row in front of them, his phone started to ring just as the curtain went up and he was so embarrassed, jumping around to get it out of his pocket.

Some of the show had been a bit boring but this part had been amazing. She listened now as more and more of the orchestra joined in, the music building and building. It sounded so sad, it seemed to fit with the wild countryside and the rain and how Scarlett was feeling. She tried biting her tongue to stop the sadness inside, a lake of sadness, but still some tears leaked out.

So she dug her nails as hard as she could into the inside of her other wrist until all she could think of, all she was aware of, was the sharp pain there. When she opened her eyes there were four curved marks pale against the brown of her skin.

The rain grew heavier, drumming down, and he switched the windscreen wipers to fast. Even then it was hard to see out, everything wobbly through the streaming water.

Scarlett remembered the way the dancers had flown across the stage. She liked doing ballet and jazz, and ballroom was OK, but her favourite was contemporary dance because you didn't have to stick to the same basic moves. You could be more creative. You could do anything that felt right for the piece. And Acro, where you could mix up gymnastics and dance. Street dance too, she loved street dance.

Nana said that Scarlett's mum used to do that. Body-popping and break-dancing. She'd even danced in a music video one time, for a band from Sheffield. Scarlett had never seen it. There had been a copy of it on an old tape, a videotape. But it had got lost or broken. Nana had helped her search for it on YouTube just in case someone had uploaded it there. But they hadn't. She wished she could have seen it. Or, even better, watched her mum dancing like that now. And Scarlett could have shown her all the moves she'd learnt. They could dance together.

I hate you!

The rush of fury burst through her and she wanted to kick out with both feet, slamming them into the back of his seat. Or twist her legs up and swing one foot round the side of the head rest, kick him in the head. *Stupid, horrible, mean . . .*

A great white flash lit up the car and threw a sheet of lightning across the sky.

Scarlett felt it crackle through her, every hair prickling.

'Christ!' he said.

There was a loud crack, like a whip, and then rumbling – it sounded like boulders tumbling over each other.

What if they got hit by lightning? They were at the top of the hill. It must be one of the highest points. Would it fry them? Would it make the car explode?

The noise of the downpour was deafening – it sounded like stones, not just water – and Scarlett couldn't hear the radio any more.

She shuddered and moved in her seat, trying to get a bit more comfortable. Her trousers were sticking to her, cold and damp.

'Christ Almighty!'

A grinding squeal, and Scarlett screamed as she was flung forward, the seatbelt biting into her shoulder and one of her ankles slamming into the bottom of the driver's seat, as he braked sharply.

'Shit!' he swore.

Scarlett, shaking, rubbing at her shoulder, sat up higher, craning to see.

The road had gone.

They were halfway round a corner, bending left, and where the road should have been there was a river of mud and stones pouring across in front of them and down the hill. The road had collapsed. Like a massive digger had carved it all away.

'Mudslide,' he said. Then he shouted, 'Fuck!'

Scarlett swallowed. She knew people swore, some of the kids at school did, but he sounded so angry. Like it was her fault.

Scarlett kept looking at the mudslide. Water was running through it in fast brown streams. What if it spread? If more of the hill started to move? It would push their car off the road. They'd fall and then be covered with a pile of mud. Or they'd bounce down the hillside, the car banging and turning over and over, then bursting into flames.

He turned round and stared at her. Then he undid his seatbelt.

Scarlett shrank back.

What now? What was he going to do now?

Chapter 5

Laura had just finished speaking to Faye when an officer going from door to door alerted her to a possible witness to the abduction. Another school friend of Scarlett's.

Jason's mother sat with him on a sofa in their front room while Laura spoke to him. The boy was skinny, all angles, knobs on his elbows and knuckles, a bandage on one hand. He wore a black T-shirt with an image of a skateboard and *This Is How I Roll* printed on it, and faded black jeans.

'Tell me what you saw,' Laura asked.

'We'd come back from school,' he said.

'You and Scarlett?' Laura checked.

'Scarlett was with Faye, till Faye's house. I'd gone past them. I was on my skateboard.' He flicked a glance at Laura from behind the hair shielding much of his face.

'OK.' Laura nodded for him to say more.

'She went up the hill. I was doing tricks.'

'Where were you?' Laura said.

'Just outside.' He tipped his head towards the bay window, the view beyond screened by shimmery grey voile curtains.

His mother gave a nod, as if backing him up. Her face was stark with worry.

'And then?' Laura said.

'She went up the hill. Then this car came. And it stopped nearby.'

His fingers were twitching, tangling as he talked.

'Where? Near Scarlett or near her house?' Laura said.

'Near Scarlett. We can't see her house from here,' he added.

'It's beyond the rise,' his mother said.

A ginger cat padded into the room and froze.

Jason's mother shot an anxious glance at Laura, and Laura smiled to reassure her. A cat in the room was neither here nor there.

'I couldn't see much then because the car was in the way. It stopped on the far side of the road,' Jason said.

'So it drove past you and up the hill, then pulled in on Scarlett's side?'

'Yes. I didn't know Scarlett had got in the car. I just thought she'd gone home.'

The cat stalked forward to the sofa, tail erect.

Jason parted his hands and it jumped into his lap, its face tilted up, head swaying, as though trying to read his expression. He stroked it between the ears.

'Did you see the driver?' Laura asked.

'No.'

'And when the car stopped? Did you see anyone get out?' Laura said.

'No. I wasn't watching it all the time. I was still skating.'

'How long do you think it was there?' Laura said.

'Not long. A minute, maybe.'

'Have you any idea what make of car it was?'

'I think it was a Land Rover.' He turned to his mum. 'Like Auntie Sarah's.'

His mother nodded. 'She has a Discovery, one of the newish ones.'

'But I'm not sure,' Jason said to Laura.

'What colour was it?'

'Black,' Jason said.

'Did you notice the number-plate? Any of the letters?'

'No.'

'Do you remember any signs or stickers on the car?' Laura said.

'No,' Jason said.

'Did you notice anyone else, any other cars come along here while that one was stopped?'

He shook his head.

The cat purred. Laura thought the animal must be daft not to sense the tension in the boy. Or was it just dogs that tuned into people's emotions? Perhaps the purring was meant to reassure him.

'And the car didn't come back down the hill?' Laura said.

'Not while I was there.'

'Were you there much longer?' Laura said.

A bony shrug. 'Ten minutes.'

'In the pouring rain,' his mother added, but there was a fond note in her chiding.

'You've been really helpful, Jason,' Laura said. 'If you think of anything else let us know.'

She stood up and the cat turned to watch.

'Is Scarlett going to be all right?' Jason said, flushing pink. He ducked his gaze.

Poor kid. 'I hope so,' Laura said. 'Thanks for your help. It's hard to know what will happen but we'll hopefully catch this person, and if we take them to court, we'll need to write down everything you've told me, as part of the evidence. Do you understand?'

He gave a nod, his mouth working, close to tears.

'We'd help you do that, and your mum would be there, too. But that's for the future. For now, just get in touch if you think of anything else.'

*

Back in her car Laura sent a request for traffic-camera footage from the junction at the top of the hill and all roads into Ashbourne to be scanned for vehicles that matched those details. Any sightings between fifteen forty and sixteen hundred. At least the tight time-frame would help narrow it down.

Then she rang Hector. 'Guess what?' she said.

'You won't make tea?'

'Or bathtime or bedtime. Possibly not even my bedtime.'

'We'll survive,' he said. 'What is it?'

'Child abduction.'

'*Ay Dios.*' Sadness in his voice.

'Yes. Wish me luck. How is he?' Laura said.

'*El tiene un humor de perros*,' Hector said. The mood of dogs. One of the phrases Hector had taught her. Meaning cranky, mardy.

Laura could hear Mateo grizzling in the background. And not for the first time she thanked the heavens she was the breadwinner and Hector the stay-at-home parent.

'You say hello?' Hector said.

'No, I—' But it was too late. Already she could hear Hector calling Mateo. She groaned inwardly. It would only make him worse when he was already in a strop.

Hector switched his phone to speaker and she heard Mateo whining.

'Mama's here,' Hector said.

'Hello, Mateo,' Laura said. 'You OK? *¿Estás bien*?' The grizzling ramped up several notches as she'd predicted.

'I'll see you later, Mateo. Bye-bye. *Adios*. Love you.'

And leave you.

A wail erupted, ear-piercing.

'Got to go,' Laura said. '*Hasta luego*. Night night, Mateo. Night night.' She ended the call and closed her eyes for a moment, gave a long breath out, trying to shed some of the tension.

OK. Work.

Laura pulled up the description she'd put together for Scarlett and checked the time. They were issuing the media release at a quarter to the hour, with or without further information about the vehicle. That way the local and national radio and TV news channels could include it as breaking news in their top-of-the-hour bulletins. National outlets didn't always carry child-abduction stories – there were too many of them – but in this case there would be extra interest. It would carry special weight given who it involved. She expected the news to spread rapidly on social media, as well.

Laura double-checked the spelling and read the piece aloud, looking for errors. Then she composed a new paragraph about the vehicle Gregory Martin was believed to be travelling in.

They might not have a great deal to go on with the car, she thought, but if Jason hadn't been out on his skateboard they'd have had absolutely nothing.

*

Dylan had driven through Birchwell, which consisted of a farm on one side of the road and two cottages on the other, and he was climbing upwards again, through the wind and rain, when the car died on him.

Just died. Total loss of power.

Fuck!

It was in danger of rolling backwards so he put the handbrake on.

'Why now? Why fucking now?' he yelled. The car had been a bit dodgy coming over Snake Pass three weeks ago on the drive down from Leeds, but after five minutes' rest it had started fine. And, yes, he was low on petrol but the warning light hadn't come on.

He turned the key. Nothing.

He tried the hazard lights. They worked, so did that mean the electrics were sound? He didn't know much about cars. Col was more into all that.

U R dead.

He'd wait. He'd wait and watch the clock on the dash (which was still an hour wrong, had been since the clocks had changed) and give it five minutes. Or ten?

Was it overheating? The temperature gauge looked OK.

He lit a fag. Something to pass the time, calm him down.

Thunder rumbled in the distance. That was all he needed. Stranded in a thunderstorm without a phone. So he couldn't even ring anyone for help.

How far would it be to a petrol station? Miles, must be miles. This was the arse end of nowhere.

He was starving. He looked out and everything was grey. Rain spattered against the windscreen. He remembered the day Steve, his mam's boyfriend at the time, had driven the three of them out for a day trip to Filey on the coast. Dylan was seven.

They'd left in bright sunshine, his mam had packed towels and Dylan wore his trunks under his trousers.

The weather had turned filthy by the time they reached the resort, rain coming down in stair-rods.

They parked looking out to sea.

Grey waves with white tops, seagulls in a line on the railings. Massive things, the birds were, with evil-looking eyes and big, sharp beaks.

Steve and his mam had been complaining to each other, squabbling about checking the forecast, and why hadn't she made any butties?

In the end they'd bought fish and chips from a stall close by and eaten them in the car. The batter was thick and soggy and the vinegar too sour, and Dylan had felt sick after he finished it. Then they'd scurried through the rain to an amusement arcade. He played penny slots, ten pence a go. He won a pound. Spent that and came away empty-handed.

Steve had driven too fast all the way home, swearing at the other drivers and sounding the horn and giving them two fingers.

When they got back Steve had gone straight out again and his mother had told Dylan to get out from under her feet, and couldn't she just have five minutes' peace for once? She'd lit a cigarette and poured another drink. He wanted to watch telly but she sent him upstairs. He thought she was crying. He didn't know what he'd done wrong. Why she was so mad at him. It wasn't like he'd made it rain.

Before then Dylan had liked fish and chips. But after that he wouldn't eat them. Not the fish. He'd pick chips and curry sauce, or chips and saveloy. Or ask if they could get pizza instead.

He'd have eaten anything at this minute, though.

If he could get the car going he'd stop at the next takeaway, chippie, Chinese, whatever, and grab something there. His mouth watered at the thought.

A tractor appeared coming towards him, uphill. A huge blue thing. Dylan waited to see if they'd stop and help him out. The tractor slowed a bit, the driver perched up high, looking either side and guiding the nearside wheels onto the verge, inches from the wall.

He ignored Dylan. Hadn't he noticed the hazard lights? Wouldn't he think to check that Dylan was OK, stranded out here in this weather? The tractor trundled past and drove on.

That's a no, then.

Then again, maybe it was for the best. It could be awkward explaining himself to people.

Dylan wondered about Petey, and what was happening at the house. Whether Col had spoken to Lloyd already, if the word had gone out. A price on Dylan's head.

Maybe he should head for Málaga. See his mam. Not that he'd expect to kip at hers or anything like that but she might know someone who'd give him a job. A job and a room.

It had been ten minutes. Dylan took a breath and drummed his feet on the floor as he let the breath out. He pressed the pedals and turned the key. The engine stuttered. *Come on, come on.* Then it started. *Yes! Get in!*

He put it in gear, released the handbrake and drove forward, knocking the hazards off.

After a dip down into another valley and a climb back up he reached a summit. The view was crazy, like something from a disaster movie. Great clouds, purple and dark grey speeding past, trailing vast curtains of rain with them, the sky behind a weird yellow colour. A flash of electric blue flared, away to the east.

Thank fuck he wasn't walking in this.

The way ahead zigzagged down the slopes. There was a lot of water on the road, some running across in streams, and he took the bends slowly.

A sign told him he was now entering Langfield. *Please drive carefully.*

Dylan kept his eyes peeled for anywhere to buy food, or even a village shop where they might sell snacks, but there was nothing. Just a dozen or so houses and a church with a tower and a graveyard. Big old headstones and angel statues.

Would Petey be buried? Or cremated? Everyone Dylan knew who'd died had been cremated. Not that he knew that many.

He'd no idea if Petey had any family about – it didn't seem so, given his living situation. Maybe it was like with Dylan: things had got complicated and they didn't want to know.

The drive up from Langfield was sheer, the cloud cover and the dense rain making it almost dark. With no markings, or cat's eyes or bollards, he struggled to figure out where the edge of the road was. That was all he needed, to overshoot and go plunging down the mountain. Was it a mountain? It was big, whatever it was.

Dylan mounted the next rise and reached a T-junction with another minor road, a warning posted about weight limits. A sign told him Matlock was five miles in one direction and Buxton was twelve miles in the other. He'd no way of knowing which would be best for avoiding Col. And the feds.

Thunder was still rumbling over to the east so he decided to go west, towards Buxton.

The route was deserted. Near the valley floor the road grew wider and the land changed from open moorland to farms with fields and dry-stone walls. He passed a signpost at a stile. A footpath.

The road narrowed again as it led him down to an old arch-shaped stone bridge that crossed a stream.

A mile or so further on there was a derelict barn, just the gable end and one side wall left standing. And soon after, a notice stuck on the verge about a car-boot sale in Monyash on 15 March. Dylan wondered who would see it somewhere as remote as this.

The next stretch was another steep, twisting climb and he hoped he wouldn't meet anyone coming the other way. His hands were aching from gripping the wheel so tightly. It couldn't be that much further to somewhere with shops and food, could it?

The final ascent was almost vertical, he had to shift into second gear to keep moving forward. As he breached the ridge he let out a sigh of relief.

Lightning flickered to his right.

He rounded the next bend, eyes locked on the road, and the engine cut out.

Dylan floored the accelerator. Nothing. The petrol light was blinking, the needle in the red zone. He braked and the car slewed to a stop, ending up diagonally across the road.

Dylan flung back his head and screamed, slamming the heels of his hands on the wheel again and again.

Chapter 6

The stew had turned out perfectly, the beef tender, the gravy a rich glossy brown. Potatoes and carrots bulked it up and the turnips added a nice tang.

Ron had bought the beef from a farmer's market in Bakewell and the veg came courtesy of the Graybridges. He had made enough to last two meals, which would save cooking again tomorrow. Although he didn't actually mind cooking, it was relaxing. Especially when it was just for him and there was no one to impress.

His mother still cooked for herself, but he knew a lot of people on their own didn't. They couldn't be bothered going to all the effort, or they'd lost their appetite, or simply didn't see the point when they'd always associated food with company, with sitting down to break bread together.

His grandma had been like that, ended up with malnutrition when she was widowed. A freezer full of food and no interest. They'd put her on energy drinks to boost her intake.

Mungo, who was lying on the floor underneath the table, hoping against all previous experience that Ron might drop him a titbit, gave a bark and scrabbled upright. He walked to the hallway, claws clacking on the stone-flagged floor.

Ron swallowed his mouthful and paused, listening, but couldn't hear anything. Not surprising with the triple glazing closed against the weather.

He carried on eating but the dog whined, pacing from the hall back into the room and out again.

The kitchen diner had windows on three sides. It was still light so Ron hadn't closed the blinds. Sometimes he didn't bother, not like the place was overlooked.

He gave a quick scan. Nothing untoward out there. The vegetable garden and chicken run to the rear, the sun terrace through French windows at the side, its patio hedged by stands of bamboo. 'Non-invasive, clump forming,' Mrs G had explained, as though it mattered to Ron what they put in their garden or how the plants behaved. The driveway out front, his camper van visible on the level parking area by the house. And in the distance, in every direction, were the peaks, visible again now the rain had eased off.

Mungo gave another bark.

'What is it, boy?' Ron said, moving to push his chair back.

Loud banging on the front door. Ferocious. Someone slamming the brass knocker way harder than was necessary.

Mungo gave a volley of barks in return.

Ron grabbed the dog's collar, pulled him into the kitchen and shut him in.

He answered the door to a young man. Mid to late twenties at a guess, wearing a baseball cap and a black hooded coat open over a fancy bomber jacket with black-and-white graffiti lettering all over it.

The man had a round flushed face, the colour of brick. On his feet Day-Glo orange trainers. Pristine. He couldn't have walked far, they were too clean, but Ron saw no sign of a vehicle.

The man looked completely out of place and it took Ron a moment to speak. 'Yes?'

'Where is he?' the man said.

'What?' Ron said.

'Where? Is? He?' Gritted teeth.

Ron saw that he was sweating. A sheen that covered his face. Beads of sweat above his eyebrows.

'Who?' Ron said.

Inside, the dog kept barking.

'Dylan,' he said. 'I know he's here.'

'There's no one here but me. Maybe you've got the wrong—'

'Don't fuck about.' His arm swung round. A machete in his hand. Big, broad, silver, savage.

He thrust it up to rest just under Ron's chin. 'Inside,' he said.

Ron felt a rushing in his head and everything tilted. 'Look,' he said, his mouth sticky, heart thudding. 'Please.'

'Inside.'

Ron felt the tip of the blade, cold against his Adam's apple. He stepped back. The man's eyes darted around, flipping to the kitchen door, the sitting room opposite. Ahead to the stairs.

'Dylan!' the man roared. 'Get down here now.' A fleck of spit landed on Ron's cheek.

Ron could smell stale sweat and some plasticky chemical fragrance on top. He was taller than the other man, broader, but with a knife at his throat what could he do?

His thoughts were scattering, tumbling, a stampede of half-formed thoughts, ideas, imaginings.

'Dylan! Now!'

The man stepped close, whispered into Ron's ear, 'Where is he?' That stink again.

'I don't know,' Ron said. 'I don't even know who he is. And he's not here.'

'Don't you fucking lie to me!' the man screamed, and his hand jerked. Ron felt a jolt of shock as the end of the knife pierced the skin at the front of his neck, a sharp sting followed by the dull burn of pain.

'Please,' Ron said. 'I swear.'

'Show me. Turn round.'

Ron did, slowly, terrified of spooking him.

The man put his free hand on Ron's left shoulder. He tapped the blade of the machete against the right side of Ron's waist. 'Feel that?' he said. 'You mess me about and I'll gut you like a fucking pig. Walk. In there.' He shook Ron's shoulder. The sitting room.

Ron did as he was told.

At a glance it was possible to see that the room was empty.

Mungo kept barking.

'Upstairs,' the man said.

As they climbed the stairs, halting and clumsy, Ron's mind chattered with fear. A wash of acid, tasting of stew, rose in his throat. *I don't want to die. Oh, please, God.*

He was humiliated by his weakness, his passivity. Shame and guilt flooded through him. *Coward.* A useless coward.

On the landing the man made him stop. Five doors, all closed. The four bedrooms (two of which were en-suite) and the guest bathroom.

Ron's neck itched at the trickle of blood flowing down from the cut to soak into his collar.

'Dylan?' the man called again. Then, 'That one.' He shoved Ron's shoulder towards the first room on the left. 'Show me.'

He walked Ron towards the door, told him to open it, barked out commands. It was the spare room where Ron had stored his things.

He made Ron lie down while he checked under the bed.

Ron looked over at his boxes. His life's possessions stacked along the wall.

What if he tried to overpower the man? Waited until there was some distance between them, like now when the machete wasn't actually touching Ron, and . . . what? Kick his feet from under him where he stood or rugby-tackle him by the stairs. Or if Ron dived and rolled and then . . . and then . . .

Ron imagined the man's fury. Ron clattering downstairs, the man after him wild with rage. The machete slashing through Ron's arm or neck, cutting through muscle and bone, a knife through butter. Amputation. Blood spurting.

Mutely, suppressing his terror, Ron went through the same pantomime in each of the other bedrooms. The man steered him back downstairs.

He was boiling with rage now, talking to himself as much as to Ron. 'Where the fuck is he? I'll fucking kill him, I know he's here. I fucking know he's here.'

Facing Ron, he held the knife under Ron's left ear. Ron was shaking so hard he feared he'd cut himself.

'Outside then. Those sheds and that, the garage as well. I know he's here and I'm not going anywhere until I've found the bastard.'

'I've not seen anyone. I've not seen him,' Ron said. He held eye contact, trying to show that he was telling the truth, but the man's eyes were hard, glassy.

Ron caught another waft of his sweat, the body odour thick and musky.

He didn't want this nutter anywhere near the horses, but if Ron misjudged how to handle things and he was killed, who would look after them? And he didn't want to die.

Big man for a poofter, aren't you? Lance tortured him. *Big man with no balls.*

Ron was back there. Smoke dense and tarry, the vicious roar of the blaze.

'Outside!' The man kicked Ron's shin, and waved the blade. He moved behind him.

Ron opened the front door.

The smell of wet grass, pure air and damp stone was so sweet it made him dizzy.

The man had his hand on Ron's shoulder again. The knife poised by Ron's kidneys.

Ron blinked. *This was insane.*

Was the man disturbed? Clinically? Deranged? Was he chasing an imaginary quarry?

'Why?' Ron said.

'Shut it.'

'No, really,' Ron said, fighting to keep his voice calm and friendly. 'Why do you think this Dylan is here?'

'I don't *think* he's here. I know.'

'Yes, but how?' Ron said.

'Because I'm tracking him. Hunting him down.' The man waved the machete.

Oh, Jesus. Images of dismemberment and gore and blood lust shuttered through Ron's head.

'How can you track him?' Ron said. At least if he kept the man talking he wasn't using his weapon. He wasn't hurting Ron, or the animals.

'With his phone! I'm tracing his phone. Now – show me those sheds.' He pushed Ron.

Ron began to laugh. He couldn't help it. He tried to stop but it was uncontrollable. Gales of it, shaking through him, bringing tears to his eyes.

'What's so fucking funny?' the man shouted. He spun Ron round and pressed the blade under his chin, forcing Ron to raise his head.

Ron choked back his laughter, his cheeks aching. 'It's in the van,' Ron said, swallowing, his saliva thick and gluey.

'Dylan?' the man said.

'The phone. Just the phone.'

'Are you shitting me?' The man kept the machete under Ron's chin and pulled a phone from his jacket pocket. He thumbed it awake. Tapped on the screen.

In the pause Ron could hear Mungo's muffled barking. And the squawking of rooks from the conifers behind the stables. The fear descended again. His bowels turning to water.

Time stretched out. The man looked up at Ron, his red face screwed up with frustration and anger. 'If you're fucking messing—'

Then he heard it.

They both heard it. A tinny burst of sound from the camper van.

'It's in the glove compartment,' Ron said.

'And how the fuck did you get it?' the man said, apparently still furious with him.

'I found it on the side of the road, on the way into Leek.'

'What?' he scoffed. 'Just lying there?'

'Yes,' Ron said.

'Give me the keys.'

Would he take the van as well?

It's just a van.

'In the hall,' Ron said.

The man screamed and Ron leant back as far as he could without moving a step.

He marched Ron into the hall to get the keys.

'Unlock it. And get me that phone.'

The man stood close by while Ron opened the passenger door and fetched out the phone. He passed it to him.

The man entered a password and scrolled through some messages, shaking his head, an expression of disgust twisting his mouth. Then he put the phone into his pocket. He rolled back his shoulders and lowered the machete.

'Keys?' He held out his free hand.

Oh, Christ! Ron's heart climbed into his throat. Was this it? Would he kill him here where he stood?

Ron swallowed. He dropped the van keys into the man's open palm. There were tattoos braceleting his wrist, twisted thorns.

A drone filled Ron's ears, a buzzing, and his vision brightened, everything sharpened, saturated in colour even as the day was ending.

'Please,' he tried to speak. 'Please?' He coughed.

He could smell fire. He was frozen. *Coward.* A moment's hesitation was all it had taken. A millisecond when if he'd just moved, done his job . . .

The man raised the knife and brushed the blade along the length of Ron's thumb, parting the flesh in a bloody smile.

'You never seen me. I wasn't here. There was no phone,' he said. 'You got it?'

Ron gave a single, slow nod.

'You don't tell anyone. No police, nothing. I know where you live,' the man said, pointing the machete at the house. 'Remember that.'

Then he ran down the drive and turned right into the road at the bottom. After a moment Ron heard an engine start.

He let out a great shuddering cry and staggered backwards. Then slid downwards, gripping his bleeding thumb.

*

Scarlett wiped at her nose.

'Don't snivel,' he snapped. He was messing with their sat nav, zooming out, making the map smaller, muttering, 'Where the hell . . . Right . . . I can back up. There's another road I can take about a mile away.'

He hadn't even asked her if she was all right after they'd nearly plunged over the edge, and she'd hurt her shoulder and her ankle. He didn't care.

'I want to go home,' she said. Then she raised her voice. 'I want to go home. I want to go home to Nana's and I need to get changed.'

'You don't need to get changed.' He was cross, deep grooves between his eyebrows. 'Why do you need to get changed? Don't be stupid.'

For a moment she didn't want to tell him but then she thought if he took her somewhere to get changed she might be able to ask somebody for help. 'Because I . . . wet my pants.'

He swore again. 'What? What are you? A two-year-old?'

She didn't answer.

'Well, I haven't got any clothes for you,' he said.

'I've got my costume.' She pointed to her bag on the floor.

'What costume?'

She didn't want to tell him about the talent show. She didn't want to share anything with him. 'For a thing at school,' she said.

'Put that on then,' he said.

'I can't get changed in here,' she said. Not with him there.

'Of course you can.'

Her eyes stung. She shook her head.

'Fine,' he said. 'Don't bother then. Stay wet.'

He moved the gear stick.

'I want to go home,' Scarlett said again. 'I want Nana.'

'That's not going to happen,' he said. 'Nana's not there any more.'

There was a lurch inside her, like something falling. What did he mean, Nana's not there any more? Nana wouldn't leave her. Not in a million years. Not if she could help it. Unless it was like Mum . . .

'No!' she said, fighting back tears. What had he done? 'Where is she?'

'She's gone. Gone for good. You'd better get used to it,' he said.

'Is she dead?'

He nodded. 'Just me and you from now on. Like it always should have been.'

'No,' she shouted. 'No!' She kicked his seat as hard as she could with both feet, once, then again pounding fast as though she could trample through it and smash him to a pulp.

He whipped around and grabbed her face, his fingers and thumb gripping either side of her chin tightly.

'Shut it,' he said. 'You keep your trap shut and you do exactly what I say.' And he shoved her away, so she fell back in her seat. Her shoulder throbbed where the seatbelt had pulled on it.

Hot tears trickled down her cheeks but she clenched her teeth together really hard and made as little noise as possible.

He shuffled in his seat and crooked one arm over the back of the passenger head rest so he could watch the road behind and he began to drive the car backwards. The windscreen wipers were still going fast. The car made a whining noise as he steered it this way and that.

Scarlett turned her face away to stare out of her window. She didn't want to see his horrible, mean, stinking face. *Bastard.* Scarlett never swore but it was true: that was what he was. An evil, stinking bastard.

She had to get away. But while she was in the car, with the doors locked, she was completely trapped. And of course he'd be careful not to let her get out anywhere where she could run for help.

'Here we are,' he said, as they reached a junction where the road divided. He took the left-hand fork and fastened his seatbelt again.

Scarlett was quiet, thinking what she could do. If she pretended to give in, to be good, she might have more chance because then he wouldn't guard her so closely.

She wiped at her face until it was dry. After a while she said, 'Can we get something to eat?'

'We'll see.'

'Please,' she said. 'I've not had any tea.'

'I said I'll see. But only if you behave yourself and stop being so bloody stupid.'

'I will,' she said, making her voice sound small, like she was truly sorry.

She decided to try not to think of what he'd said about Nana. He could be lying anyway.

She should look out for a phone box – they might have them out here in the country. There was one near school but Scarlett had never used it. She wasn't sure how they worked but there must be instructions. Did you need coins? Could you call the police for free?

If she did manage to get away it would help the police to know where they'd been. Then they could go after him.

She would look out for any landmarks.

There was a farm, halfway up the hillside, a big house and two grey metal barns. A trampoline in the garden and a tractor in one of the fields with some sheep. Scarlett would have loved a trampoline but they didn't have enough room.

They passed a row of trees, all bent the same way by the wind.

And when they came round the next hill she could see a really long rocky cliff out of the front window.

She could remember them all. The farm with the trampoline and the crooked trees and the long cliff. She'd remember everything. It would be harder when it got dark, and it looked like it would be dark soon, but she must do her best. That was what Nana always said. Do your best, and keep your wits about you.

And she would.

She'd do it for Nana.

Chapter 7

Dylan put the hazard lights on. The Astra had come to a halt across the middle of the road after a corner. Anyone coming up behind him might not have time to brake. If he was inside it at the time he didn't rate his chances. Sitting duck.

Instead, he waited at the roadside, perched on the top of a wooden ladder that straddled the wall. For walkers and that. A plastic disc with a fat arrow showed it was a footpath.

There was no shelter and the rain was pelting at him, coming sideways.

You need an umbrella.

He shook his head, trying to dislodge the image of Petey. He doubled over, arms wrapped around his knees, head down and ears alert for any sound of traffic. He could be here all night, he thought. Should he start walking?

He caught the sound of a cry, bleating. *A sheep. Or a lamb or something.* It kept on. Dylan couldn't see it. He couldn't see any sheep. Maybe it was stuck somewhere. Or lost. Maybe it was just miserable and whingeing cos of the rain.

Someone had carved their initials into the big stone gatepost in the wall. Perhaps there'd been a gate once but they'd blocked it up since. *DW, 1960.* Sixty years ago. Dead now, probably.

U R dead.

His guts cramped.

The wind quietened and the rain slackened off. Turned to drizzle.

How long had he been there? Fifteen minutes? More?

You need a plan.

He got out a cig and lit it, shielding it as best as he could from the wet. Drew the smoke in deep and held it.

A plan.

OK. First off, you get petrol. So if no one stops in the next half-hour you start walking. Fill up the car and then head for . . . His mind wound through all the places he knew: Leeds, Bradford, Huddersfield, Halifax. All of them dangerous. All of them places where Lloyd would find him.

He needed to put more distance between him and the gang.

Málaga wasn't really an option. He knew that, deep down.

Cornwall? Or Scotland or Ireland? Or Wales. Wales might work. He didn't know a soul in Wales. Didn't think he'd ever been there.

With the money he'd taken he could find himself a room to rent, scope out the local scene, see if there might be an opening.

Where are you going to source a supply?

Maybe after finding out who was dealing, he could offer his services, explain how he could help. Not just as a foot-soldier but someone to expand the business. Run some new lines.

And why the fuck would they let an incomer like you in on the business?

He took another drag, the cigarette soggy already.

The drone of an engine brought him to his feet. The sound of a vehicle coming uphill. But even standing on top of the ladder he'd no view round the sharp corner.

The motor grew louder and Dylan stepped down the ladder, practising his lines.

What if it's Col?

The blood drained from his face. He should go over the wall, hide there until he could tell if it was safe to show his face.

He was halfway back up the ladder when the car rounded the bend, an SUV with dark windows. The driver slammed on his brakes. Squealing, the car fishtailed to a stop, just nudging the off-side rear lights of the Astra. It was a Land Rover, a Discovery.

Dylan jumped down to the ground.

The driver's window opened. An old bloke with a beard. Normal-looking. He didn't say anything, just stared at Dylan.

'Run out of petrol,' Dylan said. 'If you could give us a lift? I'm not sure where the nearest petrol station is. And we'd have to move my car a bit, out the road, like.'

The man hesitated. He looked pissed off, giving him the evils. Dylan expected him to start spinning excuses, how sorry he was, why he couldn't help. But he said nothing. Was the bloke ever going to answer? Didn't he speak English?

Dylan felt his cheeks grow hot.

Then the man's face changed. Like something new had occurred to him and he smiled and said, 'Sure.' He put his flashers on and climbed out of the car, zipping up his jacket. He bent over, examining his front bumper.

Oh, fuck. If he started on about insurance and exchanging details that'd mean a paper trail leading to Dylan. Perfect for the feds.

'Looks OK,' the man said.

'Great.' Dylan laughed but still felt sick.

'Put yours in neutral and take the handbrake off,' the man said. 'I'll push the back, you steer it through the driver's door.'

Dylan did as he said. It was an effort but together they managed to roll the car forward six feet or so and onto the narrow grass verge.

'That'll do,' the man shouted. 'We should be able to get past there.'

Dylan took his holdall out of the Astra and locked it.

'Sit in the front,' the man said, getting back into the Discovery.

'Thanks a lot,' Dylan said.

There was a kid in the back, a girl in a purple coat.

'I'm Mike and that's Victoria,' the man said.

'Dylan,' Dylan said, closing the door and putting the holdall at his feet. 'Thanks. I didn't know if there'd be anyone passing.' The rain had soaked through the bottom of his trousers and seeped in the cuffs of his hoodie.

Mike tapped at the sat nav, looking for services, and said, 'There's a petrol station four miles away. The right direction.'

'And we can stop and get some food,' Victoria piped up from the back.

'Well—'

'You promised,' Victoria said.

Mike pulled out and drove past the Astra.

'Yes, we can sort out something to eat. Won't be able to drive you back, though,' he said to Dylan.

'Cool. I can get a cab or something.'

The windscreen was steaming up and Mike switched on the fan.

He could tell they weren't best pleased having to stop. There was an awkward atmosphere in the car. The kid wasn't saying much, but he could feel her eyes on him. Was she sulking maybe? Some kids were just quiet. Shy, and stuff going on in their heads. Dylan had never been like that. Plenty of stuff in his head but he didn't want to be stuck in there with it.

'Will you just shut it for five minutes?' His mam. 'You're doin' my head in. Vince [or Kenny or whoever was there at the time] can't be doing with your wittering on.'

At school too. 'If you're talking, you're not listening. If you're not listening, you're not learning.' And, 'Dylan, outside in the corridor now.'

'But, Miss—'

'Now!'

Mike turned up the radio, tried a couple of stations, obviously not wanting to chat. Dylan was relieved: he could do without being questioned. Where are you going? Where do you live? How come you're out here? Easier not to have to make up a pack of lies and keep it all straight in his head.

Mike left it tuned to Ed Sheeran singing 'Perfect'. Sort of thing Dylan's mam liked.

Wales then, that's the plan.

He really needed a phone. He'd sort something out. If they didn't sell them at the services, which was doubtful, he'd have to find some town on the way west. Or a Tesco. Yeah, one of the big ones. They'd be open late. And they were everywhere. Just stop and ask someone and they'd tell him where the nearest was. *Food. Petrol. Collect the Astra. Find a Tesco. Head for Wales.*

Sorted.

*

Laura's police radio crackled into life, 'Lima, Oscar, three seven from Control. Over.'

'Go ahead, Control.'

'We have the vehicle, Land Rover Discovery, black, captured on the A515 travelling north at fifteen forty-seven hours, leaving at the Valebrook junction. Registration: Hotel, Golf, six, seven, Golf, November, Juliet.'

Yes! This was good. This was progress.

Laura translated, HG67 GNJ. 'Can you email me a visual?'

'Will do, Sarge.'

'Do we have a registered keeper?' Laura asked.

'Checking that now.'

Laura watched while a young man, wearing a yellow oilskin, walked a Dalmatian down the hill past Beatrice's, the dog stopping to mark every other gate and lamppost.

What was Gregory Martin doing heading north? If he'd wanted a quick getaway it would have made more sense to drive west towards

Derby and the M1.

Did this mean he wasn't planning to run? That he wasn't abducting Scarlett and taking her away?

What, then?

Laura's chest tightened as she thought of the alternatives. Murder. Or murder-suicide.

But why now? What had prompted him to break cover and seize his daughter six years after his flight?

'The vehicle is a hire car, Sarge, rented this morning in Portsmouth by a Mr Alan Martin. Date of birth twelfth of July 1944.'

'What?' *Wrong name. And thirty years too old.* 'Those details don't fit,' she said.

'Used his passport as identification.'

'Alan Martin?' Then it struck her. 'He's using his father's ID! That's why he hasn't triggered any alerts. Get the hire company to send me a copy of the document.' They would have taken a scan of the passport for their records. It would give Laura an idea of the disguise Gregory Martin had adopted. And they could circulate photographs for both Scarlett and her father. 'Keep me posted on any other sightings for the car and put out a BOLO.' Be on the lookout.

'For Derbyshire?'

'Nationally.'

Police forces were stretched to breaking point. Laura knew that not even the local constabulary would be able to divert patrols to assist in the search. But they would be able to report any sightings in the course of their work.

'I'm going to move on a public appeal now,' she said, logging off the call.

She mailed through all the material for the appeal and press release. Then sent word to the border guards for assistance: could they pinpoint the arrival in the country of Alan (a.k.a. Gregory) Martin? If they could work out which ferry he'd travelled on (she was assuming he had arrived by ferry since he'd picked up the car in Portsmouth), they could find out where he'd boarded. And establish whether he was known to the authorities there.

With that set in motion, Laura snatched a moment to update Beatrice.

Beatrice opened the door quickly, her face drawn with apprehension. 'What? Come in, come in.'

'I won't. I'm about to go. But we've identified the vehicle, and now we're trying to track their location. Gregory is using his father's identity.'

'Alan? But he's dead. He died in 2017,' Beatrice said.

Laura thought for a moment. 'Was Gregory staying with his parents at the time of Jeanette's death?'

'Yes.'

'I think he probably stole his father's passport then,' Laura said.

'Wouldn't it be cancelled?' Beatrice frowned. 'Once Alan had died?'

'It would be up to his executor to notify the Passport Office and return it. If his passport was already missing it could easily have been overlooked. What about Mrs Martin?'

'Gregory's mother? She's in a home. She had a series of strokes,' Beatrice said.

'And their house?' Laura asked, wondering if Gregory still had access to it.

'It was sold,' Beatrice said.

'Thanks. I need to go,' Laura said. 'There will be news bulletins on soon, so if there's anyone you want to tell, now would be a good time. The school has been informed.'

Beatrice nodded briskly.

'I'll be in touch,' Laura said, seeing the tremulous hope in the older woman's eyes and wishing she could promise more.

*

Ahmed had reached the high point of the top road but had not seen the Astra. He'd only passed half a dozen vehicles all told, and a couple of cyclists.

Maybe the suspect had taken the old road through Birchwell. It was not much more than a cart track, single lane in places. Much slower. Why go that way? Didn't they know the area? Or did they think it'd be easier to hide along there?

Ahmed's call sign came over the radio.

'Go ahead, Control.'

'We've just had word through from Royal Stoke University Hospital. The incident at Coopers Gate you attended, the person involved was pronounced dead on arrival.'

Is he still warm?

'Received, Control,' Ahmed said.

'Major incident team have been alerted. The coroner has been informed.'

'Received, thank you. Over,' Ahmed said.

'Out.' Control ended the call.

Poor bloke. Ahmed could smell the blood. The high, meaty reek of it. He could see why people turned vegetarian. Mind, he'd miss chicken.

There had been drugs on the premises so perhaps there'd been a falling-out over that. Or maybe it was a burglary, like Ahmed had first thought. The field was wide open.

He wondered if the victim had been knifed – it seemed likely with all that blood. Ahmed hadn't seen a wound on him but it'd been hard to see anything in that mess. Knifed or shot, Ahmed reckoned. But wouldn't there have been the smell of gunpowder if a weapon had been fired?

Ahmed had never attended a shooting, but he'd an idea that that would be the case. He'd dealt with plenty of stabbings, though, knife crime through the roof. The chief constable had started knife sweeps the previous year, trying to get the weapons off the street.

'The world's gone mad,' his mother had said, when she'd read about it in the local paper.

'What's new?' his father had said, without looking up from his sudoku.

'You're such a cynic,' she had scolded him. 'How does that make anything better?'

'It's a survival mechanism,' his dad had replied, filling a number in. 'Best I can do.'

'You need to be careful,' she'd said to Ahmed. 'You're a target out there. The thought of you being—'

'I am careful.' Ahmed didn't want to set her off. Have to argue again about why he was so dead set on this career. How he liked the fact that he was in the right. He was upholding the law, protecting people. And things were clear cut. An act was legal or illegal. Ahmed understood and welcomed that simplicity. That certainty. And he liked being on the side of good. He was proud of the authority, the power that came with it.

Now Ahmed hated the thought that the suspect might already have got away. He imagined reporting to the detectives on the major incident team that he'd failed to apprehend them.

'Perhaps it's not meant to happen,' one of his aunties had said, when Ahmed failed his driving test, the practical one, for the third time.

'I'll take it ten times if I have to,' Ahmed said.

'A dog with a bone,' his father said.

And Ahmed had kept trying. He was already determined to apply for the police and no way would they take someone who couldn't drive. Hardly the sort of job where you could take the bus from A to B, even if there was still a bus.

And he'd done it. Fifth time lucky.

'Persistence,' Ahmed's head of year had told him at the end of sixth form. 'You have that. You can apply yourself, motivate yourself. I'm confident that whatever field you go into you'll make a success of it.'

'Yes,' Ahmed said out loud now, watching the black clouds gather over the fells. This was a suspected murder and he had a job to do. Several hours left on shift, and unless something even more urgent came in he'd keep searching for the person who'd killed the man from Coopers Close.

Chapter 8

Dylan, the boy they'd picked up, had pulled his hood back and he had hair that was bleached on top and dark underneath. It wasn't stripy but it made Scarlett think of badgers and skunks and lemurs. Lemurs were the world's most endangered primates. There was one called the Madame Berthe's mouse lemur, which Scarlett thought was a brilliant name for such a tiny animal, the smallest primate of all.

Dylan was staring out of the window, not saying anything. He hadn't paid any attention to Scarlett. *Victoria? Victoria and Mike?* Made-up names to hide who they really were.

If only she could tell Dylan the truth then he could get help when they got to the services. But how could she do that? She couldn't do anything in front of 'Mike'.

He wanted to be Mike? Fine, she'd call him Mike because no way was she going to think of him as her dad. After what he did to her mum, to Nana? Now to her.

A shiver ran up the back of her neck as the idea came to her.

She leant down to get her bag, lifted it onto her knee.

'What are you doing?' 'Mike' said.

'Homework,' Scarlett said.

'What homework?'

Did it matter? Was there a right answer and a wrong one?

'Maths,' Scarlett said. Her maths book was in her bag.

'Don't get car sick,' he said.

Her stomach dropped. *Him lifting her out of the car. She was crying. Sick all down her front. The horrible taste of it, the smell of it, the way it burnt her nose and her throat. Her mum saying, 'It'll be all right. We'll soon clean you up.'*

Scarlett hated that he had been there, that he'd been part of that. Being all kind and gentle. She hated that she had felt safe in his arms. She hated that she loved him. That she was part of him too. Half of her came from him. He was inside her, in her blood and her brain and her DNA.

Her voice wobbled as she said, 'I won't. I'm fine.'

She pulled out the maths book with her worksheet in it and took a pencil from her case. She had a Pantalaimon pencil case, from *His Dark Materials*. It was a shame it was polyester, which is a sort of plastic, but Nana, who'd given it to her, had said, 'It's not single-use, Scarlett. We can't change everything all at once. We just do what we can.'

Oh, Nana.

Scarlett bent over her work so if Mike looked back it would be hard for him to see what she was doing. She looked at the sum at the top of the page and filled in the numbers. Then she folded the bottom edge of the worksheet over and flattened it with her thumb. She ran over the crease again with her nail. She wrote across it, *I am Scarlett Martin. I've been kidnapped. Call the police 999. Please help me.*

She worried that Mike might hear the sound when she tore the strip off even though it was pretty noisy with Smokey Robinson on the radio singing 'Tracks Of My Tears' (Nana loved his songs) and the hissing sound of the car on the wet road and the growling of the engine, so she sucked her finger and wiped spit along the edge to soften the paper. A bit at a time she pulled the strip away.

Scarlett folded it in half. Now she needed a chance to put it in Dylan's pocket.

Glancing outside, she remembered to keep counting landmarks.

There was a pylon in a field with wires leading to another one further away. Trampoline farm, trees, big cliff, pylon.

Scarlett filled in the next sum.

On the radio the presenter said, 'The time is now five o'clock and we go over to Miriam Foster for all your latest news.'

Mike snapped off the radio. 'More of the same,' he said. 'Nearly there, anyway.'

Scarlett put her things away and tucked the note into her coat pocket.

She felt a bit like she did in the moments before a show or a race. Nerves building and everything narrowing down to the moment when she was waiting for the whistle to blow, or the music to start. Ready to run.

*

Ron knew he should move. Stop feeling sorry for himself, get off his arse, go inside and see to his thumb.

He was shaking with the adrenalin. As he stood up he became lightheaded, and half expected to faint, but the giddiness ebbed away, though he was still unsteady on his feet as he walked into the house.

He held his left hand above his shoulder, first-aid training kicking in. *Elevate the wound.*

When he opened the kitchen door, his other hand sticky with blood, Mungo came barrelling out. Ron let him go. He'd be OK outside. He'd been trained not to leave the grounds on his own.

Ron wrapped a tea-towel around his hand to absorb the blood, pressing it against the cut with the palm of his good hand. He needed to stem the flow, and get it to clot, before examining the damage.

He hooked a foot under the nearest chair to drag it out and sat down. The tide of pain was coming in waves. It had felt numb after the initial lancing slice of agony when the man had carved his hand open, but now the throbbing rolled in.

His throat was parched. Standing, he pressed his hand to his chest and used the other hand to pour a glass of water. He drank it down, ignoring a twinge in one of his back teeth sensitive to the cold.

Mungo padded back into the house. The dog stood on the threshold of the kitchen.

'It's all right, boy. He's gone,' Ron said, sitting down.

Mungo gave him a baleful look and shifted his weight on his feet. He was ashamed, Ron realised, or embarrassed, because he hadn't defended his territory.

You and me both, he thought.

'Come on,' he said. 'It's all right. Good dog.'

Mungo walked forward past Ron to the rug in front of the French windows. The sun poured in through those on fine days, and Mungo liked to bask in it.

The dog circled three times then lay down, his head resting on his front paws.

He still seemed bashful. He'd be able to smell the blood, no doubt. And sense the trauma in the air.

'Good dog,' Ron said again, but the animal looked sceptical.

A red blotch appeared through the tea-towel, growing slowly.

Ron waited, letting his thoughts wander, not settling on anything in particular. When images from the violent encounter intruded he ignored them as best he could, treating them with detached indifference. As though it had all happened to somebody else. But he could feel the tremor of shock in his pulse. He might have to face them at some point, but now wasn't the time.

The stain on the tea-towel seemed to have stopped spreading. Gingerly he unwound the cloth. The wound was deep, the flesh parted to reveal a seam of white bone at the bottom.

It would probably need stitches. But he had no van keys, and couldn't drive one-handed in any case. To get to A and E he'd have to call a cab. And this wasn't really an emergency. Not now the blood had stopped.

A few years back, places had had minor injuries clinics, walk-in centres where people could be treated by a nurse practitioner. The ones in Brum had closed as the NHS was forced to stretch resources ever thinner. He doubted there'd be anything like that near here, and certainly not open on an evening.

He looked again at the wound. Perhaps he could patch it up. He rinsed his good hand at the sink. In the cupboard there was a first-aid box, which the Graybridges kept well stocked. He picked out a sterile dressing, which would fit if he cut it in half, and a box of steri-strips.

He boiled the kettle and made up a salt solution in a measuring jug. While it was cooling he halved the dressing. Clumsily, but that didn't matter. When the saline solution was cool enough to touch he poured it over the wound, setting his teeth against the stinging pain.

He patted his hand dry with a clean tea-towel then set about sticking a line of strips across the length of the cut. It was hard to pull the edges of the wound together at the same time as applying the strips one-handed and he found himself using his teeth to grip the very edge of each strip and press it into place until he had closed the gap in several areas. Then it grew easier.

Mungo gave a snore. His back legs scrabbled. A dream, perhaps.

Ron put on the dressing and used microtape to stick down the raw edge.

There were paracetamol tablets in the kit and he took two to help with the pain, and drank more water. He considered putting the bloody towel in cold water to soak but it was saturated. He was sure the Graybridges wouldn't begrudge him ruining a tea-towel so he binned it.

He needed to clean his neck too. In the bathroom mirror he could see it was only a nick, the rusty streaks of blood down his windpipe had dried. The collar of his T-shirt was stained.

He was exhausted.

He had some cold beers in the fridge. He fetched a bottle and flipped the top off with his good thumb. A trick that Josh had teased him about when they'd first hooked up. 'Ooh, that's heavy duty. Very macho. Can you light matches on your boots too?'

'Never play with matches. Don't smoke,' Ron said.

'What do you do, then?' Josh had asked later. Prone in Ron's bed after they'd slept together.

'Whatever you like,' Ron had replied, grinning.

'Not a comedian, obviously?' Josh quipped.

'Firefighter.' He watched Josh's mouth open in surprise, the gleam in his eyes as he tried to work out whether Ron was telling the truth.

'Seriously?' Josh raised himself onto his elbows, face alight.

'Green Watch,' Ron said.

'Oh, man.' Josh laughed. Then he had frowned, tilted his head to one side and said, 'But isn't that hard?'

'Depends on the fire,' Ron said.

Josh had nudged him. 'You know what I mean. For people like us. And women. And anyone who's not white.'

'It can be . . . challenging,' Ron said. Trailing his fingers down Josh's chest, smooth, virtually hairless, unlike his own. 'And you?' He was eager to change the subject. 'What do you do?'

'Systems analyst,' Josh said.

Ron laughed. 'I have absolutely no idea what that means.'

'You're not alone there,' Josh said. 'Should I go?'

'Do you have somewhere to be?' Ron asked.

Josh had shaken his head, a smile playing around his mouth.

'You could stay?' Ron said, still stroking Josh's chest, and Josh put his hand over Ron's and held it.

God, he missed him. Even after all this time. Those early days, Ron not believing his luck that a man this funny and clever, fearless and kind, because he was kind, and young and beautiful, had chosen Ron. He'd had all that and—

Oh, pack it in.

He swallowed some beer.

He shouldn't do this. He shouldn't dwell on the past. He'd thrown it all away, hadn't he, with his fucking craven cowardice?

Maybe he should eat, heat up the remains of his—

Ron stared at the plate, licked clean. *Oh, for Christ's sake.* He turned to stare at Mungo. 'Bad dog.' Ron pointed to the plate.

Mungo opened his eyes, gave a sigh and buried his nose under his leg.

I know where you live. The man with his red face, in his stupid shoes. The knife at Ron's throat, the smell of him. Aggression and hostility. The scrote, the little thug. *You don't tell anyone. I know where you live.*

'Fuck that,' Ron said aloud, and Mungo's head flew up.

Fuck that.

Ron got out his phone.

*

If Gregory Martin had driven Scarlett up into the peaks, where there were few traffic cameras, it would be hard to keep tabs on him. Some of the pubs and shops in the villages would have CCTV but that was a long shot.

With the area so sparsely populated and few vehicles on the road, there was less likelihood that members of the public would see the car and respond to appeals for help. The timing was in his favour too. The end of the afternoon, foul weather and a storm coming in. Dark clouds already cobbled the sky. Had Martin accounted for any of that? Was the whole thing carefully planned out?

She really didn't like the thought of Martin alone with Scarlett in the wilds.

Might he be heading to a particular location? Somewhere that had some significance for him?

When she reached the traffic lights where the Discovery had last been captured she took the road up to the tops, following in Martin's tracks. And she rang Beatrice.

'Just a question, was there anywhere in the peaks that Jeanette and Gregory used to visit, any special places?'

'No. Well, they did visit. But just like anyone else, here and there. Beauty spots.'

'Can you remember any of the places they went?'

Beatrice exhaled. 'Erm . . . the Blue John mines.' Up in the Dark Peak. 'The plague village at Eyam. A well-dressing, but I can't remember which one. Heights of Abraham and Monsal Head.' Here in the White Peak. 'Oh, and Gregory used to cycle out there.'

'Racing?' Laura said.

'No, mountain biking. He went most weekends.'

'Any regular routes?' Laura said.

'I can't . . . I think there was one near Hathersage but I'm not sure.' Again in the Dark Peak.

The two areas owed their names to the geology. The Dark Peak was the high gritstone plateau in the north, moorland covered with heather and peat bogs, often bleak. The White Peak was a lower plateau of limestone. The landscape was brighter, riven with gorges, caves and valleys.

Laura and Hector had had one of their first dates visiting Monsal Head, planning a walk and a drink after. High summer and the place was crowded. Too crowded. Families and bikers and even a coach-load of Chinese, or maybe Japanese, tourists. Laura, knowing the area well, suggested they drive over to the Manifold Valley, off the beaten track.

It had been much quieter there, at least until a bee had flown into Hector's face and he'd gone into a complete panic, batting at his nose and screaming in Spanish. He wasn't even allergic. He claimed bees were the only thing he was scared of.

'Try doing my job,' Laura had said. 'You really do find out what's scary.' The brutal things people do to each other in the name of love or hate or a mix of the two. The savagery that human beings are capable of when cornered, or desperate, when they're drunk on vengeance, or delusional with jealousy, or ravenous with naked greed.

And Gregory Martin, what was he planning to do? Abduct his daughter and start a new life somewhere together? Or something much darker?

Chapter 9

Scarlett's heart sank when she saw how tiny the services were. There was a petrol station with just three pumps and a shop where you paid behind, and then a car park in front of the café. The café was a small building, like a Greggs or a Costa.

There were a couple of cars and a white caravan in the car park.

Mike parked in the corner place next to the caravan. 'Lunar Quasar' it said on the back. Quasar was some sort of space thing, Scarlett thought. Maybe a black hole. Why would you want to have a holiday in something called after a black hole?

'Thanks,' Dylan said, bending forward to pick up his holdall.

Don't leave me.

Scarlett snapped open her seatbelt. 'Are you getting something to eat too, Dylan?' She smiled when he glanced back at her. *Please?*

'Well, I . . .'

'He should, shouldn't he, Dad?' Calling him that, Scarlett felt weird. Guilty. Like she'd given in to him. Just pretending, she told herself. You don't have to mean it.

'Of course, come on,' Mike said. 'Might as well.' Scarlett was surprised to hear him so positive about it. There must be some reason he thought it was a good idea. But she couldn't work out what it was.

Dylan climbed out of the passenger door.

Scarlett picked up her backpack and tried to open the door. It was stuck.

'It's still locked,' Scarlett said.

'Ah!' Mike said. 'Safety first. Don't want you running off anywhere. Don't want to lose you.'

Like she was a four-year-old. But he was staring at her in the mirror again. A sharp edge in his voice. Did Dylan hear that from outside?

'You could get killed.' Warning her. He smiled again. Teeth all white and even.

'I know,' Scarlett said, cold inside.

He released the child lock and she opened the door, hoping her coat would hide most of the wet on her trousers.

Her fingers curled around the note in her pocket. *It's on the wrong side!* Dylan was round the far side of the car. Left of her. She pretended to tie her laces so she could swap the paper to her left hand.

Dylan had put his hood up and was waiting for them, looking awkward.

'Come on then.' Mike locked the car.

Do it now.

She felt scared, dizzy, and her stomach was churning, her heart bumping in her chest. *Do it!*

Scarlett skipped round towards Dylan. A puddle on the ground gave her an excuse to do a running jump: she acted like she'd lost her balance and bumped into him, her hand dipping into his coat pocket and dropping the note there.

'Whoa!' Dylan reared back, arms going up.

'Calm down,' Mike shouted. He caught up to Scarlett and grabbed her wrist. 'Settle down or get back in the car.'

Scarlett's cheeks flamed. 'Sorry,' she said. 'I slipped.'

Dylan was looking at them like he wasn't sure what was going on.

Scarlett said, 'I'm so hungry.' And started walking to the café and they both did too.

The place smelt of fresh coffee and something sweet, like cake or biscuits. There were only five tables and four were empty. A couple sat at the front at one side of the entrance door. They wore waterproof coats and hiking boots. Had they been walking? Why would anyone go walking on a day like this? Scarlett wondered.

The menu was behind the counter on a big chalkboard. The woman who was serving had lots of piercings and messy blue hair.

Dylan, who was first in line, ordered chilli con carne with chips.

'What are you having?' Mike asked Scarlett. 'Sausage and chips?'

She shook her head.

'Burger?'

'I'm vegan,' she said.

A flicker of annoyance crossed his face. 'Since wh—' He stopped. He glared at her, like she'd made it up to be awkward. But no one was looking.

She could hardly breathe as she waited for Dylan to find the note. But when he went to pay he took a ten-pound note from his other pocket and used that.

Scarlett scanned the list. 'Beans and chips,' she said. They had hot chocolate. That made her think of Nana.

Gone for good. Scarlett bit her lip.

Dylan took his drink and cutlery on a tray to the table at the very back.

'Have you got any plant milk?' Scarlett asked the server. Did her voice sound wobbly?

'Sorry, we had some soya but we've run out.'

Scarlett chose lemonade instead.

Mike ordered Scarlett's meal and asked for a burger and chips and coffee for himself.

'Lousy weather,' the server said. 'And they reckon it'll be really bad tonight.'

'It's global warming,' Scarlett said.

She felt him stiffen, like she wasn't even supposed to talk to anyone.

The server laughed and said, 'You're right there. You been on any of the school strikes?'

'Yes,' Scarlett said.

'Victoria,' he jumped in. 'Go and sit with your brother.'

Brother?

Then it clicked. Dylan was like a disguise for them. If anyone knew Scarlett was missing, if the police had been told, they'd be looking for a man and a girl. Not a dad with two children.

Dylan had picked the far side of the table facing the front windows and the car park.

Scarlett sat opposite him.

'I'll just nip to the shop,' Dylan said, nodding to the petrol station. He got up. He took his holdall and went back out.

Mike brought their drinks over.

'I'll go and get changed,' Scarlett said. The Ladies was visible directly opposite them at the back of the building.

'Hurry up,' he said. 'The food'll be here soon.' He was sitting facing the toilets and he'd be able to see her going in and coming out. 'And don't be messing about,' he said.

'I won't,' she said.

Scarlett took her bag with her. The men's toilet was further along the corridor and at the end was an exit. Could she run? Run out that way?

She glanced back. He was watching.

Scarlett locked the door and used the toilet. She untied and kicked off her shoes then peeled off her school trousers, her underwear and her jumper.

She kept trying to think of a way to escape, like going and asking the server for help, or refusing to come out of the toilet, or running to the petrol-station shop and telling whoever was there to call the police, but so much could go wrong with any of those ideas.

She patted her legs dry with paper towels, then pulled on her costume. Thick red stretchy leggings that she tucked her T-shirt into, and a red polo-neck sweater.

Scarlett imagined Faye worrying about her. Had Faye heard Scarlett was missing? And the show. Faye couldn't do their dance on her own. It was all ruined. He'd ruined it all. He ruined everything. He'd ruined her whole life. And now Nana . . .

Her eyes burnt and she rubbed at her nose. She looked in the mirror, a scared little girl looking back. That's all she was. Eyes full of fear. How could a kid like her get away from him? There was no way she could—

Stop it! She banged at her ears. But that hurt and tears sprang in her eyes.

Stop it. You can do this.

She had to be calm and clever.

She thought of the contestants who cried on *Strictly*, who messed up or found it all too hard. But they always tried again, didn't they? Unless they were voted off before they had a chance. And even if they were still rubbish when they had another go, people respected them because they had tried. They did their best. They didn't give up. That mattered more than winning.

Scarlett put her shoes back on and laced them up. She washed her hands and her face.

She began putting her uniform away, then froze. *Yes!*

Her heart pattered fast. She bundled up her uniform and stuffed it into the basket for used paper towels. Someone was bound to see it there. It was a clue. Like leaving a trail. As long as they didn't just throw it away. What if she left a note as well?

As she pulled out her pencil case there was pounding on the door that made her jump. 'Victoria, come on, food's up.'

'Coming,' she shouted.

She put away her pencil case and pulled on her coat.

She hoped he wouldn't notice her bag was half empty now.

He walked with her, back to the table, guarding her.

No! Dylan had taken his coat off and put it over the back of his chair. There was a carrier bag on the chair next to him. Had he found her note? She screamed at him to look in the pocket. But what if he did, and read it in front of Mike?

Scarlett swallowed and sat down.

She could smell Mike's burger and Dylan's chilli. It was like no one had ever told them beef farming caused a big part of emissions. *Avoid blaming and shaming.* That was one of the principles for Extinction Rebellion, but it was hard sometimes, especially when people were older and you'd think they'd know better.

Scarlett's mouth watered and she felt a burp in her throat. *Don't be sick. Don't be sick. Don't be sick.*

Beside her, Mike was smearing mustard on his burger.

Dylan speared a forkful of chips. He didn't look at Scarlett or Mike. He just stared out between them to the car park.

She took a sip of lemonade. Her hand was shaking but she told herself to act like she hadn't noticed. She had another sip, then put down the glass and picked up her knife and fork. Calm and clever.

*

Dylan had stocked up on a few bits from the shop on the forecourt. They hadn't got loads of choice in the snacks line but he found Pringles as well as sweet chilli nuts.

They never used to get Pringles when he lived with his mam. 'Not paying that much,' she'd say. And he'd have to make do with own-brand crisps or tortilla chips. He picked up a can of Pepsi and at the counter he asked for a couple of packs of smokes and a lighter. His was running low.

The lad on the till had his eyes on the TV, rolling news all about floods and whether the prime minister would visit or not.

They had plastic petrol containers and there was a payphone in the corner. So Dylan'd be able to buy some petrol and call a cab to take him back to the car. No point in walking, getting soaked through again. He was still drying out from before.

He smoked the last of his damp fags in a place round the back of the café where they kept the bins. A canopy shielded him from the drizzle. This was an unofficial smoking area, going by the number of tab ends all over the ground. Somewhere to hide for a quick toke.

Back in the café the server brought their food over. Mike went to get Victoria from the toilets.

The only other customers left, calling out thanks and goodbye to the server.

When Victoria sat down she kept looking at Dylan, as if he'd got something stuck on his face. It gave him the creeps. He tried to avoid her gaze, which was hard going cos she was right opposite him.

Out of the window Dylan saw the couple drive off towards the mini roundabout. Then a delivery van came along the access road and turned left into the petrol station.

Behind it a squad car.

Fuck!

The food clogged in his mouth and his heart skidded about in his chest. Panic rose through him like a blowtorch.

He set down his fork.

Don't freak.

He picked up his holdall.

He didn't watch to see what the feds were doing, he didn't want to draw attention to them. Or to himself. He just needed to disappear.

Mike looked up as Dylan got out of his chair.

'Won't be long,' Dylan said, without making eye contact.

Forcing himself to move at a normal pace, he turned, walked to the Gents, out of the exit at the end of the corridor and round to the bins. Out of sight of the rest of the services.

His pulse was thudding hard and he was sweating.

Maybe they're just getting petrol, he told himself.

Or maybe they're buying a coffee, or vape liquid. Or fucking flowers.

The trouble was he couldn't see anything from his hiding place.

It's just a coincidence. Bound to be.

Still, a feeling of dread smothered him.

He edged along the side past the bins until he reached the front corner of the building. Carefully he peered round.

The squad car was still there. No one inside. But there was a figure in the shop, in uniform.

He heard a car pass on the road beyond the rise.

He looked about. Stone walls surrounded the service area and behind them it just looked like lumpy fields. Patches of black earth, molehills. Should he go over one of the walls and hide there? *You wouldn't be able to see anything at all then.*

His mind stalled. He was stuck and he couldn't see a way out.

If you stay here, quiet and hidden, then perhaps the feds won't find you. But the lad in the shop has seen you, hasn't he? It's only a matter of time before he tells the feds and they come looking.

Dylan could barely breathe.

All he could think was that they were here, and they were coming for him.

*

Scarlett cut a triangle from the edge of her toast and scooped some beans onto it. She blew on them so she wouldn't burn her mouth.

Mike swivelled round in his chair, craning back like he was checking something. He turned back to Scarlett. He looked weird, his eyes all wild, darting from side to side, and his mouth angry again.

She hadn't even done anything. Had he guessed about her school uniform? Had Dylan found her note and shown it to him while Scarlett was getting changed?

He pulled the car keys out of his pocket and said, quietly and quickly, 'Go and wait in the car.'

'But I only—' Scarlett looked at her plate.

'Now,' he hissed. 'Get in the car now and wait for me. Don't do anything stupid.' He grabbed her wrist, squeezing it really hard. His face had gone pale and he sounded like he was out of breath. 'Don't make me punish you. You understand me?'

'Yes,' Scarlett said. Her blood ran cold.

He squeezed harder and she couldn't help but make a noise in the back of her throat.

'Do as I say. I don't want to punish you, Scarlett, but if you disobey me . . .'

'I know,' she said.

He let her wrist loose. 'Go now. Don't stop. Don't talk to anyone. Just get in the car.'

What was he going to do? Why was he sending her on her own?

She took the car keys and her backpack and went out of the front to the car park.

A police car! At the far side of the petrol station. *That's why!*

There was no one in it. Could she go and hide behind the police car? Wait for them to come back and ask them for help? Or run to the shop and ask the person in there if they knew where the police were, if she could stay with them until the police came back to their car?

Don't make me punish you.

He'd be watching, she knew he would, so she walked towards their car, a rushing sound in her ears, legs unsteady, and pointed the fob at the car and pressed the release. The lights winked and it beeped. He would think she was doing as she was told, but now she could run to the police car, or the shop.

And if he comes out now?

I'll run, I'm fast.

Was he fast too? Did she get that from him? She hated that thought.

There was a blur of movement and someone snatched at her hand.

Dylan?

Dylan grabbed the keys off her, ran round to the driver's side and jumped in.

'No!' Scarlett shouted. *Don't leave me!*

She raced to the car, threw open the passenger door and clambered in as he turned on the engine.

'Get out,' Dylan yelled. 'Fuck off.'

'No!' *Take me with you.*

'Get the fuck out. You can't stop me,' Dylan said. The car began to move.

'I don't want to stop you. I want to come with you,' Scarlett said.

'Fuck off out of it.'

'No!'

He didn't even put his seatbelt on, just reversed the car, turned round and drove away.

Scarlett was flung to one side as he swung round the roundabout. She tugged at her seatbelt to get it fastened.

There was a feeling like a balloon swelling in her chest and she laughed. She'd escaped! She laughed out loud.

She'd escaped! It was all going to be OK again. It was all going to be OK.

Chapter 10

Ahmed had spoken to the staff in the petrol station and the café and neither of them recalled seeing a silver Astra.

'It's been really dead,' the café server said. 'The weather, I guess.' She'd got that many bits of metal in her face she was probably magnetic.

Ahmed had discussed with the petrol-station lad about CCTV coverage just in case there were any cameras rigged up to catch passing traffic on the road itself. That might show him if the Astra had passed here, but the lad told him how they'd only the two cameras, which covered the forecourt and the shop.

'What have they done?' the server asked him.

Ahmed tried to imagine how she'd react if he said, 'Suspected murder,' but that would be totally unprofessional. Instead he went with the standard response: 'Just want to talk to them about an incident earlier.'

'An incident?' Her eyes shone.

'That's right,' Ahmed said, poker-faced. It might give her a bit of a kick, some excitement in her day, but this was someone's life after all. And not to be joked about or gossiped over.

'Do you want a brew?' she said.

Ahmed was tempted to sit down and have a decent break but he took one to go instead and insisted on paying for it. No one was ever going to hang him out to dry for accepting gifts and favours from the public.

The van driver he'd followed into the services came into the café. Just on the off-chance Ahmed asked if he'd seen a Vauxhall Astra on his travels.

'Couldn't tell you. Didn't notice one but, then, not like I was looking, you know?'

As Ahmed was leaving the café, he found an old grey-haired man in the car park turning frantically this way and that. Bizarre. Like some sort of slapstick.

Was he disturbed? Mental-health issues, perhaps? There was a lot of that in the job, talking people down, trying to work out if they were at risk of harm to themselves or to others. Whether to call an ambulance to deal with them.

Then there were the other people who had dementia and liked to wander. They tended to be older. The way this man was looking about, as if he was lost or confused, could be that.

As Ahmed drew closer the man saw him and stopped moving. Stood stock still. He wasn't really old, more middle-aged. Probably younger than Ahmed's dad, who was fifty-eight.

'All right?' Ahmed said.

The man broke into a smile, a huge dazzling smile. 'Yes. Yes, good,' he said.

Ahmed waited. Sometimes if you just shut up and waited, people would explain what was going on.

'So . . .' the man said, pointing at the café, '. . . I'm meeting a friend.' He nodded and smiled. He kept smiling.

Ahmed wondered how the man had got here. No vehicle and he wasn't dressed for cycling or hill-walking. He could perhaps have got a lift, been dropped off on the main road and walked here.

Was he OK? Some people were good at hiding their symptoms, at least for a short period. He remembered dealing with a woman who had been acting oddly in the centre of Leek last summer. Running up and down the steps of the Monument, slapping the walls, then lying on the floor and shouting. When Ahmed had got to her they'd sat on one of the benches round the base and had a perfectly normal conversation. She'd apologised for causing any bother, 'I'm sorry, mi duck, I really am,' and said she'd been feeling a bit odd but she was fine now.

They'd had a chat about what she'd do with the rest of the day and she said she'd go home and do a spot of gardening and, yes, she had money for the bus, and then, as Ahmed turned to go, she bolted. She would've dashed into traffic if he hadn't managed to grab her.

'It's not me,' she'd said, while they waited for the ambulance. 'It's Beelzebub. He just won't leave me alone.'

And this guy now? There was no law against waiting in a car park, in the rain.

'So . . .,' the man said again '. . . I'll . . .' And he gestured to the café as if he was waiting for Ahmed to give him his blessing or something.

Ahmed's radio came on. 'Alpha, Alpha, eight five. This is Control. Over.'

'Go ahead, Control. Over.' Ahmed automatically moved away from the man for privacy and walked towards his car on the forecourt.

'We have a report of an aggravated assault, wounding with a bladed weapon and forced entry to a residential property. Suspect has fled the scene. Over.'

Ahmed felt the muscles across his shoulders tighten. 'Give me the location, Control. Over,' said Ahmed.

'Graybridge, on the old road. Over.'

Ahmed had been expecting somewhere in one of the towns but this was out in the sticks.

Control gave him the GPS location. 'Caller at the property says the road is impassable on the southern approach. Flooded. Over.'

'Paramedics? Over,' Ahmed said, opening his car door. The guy with the beard disappeared inside the café.

'Says they're not needed. Over,' Control said.

'Copy that. On my way. Over and out.'

Ahmed couldn't ignore the call, not something as serious as assault with a knife.

It never rains but it pours, his grandma used to say. But at the moment every day seemed to be a rainy day. In every sense of the word. The wettest February on record.

He put his coffee into the cup-holder. It was too hot to drink yet. He thought he knew the way to Graybridge, would be certain of it if he could have reached it from the south, but he was less familiar with the other route so he entered the coordinates in the sat nav.

Ahmed thought of the victim at Coopers Close, all the blood – and how that might have been a knife attack. And now another on the same day – not many miles away. Not as serious by the sound of it but still . . . Could there be a connection? Was someone roaming around attacking people indiscriminately? A serial offender? His stomach lurched at the thought.

He rolled back his shoulders, put his hat on the passenger seat and launched the sat nav. Keen to get there as soon as he could and find out what the story was.

*

The call was patched through to Laura as a priority. A handwritten note had been found at a service station near the village of Longnor. Believed to have been left there by Scarlett Martin.

The jolt of adrenalin, of anticipation, cut through her fatigue. A buzz reminiscent of the high she used to get from taking cocaine, which she'd done a few times as a teenager. The artificial energy, like a sugar rush, that had left her feeling wretched and shaken the following day.

'Tell them not to handle it any more than is necessary,' Laura said. 'If they have disposable gloves, use them to put it in a clean paper bag or a plastic one. And don't disturb anything else. Ask them to close the café and for any staff and customers to remain there until I arrive. I'll be about twenty minutes.'

She wanted to be quicker, to get there sooner, but she'd be no good to anyone if she had an accident driving too fast in atrocious conditions.

When Laura arrived at the services the place looked deserted apart from the lights glowing inside the café.

She parked as close as she could to the building and took the precaution of pulling on her coat and putting up the hood to shield her from the rain beating down as she ran to the entrance.

The sign on the door read *CLOSED* and when Laura pushed at it she found it was locked.

She knocked on the glass until a young woman appeared. Chubby, blue-haired, with a number of facial piercings. 'Closed,' the woman mouthed, pointing to the sign.

Laura rolled her eyes, fished out her warrant card and held it up against the glass. They were probably expecting someone in uniform, a patrol car with blue flashing lights and siren.

The woman gave a thumbs-up and unlocked the door to let her in. 'Sorry,' she said.

'No worries. DS O'Neil, Laura.'

'Right. Jules.'

'Have you got the note?'

'Yes.' Jules gestured to the seating area. 'You want to?'

'Yes, sure.' Laura shed her coat and took a seat.

Jules brought over a paper bag, the note visible through a clear cellophane panel. 'We use them for takeaways,' she explained. 'But it is clean.'

I am Scarlett Martin. I've been kidnapped. Call the police 999. Please help me. The writing was legible, childlike.

Laura swallowed. 'Where was it?'

'In that coat.' Jules pointed to a table at the back of the room.

A black coat, not dissimilar to Laura's, was draped over one of the chairs at the far side.

'It was in the pocket. I thought they'd forgotten the coat and I looked in the pockets because I wondered if there was any ID or anything to say whose it was,' Jules said.

Odd to forget a coat in this weather.

'When I found it, I didn't know what to do so I spoke to Barney. He works in the shop.' She waved in the direction of the petrol station. 'And he told me about the news. About the kidnapping. He'd just seen it on the telly. He thought I was messing at first. Then I rang the police.'

'Who was sitting over there?' Laura asked.

'There were three of them,' Jules said.

Three?

'The little girl and her father and—'

'Hang on.' Laura woke her phone and showed Jules the two photographs from the press release. 'Is that them?'

'Yes, definitely,' Jules said.

'Who else was with them?'

'This teenager. I thought it was a dad and two kids, and that's how they acted. He, the dad, said, "Go and sit with your brother" when they were at the counter ordering.'

Scarlett Martin is an only child.

Martin had an accomplice. Laura hadn't expected that. But she was heartened by the thought that Martin had at least stopped there, presumably to get Scarlett some sustenance.

'Can you describe him? The teenager?'

'Seventeen or eighteen at a guess. About six foot, skinny. White. He had two-tone hair. Black underneath, bleached on top,' Jules said.

'Did anyone use his name?'

Jules thought for a moment. 'No. But the father called the little girl Victoria. I'm sure he said Victoria, not Scarlett.' A precaution, Laura guessed. Put people off making the connection.

'Who wore the coat?'

'The lad.'

'And they ordered food?' Laura said.

'Yes. The weird thing was they left without eating. But I think I know why.'

'Go on,' Laura said.

'We had this policeman come in after a stolen car, or a missing car, or something. They must have seen him and left.'

A police officer? 'Did you get his number? His name?'

'No – Barney might have. And Barney, he said Gregory Martin bought a can of petrol from him. Filled it at the pump.'

'A can? He didn't fill the car itself?'

Jules shook her head, as puzzled as Laura was.

'I'll talk to Barney in a minute,' Laura said. 'Did you see them leave?'

'No. Actually I didn't notice they'd gone for a while. I was in and out of the kitchen, cleaning up.' She pointed. The door to the kitchen was behind the counter, the room separate, closed off from the rest of the café.

'And, you know, people are taking turns in the toilet and with the coat being there, and the meals, it took me a while to clock they'd actually gone. And they left a bag of shopping too.'

Laura ran her hands through her hair. 'What about CCTV?'

'We've got it over the forecourt and in the shop.'

'Nothing here?' Laura said.

'Sorry.'

'I'll take a look at this coat.' Laura pulled on her disposable gloves.

'Do you want a drink or anything?' Jules said.

'I'd love a coffee, thanks. Cappuccino?' She should probably choose tea, already jittery with tiredness but she craved the kick of caffeine – she thought there was more in coffee.

'Sure.'

When Laura got close she caught a whiff of cigarette smoke from the coat. There was nothing else in the pockets. The bag on the next seat contained Pringles, chocolate bars, a can of cola, cigarettes and a lighter.

Jules fetched her coffee across. 'Thanks,' Laura said, and gestured for her to put it on another table. She needed to bag everything here for potential forensic evidence.

'And how did Scarlett seem?' Laura said.

Jules smiled. 'Fine. She asked for plant milk but we'd run out. They weren't talking much but . . .' She gave a shrug. 'Well, people often don't, they're tired of driving, all cooped up together. It felt like there was a bit of tension between the two men. Or distance. Like parent-teenager stuff. The body language. But Gregory Martin, he was friendly enough.'

'What were they all wearing?' Laura said.

'Scarlett had her uniform on, like it said on the news. And a purple coat.'

'And Gregory Martin?'

'I can't remember. It sounds so stupid,' Jules said.

'People don't notice much. That's often the way,' Laura told her. 'Don't worry.' She blew on the foam of the coffee. Took a sip.

'I think if it had been anything unusual it would have stuck but . . .' She threw up her palms, gave a shake of her head.

'And the boy?'

'Dark sweatshirt and pants. I don't remember any logos or anything,' Jules said.

'Black or navy?'

Jules shook her head. 'Sorry.'

'I'll just have a look around the rest of the place,' Laura said.

She pushed open the door to the women's toilet and glanced about. She felt all the hairs on the back of her neck tingle as she spotted the fabric filling the wastepaper bin. Navy material. *Scarlett's uniform.* If Scarlett wasn't wearing it, what was she wearing? Had they brought spare clothes with them? Something to change her appearance?

Laura lifted the trousers and saw a damp patch. She could smell it was urine without having to get any closer.

Back in the café, she said to Jules, 'I think Scarlett got changed while she was here. Did you notice her in different clothes?'

'No.'

Laura fetched evidence bags from the car for the clothes, the coat and the shopping. When they were sealed and labelled she asked Jules to go with her to the shop.

'PC Ali,' said Barney, when Laura asked him about the police officer. 'Not sure of his first name.'

'He didn't mention anything about the Scarlett Martin child alerts?'

'No, just this car he was trying to trace,' Barney said. 'But I saw him talking to Gregory Martin.'

'The police officer was?' Laura said, a chill across her skin.

'Yes.' Barney cracked his knuckles. It set her teeth on edge. She resisted the temptation to tell him to stop it.

'When was that?'

'PC Ali had gone over to the café to talk to you,' he said to Jules, who nodded. 'And then I saw him in the car park talking to Gregory Martin. And then PC Ali drove off.'

What? He just let the man walk away? A man on the country's most-wanted list? What the hell was Ali thinking? Or not thinking? *Bloody idiot. Shit!* Had PC Ali not heard her BOLO request? Or not seen the Discovery? Not recognised Gregory Martin from the description circulating?

'Do you know where PC Ali's based?' Laura said, trying to rein in her annoyance.

'Down in Leek,' Barney said.

She summarised what she'd heard from Jules, then said, 'The lad with the two-tone hair, he bought stuff here?'

'Yes, that's right.'

'Can you tell me anything else about him?' Laura said.

Barney thought for a moment. 'No.'

'What vehicle were they driving?'

'I didn't notice, I'm sorry,' Barney said.

'And it was later, *after* PC Ali had spoken to him, that Gregory Martin came in to buy a can and petrol?' Laura tried to get it all exact in her mind.

'Yes. Mr Martin – he went back in the café. And then he came here,' Barney said.

'Is any of that on CCTV?'

'I can show you,' Barney said.

The teenager looked younger than Laura expected. Lanky. His hair mostly hidden by his hood.

Her heart picked up pace as Barney fast forwarded to the footage of Gregory Martin buying a can of petrol and then filling it. 'Is that diesel he's using?' Laura said.

'No, it's petrol,' Barney said.

'What do Discoverys use?' Laura said.

'Most of them are diesel,' Barney said.

So why was he buying petrol?

'OK. Make sure to save all this and email me the files.' The system was digital, and within a few minutes the copies were in her phone.

'Did you see the teenager and Scarlett leaving?'

'No. I always have the telly on and—' He gave an apologetic shrug.

So no one had definitely seen Scarlett leave. Her clothes had been removed. Had she actually left or not? Laura's stomach shrank at the awful prospect.

'We need to search the grounds,' she told Jules and Barney. 'Make sure Scarlett isn't still here somewhere.'

Jules blanched as she understood what Laura was saying, then gave a nod. 'Yes. OK.'

Barney cracked his knuckles.

Between the three of them they covered the land around the services and peered over the walls on the perimeter. Laura checked the area where the bins were and outside the café, braced for the sight of a still form, a child's hand or leg showing where she'd been concealed. Jules searched around the back of the shop. Barney scoured either side of the access road up as far as the main road.

There were few hiding places and no sign of the missing girl.

Relief made Laura giddy. She drew in several breaths of cold air, tried to relax her shoulders, her neck. She thanked Jules and Barney and cautioned them against discussing what they'd told her with anyone else at this time. And also to call her urgently if anything more came to light.

In her car she tried to make sense of what she'd learnt. The trio had stopped, presumably in the Discovery, and ordered food. The young man had bought supplies in the shop. Scarlett had changed and left her uniform in the waste bin. Then the young man and Scarlett had gone, in all likelihood together, abandoning their food and his shopping and coat. Their departure had coincided with PC Ali arriving at the services.

Gregory Martin had spoken to PC Ali, then bought petrol, not diesel, and was last seen walking towards the main road.

Why couldn't his accomplice have driven him there?

Was there some part of the plan she was missing? Was Martin trading his daughter, passing her on to this lad to use for some godforsaken reason? If so, why was Scarlett's note found in the young man's pocket? Had he caught her writing it?

It didn't add up. All Laura had to go on for now was that Scarlett was probably in the company of this unknown teenager. Were he and Gregory Martin meeting up again when Martin had done whatever he needed to with the petrol? Fill a second vehicle? Burn something down?

Don't be flippant. Think.

She rubbed at the back of her neck, raised her arms to stretch.

Laura still couldn't see why the men had separated. Why Martin had been left to make his way on foot.

She hadn't passed a stranded vehicle or seen the Discovery or Gregory Martin on her drive up from Ashbourne, so Laura decided to head in the other direction, the road towards Leek, and see if she could catch him walking down the road with his petrol can.

And she'd speak to PC Ali, ask him what was going on, what his conversation with Gregory Martin had been about. And why the hell he hadn't reported the sighting.

Her first instinct had been relief that Scarlett was still alive, unharmed, and that she was apparently no longer with her father. But was she any safer with his accomplice? What did he want with an eleven-year-old girl?

Nothing good, to be sure.

Nothing good at all.

Chapter 11

'We need to call the police,' Scarlett said.

Dylan just shook his head, like she was annoying him.

'I can do it if you give me your phone. You can just keep driving,' she said.

'No way.'

'Well, stop, then. And you can do it.'

'No one is calling the police. Do you think I'm fucking mental?'

'Not about the car,' Scarlett said, realising why he was so against the idea. 'I won't tell them about that, I promise.'

The rain was back, heavier than ever. Scarlett had to raise her voice to be heard.

'Oh, that's all right, then. Stolen car and they're not even going to notice.' He was being sarcastic. 'You should have got out when I told you to. What are you even doing here?'

'I've been kidnapped,' Scarlett said.

'Oh, no.' He glared at her. 'How d'you make that out? That's not on me.' He jabbed a finger at her. '*You* got in the fucking car.'

He slammed the brakes on and they both rocked forward and back. This time the seatbelt dug into Scarlett's other shoulder.

'Get out!' Dylan shouted.

Scarlett flinched. 'No.'

'I'm not going anywhere until you get out.'

'You'll have a long wait, then,' Scarlett said. She crossed her arms. She was shaking all the way through.

He looked angry. His hands were balled up, like he was going to punch her. He was skinny but he was much bigger than her and he'd be way stronger.

'I'm not getting out until you ring the police,' Scarlett said.

'What are you playing at? Citizen's arrest or something? Saving Daddy's car? You accuse me of kidnapping and you expect me to call the feds and turn myself over?'

Scarlett felt something hardening inside her. He was an idiot. He wasn't even listening to her. 'Not you!' she shouted. 'Him. He kidnapped me.'

His mouth dropped open and he creased his eyebrows together. 'Say what?'

'*He* kidnapped me.'

'Mike did?'

'He's not called Mike. He's called—' The words caught in her throat. And the hardness began to melt away. Like ice being heated up.

'He's called Gregory and I'm Scarlett, not Victoria.'

'But he is your dad?'

Scarlett nodded.

'So what? Is it like a custody thing? Taking you off your mam?'

Scarlett began to cry and furiously swiped the tears away. 'No, not like that. Just ring the police.'

Dylan looked away, shook his head again, started the engine.

'Please?' Scarlett said. Did he not hear what she'd just told him?

'No.'

'Why? Why won't you?'

'Haven't got a phone,' he said.

'What? How can you not have a phone?' *Everyone* had a phone, especially teenagers like him. Even Faye had a phone but Scarlett wasn't allowed one until high school.

'Lost it.' He drove on.

'Well, a phone box then,' Scarlett said. 'We can stop at a phone box and ring the police. Yes?'

He gave a shrug. She really couldn't tell if he agreed or if he was ignoring her.

'Or a pub?' Scarlett said. 'They'd have a phone. You could leave me there. Or you could take me to the police station in . . .' She didn't know where they were any more. 'Where are we going, anyway?'

'Hell out of Dodge,' he muttered.

Did he think that was funny? Because Scarlett didn't. Maybe he didn't know where he was going. He was just a thief who'd seen a chance to steal a car. Was his own car even out of petrol or was that just like a trap, an ambush?

'Just take me somewhere I can get help,' Scarlett said. 'I won't tell them about the car, I swear, honestly.'

But he didn't answer. He just kept driving, shaking his head slowly from side to side, like he was trying not to have a meltdown.

*

Ron heard a car drive up and he peered out through the living-room window to check who was there before answering the door. Still jittery.

He saw a man in police uniform and beyond him a patrol car parked beside the camper van.

Mungo, shut in the kitchen, barked and Ron called to him that it was all right.

'PC Ali,' the man said, when Ron let him in. His eyes lit on Ron's neck and travelled to his bandaged hand. 'You reported an assault.'

'That's right. Do you want to come through?'

In the living room Ron followed PC Ali's gaze as he took in the design: the bare stone walls, picture windows at either end, log-burner, wool rugs and the large sofas in matching herringbone tweed.

'Great view.' PC Ali nodded out to the back where the limestone ridge and the pinnacle of Lovers Leap dominated the skyline.

'Beautiful,' Ron agreed. 'Do you want a drink of anything?'

'No, thanks.' PC Ali removed his hi-vis jacket and hesitated, until Ron told him it was fine to leave it on the settee.

The police officer unzipped his fleece and sat down. He took out a small notebook and pen. 'I'll get a few details first. Name and date of birth?'

'Ronald Thorpe, fourteenth of May 1971.'

'And this is your address?' PC Ali said.

'No. My regular address is down in Birmingham. But I'm house-sitting here,' Ron said.

'House-sitting?' PC Ali said.

'Yes. Looking after the place and the animals while the owners are abroad.'

PC Ali seemed disconcerted, then asked, 'Do you have a contract or anything to verify that?'

Ron felt a spark of irritation that there was the slightest doubt as to his honesty. Why would he call the police if he'd anything to hide? He could have just lied and said this was where he lived, if it wasn't all above board.

'Sure,' he said coldly.

He went and fetched his laptop, logged into the site, tapping the keys harder than was strictly necessary, and pulled up a copy of his current agreement with the Graybridges. Then he crossed the room and presented the screen to PC Ali, balancing the computer on one hand.

PC Ali took his time reading it, making a couple of notes in his book, and Ron's arm began to ache.

But at last PC Ali said, 'Thank you.' He leant back and Ron returned to his seat.

'So can you tell me what happened?' PC Ali said.

Ron ran through the sequence of events as calmly and coherently as he could, with PC Ali interrupting him every so often to ask for more details or to double-check what he was saying.

'He called out "Dylan"?'; 'And he cut your neck first and then your thumb?'; 'And the knife, how long was it?'

When Ron got to the end, to the man slicing open his thumb and threatening him, warning him not to tell anyone about it, *No police. Nothing,* he grew increasingly uneasy. Wires of tension contracted too tightly along his limbs and across his shoulders, and a squirt of fear turned his stomach, as he imagined the man learning that Ron *had* called the police. Pictured him coming back to make good his threat.

He rubbed at his beard, anxious for the sense of gnawing dread to ease off.

'You sure you don't need any medical attention? A and E?' PC Ali said.

'No.'

'OK. How did he seem, the man? Was he concerned about this Dylan?' PC Ali said.

'He was angry, raging. My guess is that there'd been some falling-out. Bad business between them. And this Dylan must have ditched his phone so the other one couldn't trace him,' Ron said.

'Can you describe the man?' PC Ali said.

'Youngish, early twenties, I'd guess. White, though he'd got a ruddy complexion, red cheeks.' Ron gestured to his own face. He remembered the man's expression, face screwed up with malice, eyes livid with aggression, skin shiny, sweating.

'Height?' PC Ali said.

'Five eight, five nine? Shorter than me. And he was stocky, not fat but heading that way,' Ron said.

'What about his hair?' PC Ali said.

'Brown, I think. Short. He had a baseball cap on and a hood over that.'

'Can you describe the cap?'

'Black and white. NYC, perhaps?' *Was it?* 'I'm not sure. He had this silky bomber jacket under his coat and that was black and white as well.'

'The coat was?' PC Ali frowned.

'No, the bomber jacket. The coat was black,' Ron said.

'Great.' PC Ali nodded, a touch of enthusiasm like that was what he wanted to hear.

'Oh, and his trainers they were neon orange, like Day-Glo,' Ron said.

'Orange?' As if Ron was mistaken.

'Yes, orange. Really bright.'

'OK,' PC Ali said, sounding disappointed. 'And the man, did you notice any distinguishing marks?'

Ron remembered the wrist tattoo and described it.

'What about his accent?' PC Ali said.

Ron thought for a moment. 'Northern, not Midlands.'

'Northern?' PC Ali looked at him.

Ron heard himself snap: 'Look, it could have been Manchester or Sheffield or Leeds. I couldn't tell you.' *They all sound the same to me.* Just like anyone from any part of the West Midlands sounded like a Brummie, according to outsiders.

PC Ali didn't reply, just wrote in his book. He gripped his pen down near the nib, reminiscent of a child learning to write. 'You didn't see his vehicle?'

'No, but I heard him drive away,' Ron said. 'He must have parked on the road.'

'Not visible from here?'

Obviously. 'No,' Ron said tightly.

'So he left with the phone, the one you'd found, and your van keys?' PC Ali said.

'Yes,' Ron said.

'And where did you find the phone?' PC Ali said.

'On the old road into Leek, on the grass verge. Before you reach those old cottages, the ones by the horse trough.' He'd ridden Patti that way a couple of times. And was pleased to find the old gritstone trough still held fresh water fed by a spring.

'OK. And there was just a phone, nothing else?' PC Ali said.

'Yes.'

'Did you look in the phone?' PC Ali said.

'It was password protected,' Ron said.

PC Ali gave a nod. Ron watched him draw a line under his notes.

'I'm going to give you a crime reference number.'

Ron wanted more from him than this disinterested practicality. Just the slightest expression of empathy, an acknowledgement of the ordeal he'd been through, or an enquiry after his welfare, but PC Ali was strictly business. Maybe he thought asking if Ron wanted to go to hospital was all that was required.

Ron knew sometimes words weren't necessary. Body language or a gesture could be enough. Like when he'd been with a man whose chip-pan fire had destroyed his flat and killed his pet dog, Shelley: he'd sat beside him on the low wall opposite the blackened building with its shattered windows, the air still reeking of smoke and white flakes of ash dancing across the pavement in the slightest breath of wind. Ron had taken off his mask and helmet and opened his mouth to speak, to say how sorry he was, but the man had given a brief nod of understanding, his eyes gleaming with unshed tears, wrinkled hands folded together, still in his lap.

They'd sat there side by side and silent for a couple of minutes or more as the world went on around them, the calls of the crew clearing up hoses, the murmurs of onlookers at their doors, until the social worker approached and Ron had left them to it, exchanging a nod of farewell with the man. That was all that had been needed.

'Have you got a pen?' PC Ali said.

'I'll put it in here.' Ron lifted the laptop onto his knee and entered the digits as PC Ali read them out.

'You'll need that if you want to apply for compensation or insurance, like for your van keys,' PC Ali said.

Ron shook his head, knowing it would be a waste of time approaching his insurers. His excess would be far more than the cost of buying replacement keys.

'If the suspect is apprehended and charged, we'll be asking you to provide a witness statement. You'd be willing to do that?'

'Yes,' Ron said. 'It's not likely, though, is it?'

'How d'you mean?' PC Ali sounded defensive.

'Well, the chances of you catching him – they're going to be pretty slim.'

'It's a violent crime,' PC Ali said, pinning a look on Ron, brown eyes gleaming with annoyance. 'All possible resources—'

'Ah, that's it, there's the thing,' Ron interrupted. '*All possible resources*. And what if there's barely any resources to go round?' A flash of heat in his veins. Then he felt like a dick. Whining on to some kid in a uniform about his thumb when God knew how many more people were in far worse circumstances. People hospitalising each other over drugs and money, women trapped with violent partners, kids being abused.

'We will be treating this with every—'

'It's all right.' Ron waved his good hand. 'I get it. I understand.' He was exhausted again. Through to his bones. Tired of it all.

'If you need to get in touch call 101 or 999 for an emergency. Just call us,' PC Ali said.

'Yes. Thanks.'

Ron closed the door after him and put the bolt on.

999. Just call us.

He felt a wave of sorrow, an undertow of nostalgia for the time when he'd been one of those people. First responders. The people you want when the very worst is happening. The people who risk everything to help. Who hold the centre. Who know just what to do.

He'd been one of them

Until he'd failed.

*

She was pecking at his head. Driving him mental with all her chat about phoning the police.

I mean, get real, no way!

All the shit about being kidnapped by her dad and fake names. It was too much. Dylan couldn't be doing with it. And there was no way he was getting involved. No more than he had been already.

Which would not have happened if he'd had any choice about it.

What if people think you've abducted her? You're in enough shit without that. How are you going to get shot of her?

The windows had begun to steam up and Dylan turned up the fan.

'Will he report it?' Dylan asked her.

'What?' Scarlett said. Or Victoria. Depending on whose story you believed.

'Me nicking the car,' Dylan said. It was a better drive than the old Astra, that was for sure.

'I don't know,' she said.

'Well, if you really have been kidnapped—'

'I have,' she said, all agitated.

'Then he's not going to want to draw attention, is he? Reporting his vehicle stolen is going to be tricky,' Dylan said.

'I don't know,' she said again.

'If you really are Scarlett and—'

'Look!' All riled up, she grabbed her bag and pulled out a book. A schoolbook. Thrust it towards him and jabbed her finger on the front. 'Scarlett Martin. Six B. Satisfied?'

'All right, then. So he won't be going to the feds, will he?'

'Feds?' Scarlett said.

'The police,' Dylan said.

'Why d'you call them feds? Acting like some American hip-hop gangsta.' All sneery. Seriously disrespecting him. The cheek of it.

'That's what they are, man. That's what *I* call them. We *all* call them that. Unless you're living in Disneyland. Like *Frozen* or somewhere.'

She glared at him. 'Stupid,' she muttered, but so he could hear.

He tightened his lips. Tempted to tell her to watch her mouth, but he needed to concentrate on the immediate situation. Think it through. 'But if they know he's taken you, your mam and them, then they'll have told the . . . feds' – he almost said 'police' –, 'won't they, and they'll be asking people to report if they've seen the two of you or the car and—' A fresh idea struck him. 'Is it for a ransom?'

'What?'

Dylan knew that when people held someone hostage for a ransom, a lot of the time it was never made public. He'd seen a documentary. The hostage negotiators tried to make contact and quite often money changed hands but it wasn't something the feds liked to advertise because of the risk of copy-cat crimes.

It was big business in Mexico. Big as drugs. But it happened here too. You took the right hostages, like a rich family's kid and that, and you could make a shedload. Dylan reckoned it would be way more stressful than dealing, having to look after the hostage and not walk into any ambushes.

Then he thought of Petey and how in a way that was like holding someone hostage. Col and Dylan moving in and invading his life, same as the woman in Grantham and the other trap houses they'd set up. Except those people were shit poor and there were no rich relatives ready to shell out any ransom, so no end in sight for them. Not until things got too hot and Dylan and Col were instructed to move somewhere new.

'Is he gonna ask for a ransom, for money?' Dylan said.

'I don't know,' Scarlett said. 'I don't think so.'

'Well, has she got money, your mam like? Big house, fancy job?'

Scarlett didn't answer.

'Well – has she?' Dylan said.

'She's dead,' Scarlett said. He could barely hear her.

'What?'

'I said, she's dead.'

Oh, fuck. It sounded like she was going to cry, mess with his head even more. And he was stressed out enough as it was.

'So you live with him, do you?' Dylan said.

'No!' she shouted. 'I haven't seen him for ages, not since— I live with my nana. And she hasn't got any money.' She sniffed.

Dylan left it for a minute, then said, 'Only if it *was* for a ransom then they'll likely be keeping it quiet.'

She sniffed again. 'It won't be a ransom.' Then she said, 'But we could listen to the news, see if it says anything, about me or about this car.' She reached a hand to the radio.

'No,' he said quickly. His hand darting out to stop her.

'Why not?' Scarlett said.

In case I'm on there.

It was a stretch but you never could tell. If there was anything on there about him, about Petey, or the county line, he didn't want to find out about it with her next to him.

The only way I'm listening is in private, on my tod.

A tractor and trailer, loaded with bags of something, pulled out of a lane ahead and Dylan was forced to slow down. The winding road made it impossible to overtake. Before long the two vehicles were joined by a Royal Mail delivery van. *Postman Pat.* Dylan was sandwiched between them and forced to travel at twenty miles an hour.

He'd loved tractors as a little kid – he'd had a red plastic one with a man you could stick in the driving seat. He could remember lying on the floor to play with it and how the dust flew up off the carpet and made these big stripes in the light coming through the windows.

But this one, big green fucker covered with mud, was a nightmare.

To be honest, it did make sense to listen to the news, work out if this car was a liability. Or if there were any reports about Petey and the house. But he needed to get shot of Scarlett, first off. Whatever he did – ditch the car and get a train, or head for Wales in the Discovery – he could do without the hassle of a kid hanging round his neck.

He couldn't stop and dump her until he could get past the tractor. How far was the bleeding thing going?

'I'll drop you at the next place we come to,' Dylan said. 'But you have to swear not to tell them who I am.'

'I don't know who you are,' she said, voice wobbling.

'You know my name,' Dylan said.

'Only your first name,' Scarlett said.

'Yeah, but don't tell them that or what I look like or—'

'Have you done something wrong?'

He glanced at her and caught a flash of fear in her eyes. Then she hid it. Raised her chin. 'Apart from taking the car,' she said.

'No. Don't be daft,' he said, but the lie hung there like a smell in the air between them.

Man, he needed a smoke. He'd left his fags at the services and the snacks he'd bought. Hadn't even eaten his chilli. One mouthful of chips, that was all he'd managed.

His mouth watered just thinking about it, and his stomach ached with hunger. It was like there was some big conspiracy to stop him eating. First with the pizza, then the food at the café. Last thing he'd had was some honey-nut flakes when he got up this morning.

Hangry. They had a word for it – hangry. And pissed off and bleeding starving.

He had to eat, and he needed to buy some smokes. So as soon as he got rid of the kid he'd work out where he could buy stuff. And then what to do about this car.

Chapter 12

On the drive back up the hill from Graybridge Ahmed reached Lovers Leap. With layby parking for half a dozen cars on the north side of the road, it was a viewing point where people could stop to enjoy the scenery below the long ridge.

In his rear-view mirror, Ahmed could see the property far below. Even in the fading light and the murky rain, the stone of the house glowed. You'd need a fair amount of money to pay for a spread like that. The road was badly flooded at the bottom. A black lake that must be a couple of metres deep. Had they considered that when they'd bought the land? Mind you, the house was several metres above the road. And when the old ford did flood you could still get to the property from the north, as Ahmed had done. And presumably the assailant had too.

Had the man been the suspect from Coopers Close? The one who'd taken off in the silver Astra? Some of the description fitted, the black hooded coat for one. The use of a blade, perhaps. But Ahmed cautioned himself that the use of a knife at Coopers Close was supposition, not fact. So he was left with just the coat.

And the trainers bothered him. Ronald Thorpe had described them as Day-glo orange. But Ahmed hadn't noticed anything like that on the person who'd run from the house. Wouldn't it have registered? Something that bright?

He tried to recall exactly what he'd seen. The open door, a

rectangle of light, a figure with a bag. A holdall, the sort of thing people use for the gym. The dark hooded coat. The DQ on the registration plate. But no zing of colour at the feet.

How could he have missed them? Perhaps he'd been focusing too hard on the figure, hoping for a glimpse of features, hoping they'd turn and look back.

Or maybe, and the thought raised his spirits, maybe the suspect had changed their shoes! They could have got blood on them – that could easily have been the case. Or they knew what the police looked for at a scene of crime. Not just fingerprints and DNA evidence but footwear impressions too – what people who weren't in the service called 'footprints'. Everyone was mad for that, these days, forensics, true crime podcasts, *24 Hours in Police Custody*, *Making A Murderer*.

From what he could tell, the man with the machete had set out to Graybridge with one express reason. To find this Dylan, the owner of the iPhone that Ronald Thorpe had found.

Ahmed gave a sigh. He had to accept it wasn't clear that there was a connection between the incidents at Coopers Close and Graybridge. He'd head back to the station and fill in two separate reports. Assume for now that they were looking for two different suspects.

But he'd take the back road through Birchwell into Leek, past where the phone had been dumped. After all, he'd not had any sighting of the Astra on the bigger road he'd used earlier. No harm in looking. It rankled that the suspect had just vanished and, despite his best efforts, Ahmed had come up empty.

So far, he told himself.

Probably long gone.

Way too late.

He crested the rise and the words died in his mouth. Two cars stationary on the far verge. The Astra and beyond that a red car – Volvo, was it? A figure in a dark, hooded coat was hunched over the driver's door of the Astra, looking inside.

Ahmed's throat closed and his spine went rigid.

Holding his breath, he steered into the roadside.

He expected them to turn, see his lights, see it was a squad car, make a run for it. Hadn't he heard the engine?

The machete! He might still have the machete. Ahmed looked at his feet – no orange trainers. Not the same guy.

He couldn't see anyone else inside the cars, not for definite. Options flew through his head. Speak to the individual or ring Control for support. But the chances of back-up coming out any time soon, when Ahmed wasn't clearly at risk, were slim to none. Never mind how he would feel if he cocked up and a van full of coppers pitched up, dragged into work during their time off, only to find this was an innocent passer-by who had stumbled on the Astra, a farmer or something. Ahmed would feel such a prat.

Besides, he had his Taser.

As a precaution Ahmed radioed Control to tell them where he was and what he was doing. He relayed the registration number of the Astra, YP08 IDQ, and asked them to find the details, the name and address of the owner.

Ahmed stepped out of the car and strapped on his equipment belt. Made sure both Taser and handcuffs were easy to access.

The figure at the Astra still hadn't reacted to his arrival and was now looking in the rear side window.

All Ahmed could hear was the patter of rain and the gushing of water from a stream somewhere in the fields.

'Put your hands on the car,' Ahmed shouted, as he drew close.

The man didn't flinch.

Ahmed's mouth was dry, he could feel the pulse thudding in his neck. He walked nearer. Only a few steps separated them now. He couldn't see any knife but then he couldn't get a clear sight of both the suspect's hands.

'Police,' he yelled. 'Put your hands on the roof of the vehicle.'

The figure turned, scowling. A woman. White, pointy nose. Shorter than the figure from Coopers Close. One hand tugging at the wire of her earbuds attached to her phone. 'What?' she said.

'Raise your hands?' Ahmed said.

'Look, I—'

'Raise your hands where I can see them.'

'Oh, for Christ's—'

'Now!' he screamed.

Shooting him a look of hatred, dark eyes flashing, she raised both hands.

'Turn around slowly and place your hands on the roof of the vehicle,' Ahmed said.

'You've got to be—'

'Do as I say!' Ahmed's hand tightened on the Taser.

She slammed her palms onto the roof of the Astra.

Ahmed stepped closer. 'Are you carrying any weapons?'

'No.'

'Do you have anything sharp in your pockets?' Ahmed said.

'No'

'Can you tell me your name and date of birth?' Ahmed said.

'Detective Sergeant Laura O'Neil, sixth of April 1984.'

What? Ahmed's heart contracted. Was it a joke? A set-up? 'Do you have any identification on you?' he said stiffly.

'Warrant card. Inside jacket pocket.' She spat the words at him.

'Could you show me, please? And move slowly.' Ahmed stepped back, his cheeks on fire. But no way was he going to back down now.

DS O'Neil made a performance of taking her hands off the car roof and turning round.

With a face like thunder, she fished out her warrant card and flipped open the leather wallet to show her ID and force badge.

Should he apologise?

Before he could decide or ask her what her interest was in the Astra, she said sharply, 'And I'm guessing you're PC Ali.'

'Yes, I am,' he said, disconcerted.

She stared, dissatisfied, until he added, 'Sarge.'

'You were at the services near Longnor earlier.'

'Yes, Sarge.' Ahmed felt like he was being walked towards a trap.

'Also present was one of our most wanted, fugitive Gregory Martin, believed to be travelling with his eleven-year-old daughter Scarlett, who was abducted after school today.' Her eyes like lasers.

'Gregory Martin?' Ahmed said. The name was familiar but he hadn't heard it recently and struggled to place it in context.

'Been on the run since the murder of his estranged wife Jeanette Martin in 2014. Now he's back and he's got the little girl.'

The ground was slipping beneath Ahmed's feet.

'I didn't see a little girl.' Ahmed remembered the lad serving in the shop, the driver in the café. The—

'You talked to Gregory Martin.' She held out her phone, a photo, the man in the car park. 'He has a beard now, and grey hair,' she said.

Words failed him for a moment. Then he pushed back. 'I didn't know, Sarge.'

'An appeal was issued at four p.m.,' she said.

'I never heard it.' He sounded like a little kid. *It wasn't me. I didn't do it.*

'Sit in the car,' DS O'Neil said. She hooked a thumb back to the red Volvo. 'I'm getting soaked here.'

Ahmed glanced back. The hazard lights still flashing on his patrol car, safe enough.

Once they were out of the rain DS O'Neil pumped him for information about the conversation he'd had with Gregory Martin. Then she fired off a load of increasingly irritated questions about a Land Rover Discovery, a teenage boy with black and blond hair, and the girl again.

He couldn't help her. And she made that blindingly obvious. Ahmed felt his resentment build at her attitude, the way she was grilling him, her antagonism. Treating him like a school kid. Not a colleague.

She wasn't the only one investigating a serious crime.

'What's your interest in the Astra?' he jumped in, as soon as he got a chance.

Her mouth tightened, before she said, 'I heard you'd been asking about that model of car at the services. So I stopped to check it out and was receiving the details when you pitched up. Registered to one Lloyd Campion, address in Leeds.'

Northern accent, thought Ahmed, remembering what Ronald Thorpe had said.

'Is it stolen?' DS O'Neil said.

'I don't know,' Ahmed said. 'I didn't have the registration before to run it through. I don't know who was driving it but they may have fled a crime scene.'

'May have?' Practically curling her lip.

'Scene of a fatality, address in Leek. A possible murder. But we haven't got a post-mortem yet so we don't know what cause of death is,' Ahmed said, left it a beat before adding, 'Sarge.'

'But you think it's murder?' DS O'Neil said.

Ahmed pictured the blood. 'It's possible.'

'If you didn't get the registration, how do you know that's the right vehicle?' she said.

'I got the last two letters,' he defended himself.

'Why dump it here?' DS O'Neil said. 'In the middle of nowhere?'

Ahmed shrugged.

Her face cleared. 'It's out of petrol!' she said, animated. 'Gregory Martin filled up a can of petrol after you'd gone. I drove this way, hoping I might find him.'

'You said he was in a Land Rover Discovery.' Ahmed felt like his brain was going to short-circuit.

'He *was*. Until the lad with him drove away from the services in it with Scarlett. So where did Martin go with his petrol if not here?'

Ahmed didn't know if she expected him to answer that. The whole story was getting more confused.

'And how come it took you so long to get here?' she said. 'You left the services before I got there.'

'I'd another call-out, an assault—' He was interrupted by her police radio.

'Lima, Oscar, one nine. This is Control. Over.'

'Go ahead, Control. Over,' DS O'Neil said.

'Sighting of Land Rover Discovery, Hotel, Golf, six, seven, Golf, November, Juliet. Captured seventeen oh-five, heading east on B5054 towards Matlock. Reported by a Royal Mail delivery van. Over.'

'Understood. Over and out.' She turned to Ahmed, said quickly, 'I've got to go.' Her face sharper, eager.

She buckled up. 'You see Martin again, any sign of him, please do me a favour. Let me know. You could even arrest him.' More than a touch of sarcasm there.

They swapped call signs.

Ahmed climbed out of her car and moved so she could leave. He was still smarting from the encounter. And his head was muddled, puzzling over how it all fitted together. If it did.

Just think if he *did* find Gregory Martin . . . 'One of our most wanted,' she'd said. Imagine ringing DS O'Neil to let her know that PC Ahmed Ali had Gregory Martin detained in custody. That'd show her. That'd show them all.

He swung his head from side to side to try to shake the tension and felt his neck crick. Then he straightened his jacket, secured his Taser and cuffs, and went to have a proper look at the abandoned Astra.

*

They'd been following the tractor for ages, and even though Dylan wasn't saying much about it, Scarlett could tell he was really stressed. His hands gripped the steering wheel and all his knuckles had gone white. There was the atmosphere too. Even with her eyes shut she could feel it. How he was all wound up. Animals had all these signals to communicate without talking. And people did that, too, without realising it.

The tractor was huge, mud thick on its wheels and bits of dead grass or straw or something. Sometimes a bit would fly off when it went over a bump and land on the low trailer or bounce off onto the road. The post van that had been following them had turned off and gone down a narrow track.

Scarlett didn't like going slow either. She imagined Mike coming after them. How angry he'd be, and the thought of that, of him catching up to them, made her feel so sick, her mouth filled with spit. She pressed her hands onto her knees and clamped her teeth shut.

She's dead. It had been so hard to say it out loud and then she'd felt guilty, dirty somehow for telling Dylan. And she didn't want to think about it, to remember any of it. It was like a hole opening up to swallow her. An awful feeling inside. They'd always said she didn't have to talk about it, didn't have to think about it, that it was up to her. That no one would make her remember if she didn't want to.

She's dead.

And now Nana was too. She wanted to cry.

Dylan braked hard. 'You're shitting me.'

The tractor had stopped, blocking the road. As they watched, the farmer jumped down and went to a gate in the wall.

'He's just opening the gate,' Scarlett said.

'No shit, Sherlock,' Dylan said, which was just mean.

The farmer pushed the gate back into the field and walked over to the tractor.

'Could you not go any slower?' Dylan muttered.

The tractor rumbled loudly as it turned into the opening, pulling the trailer through.

'Finally!' Dylan said.

Scarlett wondered what Dylan had done wrong. She was pretty sure now that he *had* done something wrong and not just stealing the car. She couldn't wait for him to drop her off.

'We could check the sat nav,' she said. 'See what's nearby.'

'Nothing's nearby.' He stared at her like she was stupid. Why was he so angry?

'Well, where the nearest shops are or a pub or—'

'Try it, then,' he said.

Scarlett reached out and switched it on. She wasn't sure if she could make it work but she'd try. She sometimes followed Nana's maps when they went anywhere new. 'You navigate,' Nana would say. 'I'll cogitate.'

'You cogitate, I'll aggravate.' A game they played, coming up with as many rhyming words as they could. And they had to have three syllables.

She wanted to go home so badly it was like her whole body was hurting, aching with missing Nana. But if Nana was gone. If that was true—

Don't! Think about something else.

'What the fuck?' Dylan made her jump. He was doing something weird with his head, whipping round and then looking in the wing mirror, then back again.

Scarlett turned to see. A car was following them. A red car. And it was flashing its headlights.

Was it him? Her heart flipped over.

Dylan accelerated so fast that Scarlett was thrown back in her seat.

He swore under his breath, tearing round the bends even though they couldn't see whether anything was coming.

Oh God oh God oh God.

The car behind kept coming fast.

She shrank down in her seat.

Outside, the walls and the fields and the trees streaked by.

At the summit of the hill the car left the ground. It actually left the ground. Scarlett's stomach dropped and she screamed. They landed with a thump and she bit her tongue. A horrible throbbing pain filled her mouth and she tasted blood.

Dylan only went faster, but the car behind came closer. Now it was sounding its horn as well as flashing its lights.

'Fuck off!' Dylan yelled. They screeched round a zigzag, right then left then right, almost grazing the walls.

Scarlett couldn't look. She was going to be sick or wet herself again, or both. She leant forward and put her hands on the door of the glove compartment to steady herself.

Dylan roared. With a horrible grinding snarl of brakes the car slewed to a stop, spinning round side on. Scarlett was hurled to her left, smacking her temple on the window.

Before she could speak, there was a smash, a violent jolt, and Scarlett was punched in the head.

Stunned, her ears ringing, it was a second or two before she could open her eyes.

She was being swallowed by a massive white balloon, a bouncy castle. She tried to raise her arms to push it away. It was smothering her.

Airbag. It was an airbag, at the side of her.

She could smell burning rubber.

Dylan's side airbag had puffed out too. He was pushing it down and his nose was bleeding. The red car's bonnet was sticking up and all crumpled. It had crashed straight into their driver's side. Scarlett still couldn't see if it was Mike. But who else could it be?

Movement and she heard their car engine growling. 'Come on,

come on!' Dylan was saying, as he tried to start it. When it caught, he twisted the wheel and there was a rocking sensation and more grinding noises, metal tearing metal. The cars were stuck together!

Dylan managed to wrench theirs away from the red one and steer them down the road.

With a shock, like another punch, Scarlett realised that he'd stopped across the middle of the road deliberately so the red car would run straight into them. *He crashed on purpose!*

They could have been killed!

'I'm going to be sick,' Scarlett said. Her voice was all blurred because of her tongue and being punched in the head. 'Can you stop?'

'No way.'

Dylan drove on. The airbags were going down like burst balloons.

'But I'm going to be sick,' Scarlett said. Vomit filled her mouth, burnt the back of her throat. She gulped. She couldn't stop it. Retching, she leant forward and opened her legs, hoping to miss her knees. It burst up through her nose and spurted out of her mouth, splattering over her bag in the footwell. Her eyes watered and she was coughing and choking.

'No!' Dylan roared.

She thought he was yelling at her until she looked up, wiping her mouth, and saw the water ahead. A big pool of it, like a lake.

They hit it. And waves smashed up and over the car from all sides. Water and bits of plant and mud and stones smacking on the windows. The engine spluttered and died and the car bobbed and turned. It was floating. They were going to sink. They were going to drown. They were going to drown, trapped in the car.

I don't want to drown.

I don't want to die!

Scarlett started to scream.

Chapter 13

The pillow wasn't right, squashing her face like this. Laura never slept on her front.

Move.

Was Mateo crying? Was that him? She was so tired. Too tired to turn over and open her eyes and check the time. Perhaps Hector would see to him if she left it, if she stayed where she was. Even if it was her turn.

She woke again, her lips, her mouth parched, a crackling in her throat when she tried to swallow. Had her alarm gone off? Was Mateo crying?

It was hard to breathe – her nose was blocked. Pins and needles in her hands. She began to raise her head, to roll onto her side, but a shooting pain lanced down her neck and into her shoulder. She tried to call out, to call for Hector, but the words were already gone. And she was sinking.

Drool tickled the corner of her mouth. *What time is it?* The pillow was flat, dusty, the mattress hard underneath it, digging into her forehead. *I'm so thirsty.*

Wake up. Groaning, she lifted her head an inch, then another. *Oh, that hurts!* She must have slept funny.

When she turned to look at the clock she swooned with pain. *Something's wrong. Really wrong.*

Mateo? Her mind darted to him, searching for clues, for recall.

Fishing for an answer to her dread. Had something happened? Was he OK? She came up blank.

She opened her eyes and the world swam. A blur of white.

The smell of rubber and petrol.

A crazed windscreen, the car bonnet upright, dented.

A crash! Collision. Head-on.

Move!

It was almost dark, the colours outside fading to monochrome. She was alone. Raindrops silver on the windscreen. Her ears whooshing and whining. A chemical smell scraped at the back of her throat. She coughed and needles of pain stabbed through her face and neck.

Slowly she shuffled, mouthing, *Ow-ow-ow* as she did, until she could reach the seatbelt, her hands still smarting. Her movements were clumsy and it took her four tries to release it. She had to rest then.

Laura stared at her hands. There were red blotches in her vision. But when she moved her eyes she understood the blotches were on her hands. Burns. Airbags can do that.

Bruised, burnt. Maybe whiplash. Was anything broken?

Laura coughed and the answering pain brought tears to her eyes. A rib, maybe.

Move.

Get out.

When she could bear to act again she tugged the door handle. It wouldn't budge. The door was completely stuck. The metal crumpled. A gap along the bottom edge, wet tarmac gleamed below it. The door was buckled and she was stuck inside. The car crushed like a can. Cold fear clutched at her heart. *Hector! Mateo!*

Breathe.

She steadied herself. Sipped in a breath through her mouth, and another, nose still stuffed up. Breathed again.

Then came anger, rolling through her. She was seething. Because that pillock, that stupid bastard, had deliberately blocked the road, knowing she would slam head-on into the side of him.

He could have killed her! Killed them all. And when Laura found him, when she got her hands on him, she would rip his bloody head off. See how he liked it.

*

Peering in through the windows of the Astra, Ahmed found nothing that shed any light on who'd been driving it, no luggage or personal belongings. He banged on the boot and listened, waiting for an answering tap or muffled cry. None came.

From his patrol car Ahmed spoke to Control, relaying the details that DS O'Neil had given him about the Astra's owner, Lloyd Campion. Was Campion on the police database?

'One conviction in 2007 for conspiracy to supply crack cocaine and heroin. Served three years. Over.'

A dealer, then. Or he had been dealing back then. 'Is the car insured? Over.'

'Checking for you now.'

Ahmed wound his window down and wiped the wing mirror clean while he waited.

'Car insured for Dylan Ellis, date of birth eighteenth of August 2002.'

Ahmed felt a thrill of excitement, a tingle along his forearms. The man with the machete who had assaulted Ronald Thorpe had been hunting for Dylan. Dylan Ellis had almost certainly been driving the Astra. An Astra that belonged to a dealer based in Leeds. So was Dylan Ellis working here for the Leeds gang? County lines? And was the man with the orange trainers part of the same enterprise? Either that or a rival.

What about the victim at Coopers Close? Another dealer? A customer who'd got into a fight with Dylan Ellis? Or someone whose house was being used by cuckoos?

Once Ahmed was back at the station, it'd be a matter of moments to check who was officially resident at the property. A flush of triumph lifted his spirits. This was a serious catch. Serious crime.

He was about to set off but DS O'Neil's parting shot niggled at him. *You see Martin again. Let me know. You could even arrest him.*

No sign of Gregory Martin on the road from the services, according to DS O'Neil. But he'd left there carrying petrol. So where had he gone?

Ahmed consulted the map. He saw that there was a footpath, part of the Arbor Low Trail, that ran from near the service station over the fields and crossed the road a few yards from where he was parked. It was a more direct route than the road, so anyone walking it would shave half a mile off the distance. And would be out of sight.

Worth exploring.

Ahmed climbed the stile by the signpost and saw there was no way to avoid the thick mud at the bottom of the ladder, likely churned up by walkers in the wet weather. He took two large strides through it, then followed the path down a steep incline between bushes bare of leaves.

Rabbits scattered as he approached.

Ahmed thought of Bolly, the pet rabbit he'd had. He'd brought him into the house to play, but when Bolly had chewed through the washing-machine's cable his mother had banned him from inside.

A fox had taken Bolly. Ahmed had gone out one morning before school to feed him and the hutch door was broken, the chicken-wire torn away. No sign of the rabbit.

'You don't know it was a fox.' Ahmed's mother had ticked off his dad while Ahmed sniffed over his Weetabix.

'What else would it be? You think Bolly launched some great escape plan all on his own? Suddenly found the skills, the brain capacity—'

'Enough!' Ahmed's mother had said. Then to Ahmed, 'Go and wash your face. You'll feel better.'

Ahmed hadn't asked for another rabbit: he hadn't wanted to lose a second in the same way.

One Saturday while he was round at his friend's playing video games, his father had broken up the hutch and replaced it with a garden bench.

These wild rabbits were half the size of Bolly. And greyish brown while he'd been a rich chocolate colour.

Runnels of water poured down the slope, forging new streams. At the bottom of the valley the brook hissed and frothed and had flooded the banks either side. Ahmed slipped and grabbed at the bushes, his glove snagging on the spiky black thorns.

Here the path had been swallowed by flooding so Ahmed had to go across higher ground. Clumps of reeds showed him where the wettest patches were and he skirted round those.

The valley twisted and narrowed and Ahmed headed for the wooden footbridge where the footpath crossed the water. The planks were slick, green with slime, the handrail worn with use.

As he reached the other side, a clatter in the trees made him jump.

Just a bird.

More frightened than you are, his mum said.

The copse he entered smelt strongly of rotting leaves and old wood, a mushroomy smell. Everything was damp. Moss coated the tree trunks and the ground squelched underfoot. Fungus big as dinner plates grew out of one trunk.

Ahmed heard a sound. A cough.

Was it?

He stood still, ears straining. But there was just the drip-drip-drip of rain.

The path wound through the dank wood, then took him back across the stream. Someone had laid boulders here, stepping stones.

But with the water level so high they were submerged. He crossed as quickly as he could, hoping his boots wouldn't leak. He used dubbin on them regularly so they should be OK.

Presentation – that was important in the job. A neat, clean appearance. Professional. No one wanted a police officer to turn up looking like a slob. He'd have to clean all the mud off them before tomorrow's shift. And change his trousers.

The next stretch of path was quicker: flagstones ran parallel to the stream. They were large and grey, slippery if you weren't careful. At the end of the run more mud and—

Ahmed stopped. Stared. *A shoeprint.* The cleats clear. A shoeprint pointing towards him: someone had gone in the other direction. It must be fresh, today's. With all the rain, a mark like this would soon be washed away.

Ahmed walked a few yards further on and saw another impression, the front part of a sole.

But he hadn't passed anyone.

Unless they were hiding . . .

He looked round, listening again. A bird squawking, the rush of the stream, the sizzle of rain.

Checking the time, Ahmed reckoned he was probably a third of the way back to the services but there didn't seem much point in carrying on. If Gregory Martin *had* taken this route Ahmed would have seen him by now.

Or missed him.

It'd been a long shot anyway, thinking Martin had walked this route. After all, it was only a hunch of DS O'Neil's that the Astra was out of petrol. And another leap to think Gregory Martin was coming to fill it up. She could be way off the mark. That shoeprint could have been made by someone earlier in the day, he told himself, this morning perhaps.

Ahmed took a photograph of it, anyway.

Covering your tracks? His dad.

Ha-ha.

Retracing his steps, Ahmed scanned the ground for more shoeprints but didn't see any. Not even in the swamp around the stile, which was just a mess.

He climbed the ladder and his stomach lurched.

Ah, shit! Oh, man!

The Astra was gone.

*

The car was sloshing about, dipping and rocking, like a boat. The engine had died. Dylan didn't like to try starting it – he'd probably get electrocuted or something. And with the wheels not gripping the ground, it wasn't like it could take them anywhere.

Time to bail.

But his door wouldn't open. Damaged in the crash.

'It's stuck,' he said to Scarlett. 'Try yours.'

She pulled at the handle but shook her head. 'Too much water. Pressure on the outside.'

Einstein.

His heart was banging hard. 'We can't stay here, can we? Sitting ducks.' He screwed up his face. The car reeked of vomit, sharp and cheesy. Made him gag.

Her face was dusty, from the airbag, he thought. She was gulping air like she was drowning already.

He imagined the water coming in, his head trapped against the car roof, last inches of air. Fuck!

He caught sight of his face in the mirror, blood smeared round his nose, red mark on his right cheek from the impact, panic in his eyes.

'The boot,' she said, and, quick as a flash, she unstrapped her seatbelt and slipped between the seats into the back, no messing. Like an eel.

He was skinny but he'd never fit through like she could.

'Tip your seat back,' she said, as if she knew what he was thinking.

Dylan managed to crawl through, twisting and turning, until his foot got stuck and he had to wiggle it about to free it.

Scarlett was fiddling with the button that released the rear seats to lay them flat and getting nowhere, so he told her to move out of the way and let him have a go.

The smell of chunder and the rocking of the car made him feel seasick.

He pulled hard on the orange lever and tugged at the rear seat, which gave way. He shifted to fold it forward so they could get through to the boot.

'We're going to get wet,' Scarlett said.

Not wrong there. Dylan reckoned the water stretched a good ten or twelve feet in every direction. Would they have to swim? It couldn't be that deep, surely. Dylan could swim but he'd have to find a way to keep the holdall over his head or all that cash'd get wet.

He opened the boot and raised the door.

The sick stink was replaced by the smell of river water. Soil and crushed plants and something rotten, like drains.

Dylan put his holdall on the floor of the boot and turned so he could grasp the sill of the door, then lowered himself into the water.

He gasped at the cold. He felt the shock shrink his balls, ripple goosebumps over his skin. But at least he could touch the ground. The water came up to his chest. Thick murky brown with loads of twigs and straw and stuff floating on it.

'This high.' He showed her.

He grabbed his bag from the boot and held it up on his shoulder.

'You coming?'

She followed him, huffing as she slid into the water. Holding her head up high, the water reaching her neck.

Dylan waded forward. It was impossible to see the ground, but it was lumpy, strewn with hidden obstacles that could trip him up. He made it to the edge and onto the road surface, water streaming down his pants. He felt filthy, cold and rank and mucky.

Scarlett stumbled as she neared the water's edge, pitched to the side and yelped, but righted herself in time to avoid going under. When she reached solid ground she was limping.

'There's a house up there,' she said, pointing ahead. 'I saw a chimney and smoke.'

'No.' Dylan shook his head.

'But we could—'

'No!'

'What's your plan, then?' she shouted. 'We're soaking wet and a storm's coming, so what's your plan?'

Dylan gritted his teeth. He looked up the road. Hills, rain, more hills. If he had a phone, he could call a cab, get to a train. If he had a phone . . . *Fuck.*

'We need to get out of the rain,' Scarlett insisted. 'We could ask them for help.'

'No,' he said.

Her face crumpled and she tossed her head and turned her back to him.

Dylan shuddered, his teeth chattering. It was freezing.

She looked around at him. He could tell she was trying not to cry, her eyes all hurt-looking, mouth pinched. 'You do what you like,' she said. 'I'm going to get out of this rain.'

'Don't go to the house,' he said.

'Why not? And why should I listen to you, anyway? You crashed the car and then nearly drowned us.' Her words were breaking up, her face darkening. She was going to start crying again.

He walked closer, feet squelching in his trainers. 'We're not going to the house,' he said. 'I have to stay under the radar.'

'Well, I'll go on my own, then,' Scarlett said.

'No,' he said. Deadly serious. He couldn't let her ruin everything. 'We stay together until I can find a way out of here, right?'

'Why? Cos you don't trust me?' she said.

'I don't trust anyone,' Dylan said.

She turned to go.

'Stop,' he said. 'You're staying with me.' He grabbed her arm and she yanked it away. A dart of fear in her eyes. Petey had looked at him that way. It made Dylan want to lash out. Give them a good thumping. *Something to cry for.*

He hawked and spat a gob of phlegm. God, he'd kill for a smoke.

'We'll check it out,' he said. 'Not the house, but see if there's somewhere to shelter, somewhere they won't see us. We can wait there till—'

'Till what? Till when?' She shivered, crossed her arms, hugging herself.

All the fucking questions. His skull was going to explode.

'Till I can get away,' he said. 'Got it?'

She gave a quick shrug, mardy.

'We need to be careful. They might have security gates or cameras or dogs,' Dylan said.

She rolled her eyes. Gave another shrug. Her chin quivered.

'Stay close. And do what I tell you to,' he said.

'Fine,' she said, in a strop, and began limping up the road.

Dylan looked back as they reached the turning for the driveway up to the house.

The car was still swaying and bobbing in the brown floodwater.

Chapter 14

Ron was sprawled on the sofa, half asleep and more than halfway drunk. He'd followed that first beer with two more, then moved on to spirits. The Graybridges had an impressive cellar.

Was it called a cellar if it wasn't wine? And if it wasn't below ground?

Bottles arrayed in a glass and beechwood cabinet. She liked gin and he liked whisky. Ron would settle for whatever was going. Anything that got the job done.

Mungo, stretched out in the middle of the rug, gave a shuddery sigh and twitched a leg.

Josh had always preferred white wine. 'I only have to look at forty-per-cent proof and I get a headache,' he said.

'Aren't hangovers par for the course at your age?' Ron had said. Josh was twelve years younger than him.

At twenty-six Ron had been a regular at the clubs, pulling all-nighters, poppers and Es giving him the energy to dance till dawn. That had changed when he joined the Fire Brigade. Reined it in. Several nights a month on call at the station and no alcohol allowed, of course.

The peculiar intimacy of eating and sleeping with a group of strangers took time to get used to, trying to navigate the existing routines, to fit in with the group, negotiate the petty rivalries and the allegiances.

Ron was moved to a new station as part of the service reorganisation and it hadn't taken him long to work out that Lance was pack leader, even though he wasn't the most senior watch member. Lance had charisma, helped by his classic good looks and infectious laugh. A lover of humour, not only the practical jokes that seemed to be a long-standing tradition in the service but word play and slapstick, jokes and gags, even impressions. He'd have them in stitches, wiping their eyes. None of them objected to the fact that half his material was hate-filled malice. Always punching down.

The first time it hit Ron, really hit him, they'd just finished a roast chicken dinner and a card game was under way with Lance pontificating on the prospect of equal-opportunities training that the service would be running in a bid to increase diversity. 'Load of bollocks,' he'd said, dealing a fresh hand. 'Who wants some limp-wristed fudge-packer giving you a fireman's lift, eh?' A couple of the men sniggered. 'Unless it's another shirt-lifter.' Lance went on, his voice changed to a high, mincing register: 'Ooh, Jeremy, you can stick your hose in my chimney anytime.' A burst of laughter. Ron hadn't joined in. And Lance had homed in on him, in an instant. 'You not amused, Ronnie boy? You disagree?'

Say something.

'I don't have a problem with it,' Ron said, trying to hide the tension running through him. *Being gay.*

Lance had eyes locked on him, and Ron was aware of the others poised to take their cue.

'Diversity,' Ron said, bottling it.

'You want to watch him, Jimmy, bunk next to yours,' Lance said. 'Sleep on your back, I would.'

In the twisted, logic-free world of rampant homophobes, gays were both ineffectual limp-wristed pansies and raving sexual predators. And they were all paedophiles.

Jimmy laughed, blushing. Fair-skinned and freckled. The same age as Ron.

'Fuck off,' Ron had said, picking up his cards, trying to smile and shrug it off. Not having the guts to make a stand. Fearing that if he did come out, they'd make his life hell, drive him out of the job. He sifted through his hand, waiting for Lance to have another dig, sensing that Lance had guessed his orientation and was ready to out him.

But Lance had just tapped his cards on the table, knocking them together and said, 'Not that I'd object to a couple of birds on the watch. A quick shag now and again on a slow night, eh?' And had given a big throaty chuckle.

The sound of banging and Mungo barking broke into Ron's memories. He felt a moment's relief that all that was behind him, in the past. The relief soon soured with the taint of what had come afterwards. For him. For Lance.

Heart in his mouth, palms sweating, Ron crept to the window and peered out from behind the curtain.

He saw a middle-aged man, grey hair and a neat beard.

Now what?

Ron moved to the hallway, called from behind the front door, 'Who is it?'

Mungo barked again and Ron turned to shush him.

'I'm sorry to bother you,' the man replied. 'My name's Mike Carter. I'm hoping you can help me.' Well spoken. Nothing like his earlier visitor.

Ron felt foolish, hiding behind the door. And woozy from the booze.

The man sounded pleasant enough. And he was asking for help. You didn't turn away someone in need, especially not out in the country.

Still, Ron didn't shut Mungo away. He wanted to have the dog there as a precaution, even though he was a pet and not a guard.

'Sit,' Ron instructed, and Mungo did.

Ron took the bolt off the door and opened it, moving back.

'Thank you so much,' the man said, stepping inside. He sounded a little out of breath and worry lines made deep grooves between his eyebrows. 'I'm sorry to bother you.'

Ron shut the door but didn't invite him any further in. He'd had enough of people for one day. The sooner he got rid of him the better.

'Only I'm looking for my daughter.'

'Your daughter?' Ron hadn't expected that.

'She's run away,' he said. 'She's been groomed by this older lad she met online. She's gone off with him. She's only eleven.' His face was drawn, eyes avid with anxiety.

Oh, good God. 'But what makes you think they're here?'

'Sorry.' The man held up a hand. 'I'm in a bit of a state. Only the car they were in, it's stuck in the flood down the hill.'

'Here?' Ron said.

'Yes. They've abandoned it. Have you seen them? Seen anyone? She's wearing a purple coat.'

'No,' Ron said. 'Do the police—'

'They know,' he said quickly. 'They're out looking too.' He was frowning, shaking his head. 'The car's here but . . . I don't know.'

'I haven't seen them,' Ron said.

The man grimaced, straight white teeth. Ron still had an after-image of Lance in his head, Lance laughing. Ron felt muddle-headed, slow from the drink.

'Without a car,' the man said, 'they must be on foot.'

'Or they could have called a taxi?' Ron suggested.

'Maybe.' A flash of intent lit his eyes. 'Where's the nearest train station?'

'Matlock,' Ron said. 'About ten miles.'

'OK. Thank you and I'm so sorry to bother you. But in this weather . . . Thinking of her with . . .' The man was still breathing unevenly. Panicking. Ron felt for him. Almost enough to offer him a hot drink. But not quite.

'I'm not sure what trains'll be running. With the floods,' Ron added. 'There's lines closed.'

The man nodded. 'I'll try there, anyway. If you see them, he's eighteen, skinny, hair bleached. White lad. She's mixed race, got a little Afro.' He demonstrated, hands either side of his head, and faltered. Took a breath and wiped at his beard.

'Purple coat,' Ron said.

'Please, take my number, just in case.'

Ron typed it into his phone and promised to call if he saw either of them.

'I hope you find her,' Ron said, as he showed him out.

Piccadilly Circus, his mum's voice. *Without the clowns.* She'd always added that and he'd never really known what it meant, or where it came from.

He'd give her a ring, tomorrow or the day after. Once he was feeling more like himself.

Not feeling yourself? Lance sneered. *Too busy groping someone else?*

'Piss off,' Ron muttered.

He felt unsettled. Should he have done more, asked more about Mike Carter and his daughter's situation?

It was as if something was missing, something he'd forgotten to say or do.

Then he reassured himself: he had done everything that was asked of him. The man had been in such a panic, and only anxious to continue his search as soon as he knew Ron hadn't seen her. He must be insane with worry, Ron thought.

The day had been so bizarre, one thing after another. Violence exploding in the backwater where he'd always felt at peace, cocooned as much as he ever could be. No wonder he couldn't think straight and was second-guessing himself, the residue of shock still poisoning his system.

Nothing to do with the Scotch, then? He smiled, thinking of Josh. Thinking of him too much, these days. Not healthy. *You can't go back.*

He walked down the driveway to the road, and there at the bottom of the hill was the abandoned car, plumb in the middle of the flood. A Land Rover Discovery. It would cost someone a pretty penny, recovering a vehicle like that and making it roadworthy. Idiot must have thought he could drive straight through, no idea how deep the water was.

Ron looked up to the hills in the north. Clouds like galleons swept past Lovers Leap. Beyond, the land was shrouded in cloud the colour of steel wool in the encroaching dusk.

Ron wondered if he'd be left to report the vehicle. The lad who'd driven it wasn't going to be hanging around waiting for the AA or Green Flag if he was eloping with a minor. Statutory rape that was. Ron didn't like to think about it, about the girl. Any of it.

He belched and tasted sour whisky. He probably ought to eat, line his stomach. It was only a quarter past six but it felt like the middle of the night.

The horses would be OK till morning and the hens were safely away. Mungo would need another trip outside before Ron locked up for the night. He should turn in early.

There was a portion of stew left in the slow cooker. But he'd have another wee dram first. After all, who was counting?

*

There had been someone at the house. All the lights were on as they'd crept past and Scarlett had caught sight of a man, a big man with red hair. Then a dog had barked and Dylan hissed at her to move it.

They were looking for somewhere out of the rain. There were lots of different buildings. First there was a double garage, which Dylan had tried to get into, but the door was locked on that.

Scarlett had gone to the next one. Hopping part of the way because her left ankle hurt with every step. The building was single-storey with big wooden doors. Was it a barn? Was it big enough to be a barn? The rain was dripping into her eyes and she brushed it away with the back of her hand.

'Try this?' Scarlett said to Dylan. A bar kept the doors closed and it made her think of castles and forts in films in the old days before they had locks and keys. The wood was heavy, and lifting it brought the pain to her shoulder, but she managed. She propped it against the wall further along.

Dylan pulled open the doors.

There was a strong dusty-sweet smell, like grass in summer, mixed with something else, something sharp. Then a snorting noise and Dylan reared back, knocking into her.

'Shit!' he whispered.

'What?' Scarlett edged past him. She heard the noise again and saw a flash of white in the gloom, the roll of an eye. Then she made out the silhouette as it shifted in the shadows.

'It's a horse!' she said. She stepped further into the space and found another. 'Two of them. Horses.'

The second nickered at her. Slowly Scarlett lifted a hand and patted its neck. She turned round, surveying the stable, her eyes adjusting to the dim light. There was space opposite the stalls, and bales of hay. 'We can sit on that.'

'No way,' Dylan said.

'Why not?'

'We'll find somewhere else,' he said, still hovering at the door.

'But why?' Scarlett said.

'Cos someone might come and feed them or whatever.'

Scarlett didn't think that was the real reason. 'They won't hurt you,' she said. 'They're shut in.' She saw a flashlight hanging by the door. If she jumped she could reach it, but Dylan was nearer. 'Get that,' she said, pointing.

'Why?' he said.

'Because we might need it to see. It's nearly dark.'

He unhooked the strap and flicked it on. A yellow wash lit the stable and the two animals. One was chestnut and the other was black, the one she'd stroked.

Scarlett had been horse-riding a few times, with a class on Saturday mornings, but when she'd started dance school she'd had to stop.

'We could stay here,' Scarlett said again. 'It's dry and there's—'

'Come on,' Dylan said. He turned off the torch and Scarlett was momentarily blinded. Her heart jumped. She didn't like the dark. Couldn't bear the dark.

'Wait,' she called.

'Shut the fuck up,' Dylan said harshly.

She thought about the man in the house. She wondered what Dylan would do if she just left now, ran back and banged on the door. She'd be able to get dry and have a drink. She was so thirsty and soaked through and she ached all over. She could use the man's phone to ring Nana.

But Nana's— Little shocks of fear bit at her fingers.

Scarlett couldn't run properly with her foot like this anyway. Dylan would easily catch her. Tears stung the back of her nose and behind her eyes. She sniffed them away.

Outside Dylan told her to put the wooden bar back on.

He stopped by another shed next door to the stables. Stone walls at the bottom part and wooden planks above. A water tap on the wall.

Dylan worked at the bolt on the door, which squeaked when he slid it back, and Scarlett thought she heard the dog bark again.

He shone the torch. It was like a storage place. Saddles and straps hanging up. Cubbyholes with brushes and things. Sacks and bags piled up along one wall. A long wooden bench and a wooden chair that looked like it was made of old sticks.

'This'll do,' Dylan said.

It wasn't as good as the stables, anyone could see that. Not as big, no hay bales to sit on. They could have used some hay to cover themselves and keep warm, like a nest.

Scarlett went back out.

'Where are you going?' he said, following, looking like he was ready to chase her.

'Drink of water,' she said. She turned on the tap and rubbed her hands under the cold water until she got rid of the worst of the dirt, then crouched down, ignoring the stabbing in her ankle, cupped her hands and took several mouthfuls. Her tongue hurt when she swallowed. The water tasted funny, rusty, not like normal water, but she didn't mind. She was so thirsty.

Dylan had some too, but he spat it out. 'That's well rank.'

Then they went into the shed and he pulled the door shut. Dylan sat on the long bench and Scarlett tried the chair made of sticks. It was more comfortable than it looked. And it rocked. But she was still so shivery and her feet were numb. Her legs ached with the cold.

'Now what?' she said.

'We stay here till it gets light. Can't go anywhere in the dark,' Dylan said.

Scarlett coughed. Her lips stung. She ran her tongue over them – they were cracked and she tasted blood. She rocked in the chair. She thought of the collision. The massive bang. The red car with its bonnet all crumpled.

'Do you think he's dead?' Scarlett said. The question was like a stone crushing her chest.

'Who? Dylan said.

'My dad.' Her voice dipped.

'Why should he be dead?' Dylan said.

'From the crash,' Scarlett said.

Dylan laughed. How could he laugh?

'That wasn't your dad,' Dylan scoffed.

Scarlett felt prickles on the back of her neck, a dizziness in her head. 'What? Are you sure?' *He's still out there!*

'Yes. Didn't you see her?' He was scowling at Scarlett like she was thick.

Her? 'Who was it?' Scarlett said.

'I don't know,' Dylan said, spreading his arms and making the torchlight bounce around the walls.

Scarlett was hot all over. He was so mean and stupid.

'So you made someone crash and you might have killed them, actually killed them, and you don't even know who it is?' She was nearly shouting.

'She was coming after us,' Dylan said slowly, a threat in his voice, his face set. 'She was going to stop us. Stop me.'

'Well, I wish she had,' Scarlett told him.

'Fuck off.' He switched the light off.

'Turn it on,' Scarlett said quickly.

'We'll waste the—'

'Turn it on! I'm not sitting in the dark.'

'Scared, are you?' he sneered.

'At least I'm not scared of horses,' she said.

Dylan snapped the light on, pointing it straight at Scarlett so it dazzled her. She jumped up, limped over and snatched it from him. And he gave another laugh. She set it on one of the shelves, angling it so it lit the space but shone away from them and softened the light.

Scarlett picked up a couple of the empty sacks, coughing at the dust that flew from them. She went back to her chair. She wrapped one around her shoulders and the other over her knees. They smelt of horse, a hairy smell.

Scarlett shuddered again, and wrapped her arms around her chest. 'You can leave me here,' she said. 'In the morning. You set off and I'll wait here and count to a thousand or whatever, then go to the house for help.'

He didn't say anything.

'Dylan?'

'Yeah, I heard you,' he snapped. 'Let's just drop the chat, right? Bit of peace?'

Pig.

Scarlett closed her eyes. The rain falling sounded like crackling, like a fire starting with those snapping, spitting noises.

She didn't want to think about the woman's car. Or Mike somewhere out there, hunting for Scarlett.

Her foot didn't hurt unless she moved it. It must be twisted or sprained. Scarlett wasn't sure what the difference was.

She was so cold. Her insides were cold all the way through, but her face was hot. Nana would always put her hand on Scarlett's forehead to check for a fever. Then she'd feel under each side of her ears at the edge of her jaw. *For the glands.*

Scarlet hated being ill. That wobbly, dizzy feeling when things seemed to be growing and shrinking and what she could see was tilting, the colours too bright and noises suddenly louder than they should be. And the dreams that came with a fever. Like her nightmares.

Dylan coughed and her heart gave a jolt. He must be cold too. He didn't even have a coat on. What had he done that was so bad he'd crash a car and hide out like this and not even let her go to get help? Had he actually hurt someone— *Don't! Stop!*

Her stomach ached and she pulled the sacking tighter around her. She could sense the questions, all the awful questions, bubbling away. The ones she'd never dared to ask, never wanted to say out loud because if she did she'd have to hear the answers and she didn't want to know. She couldn't bear to.

Scarlet wriggled and rocked the chair, trying to get away from the voices in her head. *Think about something else!*

When all this is over. A hot bath and a huge plate of pasta with lentil sauce and pineapple cake and hot chocolate made with oat milk and seeing Faye and— *But Nana . . .*

A lump filled her throat. What would she do? Where would she live and— She gulped with panic, fierce and wild. *Stop it!* She squeezed the wooden arms of the chair as hard as she could.

Her dance. Her and Faye's. She'd go through it in her head, every single move. And when she'd done it and got to the end she'd do it again. And if that didn't work she could go through all the words for all the songs she knew by heart.

Dylan made a noise again, like a snort. His eyes were closed. Was he asleep? How could he sleep?

She moved, rose up, thinking of the door, of stealing out and creeping away. But his eyes opened and he looked at her. He gave a shake of his head, got up and hauled the bench across the stone floor, making a scraping sound as he dragged it, until he had it in front of the door. Like a barrier. Then he stretched out to lie on his back like he was going to sleep.

Scarlett wouldn't sleep. There were lots of time she couldn't sleep, when the dreams came back. When all the horrible feelings crept around her, all the terrible thoughts, like poison. Snatches of memory: the dark and the cold, a blue light, the bottom of the sofa and a row of fat shiny studs like beetles with dull, silver shells, a humming noise, and rattling. *Mummy? Mummy?*

Scarlet moaned and pressed her fists into her eyes. Shut up, she told herself.

She didn't always wake Nana. Less as she got older. Instead she'd read something, look at her books about ocean mammals or how bees talk to each other. And wait for it to get light outside. Wait to feel safe again. Just like now.

But would it really be better in the morning? Would Dylan really let her go?

The shadows in the room dipped and there was a patting noise.

Scarlett gripped the arms of the chair and looked about before she realised that it was a moth, a big furry pale brown moth flying onto the torch over and over again, its wings fluttering as fast as her heart beat in her chest.

Chapter 15

Laura heard the engine before the car came into view.

Taken you long enough.

PC Ali pulled in behind her and left his headlights on, the beams lifting the dull grey twilight.

Laura narrowed her eyes, the light was too harsh in the mirror. She turned her head to the side, wincing. Her skull was pounding still.

'Sarge?' PC Ali called through the window. In his alarm, he looked even younger,

Laura pressed the window switch, not expecting it still to work, but it edged down a few inches and grated to a halt. 'Come the long way?' she said, voice rasping, like a chain smoker's. Words slurring. 'The door's jammed.'

'What about you? Are you OK?' He was shaking his head, obviously shocked by the damage. She'd given him the code for needing assistance and her location when she radioed for help but told him nothing else.

'That one might open.' She pointed her thumb to the back seat behind her, sending a wave of pain like a flamethrower through her temples, making her nauseous, leaving her drained.

'I should get an ambulance.' He was staring at her hands.

'Looks worse than it is,' Laura said.

'Yes, but still if—'

'Just try the bloody door,' Laura said.

PC Ali set his jaw and moved to pull at the door behind her. The car rocked with each tug. *One. Two. Three.* The motion made her grit her teeth.

'It's not going to do it,' PC Ali called.

'Try the other side then.'

Laura listened to the scuff of his feet on the road. He began to yank at the front passenger door.

'Not that one,' Laura said. He stopped and looked at her, disconcerted. 'Any fool can see that's buckled too. The back.' She closed her eyes.

The car was tipping again and on the second pull the rear passenger door flew open.

Now all she had to do was gather enough strength to clamber back there.

'Can you get through?' he said. 'I could call the Fire Brigade.'

Up to their eyes rescuing people from the floods? Great idea. 'I can do it,' she said. *Could she?* Laura was fit generally, a bit overweight but she kept in shape by swimming. She twisted round. And everything rippled.

'Do the seats recline?' PC Ali said.

'Yes.'

'That might be easier.'

Laura didn't waste any energy replying. Her chest and lungs felt frail, as though she had an infection. *Or maybe been in a car crash.*

She bent down to reach the release lever under the passenger seat, head spinning. The seat flipped back and PC Ali reached in to remove the head rest.

Laura rolled to her left and onto the passenger seat, got onto her hands and knees. The burns on her hands blazed as she took on weight, ready to crawl. *Like Mateo.* Though he could walk now, little trots before pitching over. *If the crash had been worse, if the airbag hadn't—*

'You OK?' PC Ali said.

Laura gave a grunt, braced herself and shuffled forward, head first. Reaching the end of the seat, she didn't have the space or even the strength to swing her legs round. She was beached by the door.

'Can you?' She raised her arms, feeling like a right tit, a child asking to be picked up.

PC Ali blushed and stepped forward. 'Yes, sure.' He crouched and slid his arms under her armpits then took slow steps backwards, lifting her out of the car.

She could smell something astringent, minty, this close up. Hair gel, perhaps, shave foam?

She gained the ground and he released her. Her throat was parched. 'Have you any—' She swooned, stumbled on the grass verge, lurching towards the dry-stone wall. *Shit.*

He caught her again. 'You need an ambulance, Sarge.'

'No.' She coughed and the band of iron cinched tighter around her head. She put out a hand to steady herself on the side of the car.

'I think you've got concussion,' PC Ali said.

'No ambulance.'

You said no to an ambulance? Are you insane? Hector's face pale with fury. ¡Madre de Dios! ¡Puta loca! *Mad slag. You think of us?*

But Scarlett was near, had been near. Laura *had* to follow her, find her.

'Is anything broken?' PC Ali said.

'No.' But the stabbing pain in her side, agonising when she breathed out, must be a cracked rib.

'Come and sit down,' PC Ali said. 'I'll move your car.'

She watched from his patrol car as he leant in through the back passenger door of the Volvo and twisted the steering wheel, then took the handbrake off and made use of the camber to roll the car to the roadside. Laura heard him swear as it knocked into the wall. What did it matter? It was a write-off anyway.

'Who crashed into you?' he asked her, once he'd joined her and she'd taken a drink from his water bottle.

'Other way round. It was the Discovery,' Laura said.

'You found them?' He sounded surprised.

'He wouldn't respond. I was flashing my lights. He wouldn't . . .' She tried to clear her throat. She stared out at the wreck of her car. Only two years old. 'But he speeded up and then he stopped sideways on.'

PC Ali whistled, shaking his head. 'And he could drive away?'

Obviously. She threw him a look.

'I could take you into Chesterfield – they have an A and E department,' PC Ali said.

'I'm not going to hospital. We're going after them.'

'But they must be twenty minutes away by now,' he said.

She wanted to shout at him but it would only make her head worse. 'I don't care,' she said. 'I want to follow them.'

'I was due back at the station—'

'Did you find Gregory Martin?' Laura said.

'No.'

'And your suspect? The one in the Astra?'

'Dylan Ellis,' PC Ali said.

'What?'

'That's the name on the insurance.'

'I'm not sure how signific—'

'No, listen, Sarge. I had another callout. Aggravated assault.'

'You have been busy,' Laura said drily.

'Just down here.' PC Ali waved to the road ahead. 'The perpetrator was looking for someone called Dylan. They attacked the householder with a machete.'

'Ouch.'

'I think Dylan Ellis was working a county line,' PC Ali said. 'The house in Leek – I think it was a trap house.'

'Set up for dealing?' Laura said.

'Yes.' He gave a sigh, then said, 'It was gone.' He sounded embarrassed.

'What was gone?' Laura said.

'The Astra.'

'How can it have gone? Where were you?'

'I went to see if Gregory Martin was on the footpath. It's a short-cut if you're walking. He must've been hiding.'

'If it was him then he must've had a key for it,' Laura said. *The coat in the café, the note in the pocket. That was in the teenager's coat.* It was hard to line it all up, her head full of fog, but she persisted. 'The teenager at the services had to leave his coat there when he ran, when he took the Discovery. I reckon his keys were in the coat and Gregory Martin, who'd been stranded, took them, stocked up on petrol and went to retrieve it.' She thought for a minute. 'Can you describe Dylan Ellis?'

'No.'

'Look.' She showed PC Ali the CCTV from the shop. 'I think this is Dylan Ellis. And now he's got Scarlett.'

Why? What was he doing with her?

'We need to stop him.' She flexed her fists and stings streaked through her hands, taking her breath away. 'So let's go and find them, shall we?'

He started the engine.

'They won't have got far if they carried on down here,' PC Ali said. 'It's flooded in the valley, about a mile on. When I came earlier I had to go round the long way, approach from the north. But there's a couple of lanes, turning off before the ford, to farms.'

'We'll check them out, then,' she said.

A wave of vertigo rippled through her and she closed her eyes. When she opened them PC Ali was frowning, mouth opening, no doubt going to bleat on about hospitals and ambulances again.

'Quick as you like,' Laura said. 'We've wasted enough time already. And there's a child at risk out there.'

*

Ron let Mungo out and the dog hared off around the side of the house. Ron called him back. Usually the dog peed against one of the trees that skirted the garden at the front of the house and didn't venture further in the evening. He whistled for Mungo, then resigned himself to go and fetch him. He trudged past the sitting-room windows and turned to follow the path that ran to the stables. 'Mungo. Come here.'

The dog was whining now, over by the outbuildings.

Ron's eyes were drawn to a yellow glow, a lozenge-shaped light coming from the small skylight on the tack-room roof.

As he looked, it vanished.

Someone was in there.

The man with the machete?

Sweat broke across Ron's back, around his brow.

But hiding wasn't that bloke's style, was it? If he'd come back he'd already have dealt with Ron, surely.

Mungo was patrolling in front of the building, snuffling at the ground, turning back to Ron, eager to enlist him in his hunt.

'Here, Mungo. Come on, boy. Come now!' Ron shouted.

The dog returned to him, rump and tail wagging, wary of being scolded.

'Stay!' Ron commanded. The dog did as he was told.

Ron moved quietly across the grass to approach the outbuildings from the back. The sound of rain would cover any noise he made brushing past the shrubs and picking his way between the silver birch saplings. Their pale grey bark catching the last of the light acted as way-markers.

Cautiously he drew closer to the tack room. He edged up to the back wall and leant close, ears pricked for the slightest sound within.

An owl hooted from down in the gorge.

Ron stilled himself, breathing as shallowly as possible, his heart thudding loud in his ears.

He heard a shuffle, the creak of timber. Waited.

A cough, small and breathy. A murmur, a child's voice making some request.

'No,' the second voice, low.

The child again, slightly louder. Ron couldn't make out what they were saying, though he heard pleading in the cadence.

'Wait,' the male voice.

Then a rush of words from the child, hysteria, movement too. Ron caught odd words: 'I'm not going' . . . 'the light' . . . 'please.'

'Shut it!' A shout from the man, the boy. The skin on Ron's head tightened. They were here! The child and the paedophile who had groomed her.

Silence from within.

Is it them? Who else could it be? He had to make sure.

Ron walked away, deliberately crunching his boots on the path and calling to Mungo, 'In we go, there's a good dog. Inside now.'

He put Mungo into the house, then walked quietly back until he could see the outhouses. He stood in the rain, waiting. His thumb throbbed, and he could feel heat creeping up his arm. He'd need to keep an eye on it, watch for any sign of infection.

Ron saw the diamond of light reappear from the tack room and stole back there. In the rear wall a knot of wood was missing in the panelling, the size of a two-pence piece. It was on his list of little jobs to fix, not that it caused much damage. The rear wall faced south and was shielded from the worst of the weather.

Holding his breath, he put an eye to the hole and could see the girl side on, her halo of dark hair and a glimpse of purple coat at her knees. She was in the rustic rocking chair, her abuser beyond her, sitting on the bench by the door, a torch in his hands.

Ron didn't linger.

He walked as lightly as he could back to the house.

Once inside, he rang the number Mike Carter had left.

'Your little girl, she's here,' he said. 'They both are.'

'Oh, thank God,' the man said, in a rush.

'I'll call the police?' Ron said.

'No, no, I will. Thanks. I've a direct number. Listen, keep them there, please. Make sure she doesn't leave. I'll be there as soon as I can. Just keep her there. Please.'

Ron agreed and rang off.

He rubbed at the back of his neck. Anxious. Unease broiled in the pit of his stomach. What if Ron had spooked them? Or Mungo had? What if even now they were leaving the grounds? *Eleven years old and she's probably head over heels in love with this lad. She's a child.* His stomach turned.

He had to make sure she didn't leave, keep her safe.

Ron zipped his waterproof back up and activated the torch on his phone, then walked back to the tack room.

When he'd rounded the building and reached the front, he shone his torch on the bolt. *Slide that shut and they're trapped. No way out. No chance of escape.*

But a sense of revulsion filled him at the thought of sealing her in there with her predator.

And what might the man do if he realised they were caught, that his time was almost up? What might he do to her then? Cornered, desperate, sexually deranged.

Ron couldn't risk it.

With one swift movement he flung open the door, blocking it with his body. Eyes taking in the startled youth leaping up from the bench just inside the door. The little girl crying out, wide-eyed, shivering and swaddled in sacking.

Ron smiled and said, 'Now what on earth are you doing here on a night like this, eh? Come on inside. Get dried off. Have a hot drink. You'll catch your death out here. Come on. I don't bite.'

Chapter 16

Scarlett stood up, shaking off the sacks, panic flashing through her. The big man, Ron, was still talking as he slid the bench back, telling them to come with him.

Scarlett looked at Dylan. Dylan didn't say anything, he just grabbed his bag and, still holding the flashlight, which he'd snapped off when the door opened, followed Ron outside, his face set and his eyes hard.

Scarlett went after them, trying to keep the weight off her bad foot. Her thoughts were whirring, wild. What was the man going to do? Would he help her? He had a phone so he could ring the police and tell them where she was. That was good, wasn't it? Better than sitting in the cold shed with Dylan all night, not knowing if Dylan would really let her go in the morning. He hadn't exactly agreed to Scarlett's plans, had he? Just told her to shut up.

They came past the stables and round the corner and the house was all lit up. Scarlett felt a lump in her throat, seeing it like that, like she was coming home, even though it was a stranger's house. And then thinking how kind this man was when he could have just shouted at them for trespassing.

She wondered how he'd known they were there. Was it the dog barking? Or had he heard voices when they were arguing about the stables, and seen the torchlight? He didn't seem angry at all and he had a friendly face and had spoken to them gently so hopefully—

A sudden scuffing sound, a change in the air, and Dylan was running away.

Wait! Had Dylan seen something was wrong? Spotted some danger that Scarlett hadn't noticed? Her skin prickled and she wanted to run after him. Was that stupid? She needed help and Dylan wasn't going to let her get the police so . . .

Anyway, she couldn't run.

'Let him go.' Ron gave a shake of his head, looking disappointed. But he didn't make any move to stop Scarlett and that reassured her. He wasn't forcing her to go with him.

She shuddered.

'Let's get inside where it's warm,' he said.

They carried on walking.

'You've hurt your foot?' Ron said.

'Yes, twisted it.'

'I should have an elastic bandage inside,' he said.

She thought he would ask lots of questions, like what were they doing in the shed, and where had they come from, and who were they and why were they wet through. Though maybe he just thought they were wet from the rain. Or he'd seen the car in the flood and worked out they'd been in it. But he didn't say anything else until they got inside, where a big black Labrador greeted them with a little dance.

'That's Mungo,' Ron said.

'I'm Scarlett.' She patted the dog.

'So, what first?' Ron said. 'Food, hot drink, clean clothes. I should have something . . .'

'I need to call the police,' Scarlett said.

He smiled. 'No worries, they're on their way.'

'Really?' A lightness rose, a bubble in her chest. It really *was* going to be OK. The police were coming. And knowing that was like a dam breaking. All the things she'd been so frightened of came flooding up and she began to cry.

'Scarlett? Hey, sit down.' Ron pulled out a chair. He had a bandage on his thumb.

He crouched in front of her. His hair was all red and straggly, and with his big beard, he looked like a pirate. Or a heavy-metal musician.

'Did he hurt you?' Ron's breath smelt bad.

'No,' she said, wiping her face and wincing when she touched her cheek where the airbag had punched her.

'You sure?'

She nodded.

'Your face?' Ron said.

'Oh, that was in the crash.'

'You had a crash?'

'Yes, before we came down the hill.'

He shook his head. 'But you're OK?'

'Yes.' Scarlett sniffed.

'How about I make you something to eat while you get dry? Mrs G should have some clothes that'll do in an emergency. And I think this counts.'

Scarlett was glad to hear he was married. But she wasn't sure why that mattered.

'Is she here?' Scarlett said.

'Away at the moment. OK?' He looked at her so kindly she nearly started crying again.

She took a shaky breath and said, 'OK.'

'So, I've some beef stew I can heat up . . .'

Scarlett felt tired all over again. 'I'm vegan,' she said.

'Oh. Right.' He went to the fridge and looked in it for what seemed like ages. Then sighed. He opened one of the kitchen cabinets.

Mungo had come over to Scarlett and she stroked his head. He had a wet nose and big black eyes.

'Beans on toast?' Ron said.

‘Yes, please. Dry toast.’

‘Dry toast?’

‘Unless you’ve got any vegan margarine.’

‘Ah, right.’ He gave a nod.

‘Now, I’ll show you her clothes, or would you rather I brought things down?’

Scarlett was going to say she’d go up but then she remembered her ankle. So she said, ‘Can you get them?’

‘Course.’

He came down in a couple of minutes with arms full of clothes. ‘I’ve drawn the curtains in the living room. Give you some privacy,’ he said. ‘There’s a towel here, too. Not sure about shoes, but these are probably the best.’ He held up a pair of suede bootees. ‘Just give me a call when you’re done. Now I’ll get those beans on. What about a drink?’

Scarlett knew he wouldn’t have any plant milk so she said, ‘Some juice?’ And he said he had orange or tonic water so she picked orange.

In the living room Scarlett sorted through the clothes. Everything was way too big for her but she found some yoga pants which had a drawstring and if she pulled that really tight and tied it they didn’t fall down.

She dragged off her top, which stuck to her damp skin, and chose a long-sleeved, white T-shirt and pulled it on. A thick roll-neck fleece with red and pink zigzags on it would go on top. The sleeves of both covered her hands so she pushed them back.

The suede bootees were big, too, but she hoped they’d stay on. She tried not to think too much about what they were made of. *Priorities, Scarlett.*

Oh, Nana.

The falling feeling came rolling through her. The flash of blue. Her voice echoing in the quiet house, ‘Mummy? Mummy? Please, Mummy?’ No answer; just that humming noise.

Breathing? Had she been breathing? The notion was like a fist in her stomach.

Scarlett just wanted it to stop. Wanted everything to be all right again. Well, as all right as it could be.

'Everything OK in there?' Ron called.

Scarlett cleared her throat. 'Fine,' she said. She snatched up her wet things and carried them into the kitchen. 'I don't know what to do with these.'

'I'll find you a bag,' Ron said. 'Just put them down there.'

'You hurt your thumb?' Scarlett said.

'Ah, yes.' He looked a bit embarrassed. 'It's nothing,' he said. 'Cooking accident.'

The beans on toast were on the table. Mungo was close by, nose raised, sniffing.

'You sit down,' Ron said to the dog. 'You've had your lot today.'

Scarlett hopped over to the chair. She felt warm now. On the outside anyway. Still shaky inside and every so often a shiver ran through her, reminding her that she was still scared even though she'd found someone to help.

'Will the police be here soon?' Scarlett said, as she sat down.

'Any time now. Your dad said he'd call them when I let him know you were here. So they can't be far away.'

Scarlett's blood turned to ice. The room, the dog, the food all faded away, leaving only darkness.

*

Dylan had run until he couldn't breathe any more, a stitch stabbing in his side. And he had blisters on his heels where the wet trainers had rubbed. He crouched and switched off the flashlight. It had been impossible to see where he was going without it. Rocks and trees all over the shop, could have knocked himself out.

He listened and looked, trying to quieten his panting, but no one seemed to be following. The Ron bloke hadn't come straight after him when he'd legged it and there was no sign of him now.

Dylan coughed and spat. Listened again. It was weird, the quiet. The only sound was the rain, like lots of ticking.

The path he was on led away from the buildings and into a steep valley, a sort of canyon. When he shone the light he could see the sides rose up, scrubby bushes sticking out here and there but most of it was stone. He hadn't seen any notices or footpath signs so it was probably private property.

Imagine owning a hill, a valley.

When he got his breath back he'd go on. He still felt too near to the house.

And now he'd been discovered he needed to make tracks. The path must go somewhere, right? Eventually he should reach a road or something. It wasn't overgrown, not the main part, so someone must use it. He couldn't go back the other way: this was his only option.

At least he'd got shot of Scarlett. Would she keep her mouth shut about him? How could she when she'd been found with him? Not like she could pretend she was on her own.

His pulse speeded up as he thought of her answering all their questions. She was a bright kid – she'd probably memorised everything he'd said. *Shit!* He banged his fist on his forehead. *Wait. What does she know? Actually know?* What had he said?

He flashed back to the Astra dying on him, blagging a lift off them. She knew his name, his first name, and what car he'd been in. *What else?*

The service station.

Following the tractor.

The crash.

The flood.

His mind jumped from one thing to another, sifting through for any conversation they'd had, anything he'd let slip.

She didn't know anything else. Not his surname or where he'd been or what he'd been up to. What he carried in his bag.

Have you done something wrong? She'd got some stones, the situation she was in and still arguing the toss. Laying into him about the crash. Standing up for herself. Even if that was a pain in the arse.

She reminded Dylan a bit of Kayla. He hadn't thought of Kayla for ages. She'd been at the pupil referral unit with him. Mouthy but dead clever. She'd made him laugh. Eyes that were dancing all the time. And she couldn't stand still for two minutes together. They'd hung out for a while, even got it together a few times round at hers when her mam was out at work. She was sweet, Kayla. Sharp and sweet.

His stomach twisted as he remembered hearing the news about her at the unit. Dylan had been off sick with a bug. Kayla hadn't been answering his messages. Or his calls. He thought maybe she was breaking up with him but he didn't know what he'd done wrong. Fair enough, though. Not like they were married or anything. 'Overdose, Miss,' one of the other kids had said. And just like that she was history. Someone else who'd disappeared from his life. Hard to believe he wouldn't see her again, all lippy but soft too, with Dylan anyway, when she got the chance. It had made him want to punch something. That was all before Dylan had fallen in with Lloyd and Col.

He rubbed at his nose. The blood had dried inside, making it itch.

There was a screech, a screech in the dark, and his heart gave a jump. Owl. Must be an owl. Keep moving.

As he continued into the gorge, the path was bare rock for stretches. The ground at either side was uneven, strewn with stones. Here and there the beam of the flashlight picked out holes. *Broken ankle's the last thing you need.*

He was dying for a piss. He swung the torch round again, checking he was alone, then set it down and took a piss on a bunch of grass.

Could be worse, right? he told himself. Col hadn't found him, he'd got away from the Ron bloke, and he still had all the money. Freedom, a new start, all still possible. He just needed to get to civilisation, sort out the necessaries: phone, fags, food and a ticket to ride.

This time tomorrow he could be sorted, home and dry. Not 'home' home but a fresh beginning. Clean slate.

*

'Nothing,' Ahmed said, frustrated, as they reached the farm at the end of the lane. 'They've not come down here, either.'

'So we go back up to the main drag?' DS O'Neil said.

'Yes.' Ahmed did a three-point turn. He picked up speed and ran through the gears, hoping they wouldn't meet anyone coming the other way along the single-track route and lose more time waiting for them to reverse.

He pulled out onto the B-road. Ahead of them the limestone ridge dominated the skyline and before there, tucked out of sight in the valley, lay Graybridge.

Ahmed wondered if Dylan Ellis was deliberately heading to Graybridge. Like the machete man had done earlier. But according to Ronald Thorpe, the machete man was searching for Dylan Ellis and was livid about not finding him. So why would Dylan Ellis go anywhere near the place? Ahmed's thoughts were interrupted by the sound of DS O'Neil's radio crackling into life.

'Lima, Oscar, one nine. This is Control. Over.'

'Go ahead, Control. Over,' DS O'Neil said.

'We've received word from authorities in Tenerife. Alan Martin has been accused of domestic violence. A complaint made by his partner, Alicia Hernandez. Over.'

'Good work,' DS O'Neil said. 'Email me everything you've got and any further details they can give us. Over and out.'

Ahmed changed down a gear as they neared the crest of the hill. 'You think that's why he's come over here?' he said. 'To get away from the Spanish police? But it's risky, isn't it? And taking his daughter. That's just drawing attention to— Whoa!'

At the bottom of the incline sat the Discovery, half submerged in the flooded ford, the boot door open. Ahmed slowed the car to a halt.

'Can you see if anyone's in it?' DS O'Neill said.

'Hard to tell from here. I can't see anyone. Looks like they climbed out the back. That's Graybridge, the house, over the far side. If I'd ended up in the water, I'd make for there. Nowhere else in these parts.'

'We should check the car,' DS O'Neil said. 'Dylan Ellis was well enough to drive away after I'd rammed into them, but Scarlett? She might have been hurt. She could still be in there.' She unsnapped her seatbelt. 'We go down and—'

He interrupted. 'We need to drive round and come in the other way.'

'And how long's that going to take?' she said hotly.

'Ten minutes. Fifteen,' Ahmed said.

She looked appalled. 'It would be quicker to walk.'

Why wouldn't she listen to him? He knew what he was talking about. 'No,' he argued. 'There's no clear way through. We'd have to get around the water in the first place, go over the walls, through the fields. Then we'd be stuck without a car. That would be stupid. And unsafe.' Had he just called a senior officer stupid? Ahmed swallowed. He tightened his hands on the steering wheel. But he was right, he knew he was.

'Oh, for God's sake,' she said, tugging at her seatbelt.

Which he took for a yes.

While he turned the car around, DS O'Neil got on the radio to report the location of the Discovery. 'Still be on the lookout for Gregory Martin . . .'

'Driving an Astra,' Ahmed whispered at her.

'What?' she said.

'He's in the Astra.'

'We *think* he's in the Astra,' DS O'Neil said.

It was a bloody good guess, as far as Ahmed was concerned. 'It can't hurt,' Ahmed said. 'The more information out there the better.'

'Unless it's the wrong information.' There was a pause, then she dipped her head. 'Also looking for an Astra, registration . . .' Ahmed recited it to her and she relayed it. 'Which Gregory Martin may be in possession of. Over and out.'

Ahmed heard her take a breath.

'OK,' she said. 'So we check the Discovery when we get there and—'

'How are we going to do that? It's in the middle of a flood,' Ahmed said.

She gave him a stare. 'We wade out, carefully, until we can see inside.'

We? Yeah, right.

Ahmed could tell who'd end up soaked through, up to his chin in mucky water. But then again . . . if the girl was lying injured in the footwell, or whatever, and Ahmed saved her . . . then caught Gregory Martin and Dylan Ellis.

'Right,' Ahmed said. 'And if there's no sign we ask the guy at Graybridge, Ronald Thorpe.'

'But if he's not seen her how do we search in weather like this?' DS O'Neil said. 'We can't use drones. The helicopter would struggle, even if they did agree to the expense. It's probably occupied with all the flooding.'

'I don't think they'd OK that, anyway, Sarge. Not unless we had a definite recent sighting.'

'I'll liaise with the search advisers once we've spoken to Ronald Thorpe. See what they say.'

It was fully dark and the road was unlit and unmarked so Ahmed switched his headlights to full beam. Now and again he caught a distant glimpse of an isolated farm in the gloom. Tiny yellow daubs of light.

'Alpha, Alpha, eight five. This is Control. Over.' Ahmed's radio.

'Go ahead, Control. Over,' Ahmed said.

'Report of a mudslide breaching an unclassified road, west of Tintley Hill Farm, near the junction with the B5054. Over.'

'Copy that. Over,' Ahmed said, picturing in his head where it must be.

'Can you attend? The road needs to be closed and warning signs erected. Over.'

No! No. No way was he going to drop the hunt for Dylan Ellis and Scarlett Martin to put up traffic signs.

'Not at present. In pursuance of a child rescue alert, victim Scarlett Martin. Assisting DS O'Neil. Over and out.'

'I must have passed that junction earlier,' DS O'Neil said, 'coming up from Ashbourne.'

'It's not used much. I can't see anyone going that way tonight, not in this.' He hoped he was right. Ahmed would hate for anyone to be hurt, ending up with the road gone from under them, car plunging down the hill. But that was just speculation. It might never happen, while this – the hunt for Scarlett, for Dylan Ellis and Gregory Martin – this was *live*. This was now. And it was happening to him.

'Tell me again about Ronald Thorpe,' DS O'Neil said.

Ahmed did, everything he could remember, even that he was house-sitting and had picked up Dylan Ellis's phone.

'Dylan Ellis,' she said. 'Do we think he's armed?'

Ahmed wanted to say yes, thinking of Coopers Close, the blood, but there was no firm evidence he was carrying a weapon. 'Don't know, Sarge,' he said.

'OK. If we find him, we assume he is until we establish otherwise, clear?'

'Yes.' Ahmed swallowed. And took a breath. Anticipation and anxiety prickling him from head to toe.

Chapter 17

Scarlett moved so quickly that the chair toppled over and crashed to the floor.

Mungo barked.

'What did you say?' Her face was wide with horror.

Keep her there. Please. Ron held up his hand, palm out, placating her. 'Look, I know you might be upset but—'

'How could you do that? How could you?'

'You're only eleven,' Ron said.

'What's that got to do with it?' she said.

'You're a child.'

There were tears on her cheeks, her forehead crazed in a frown. She shook her head, turned away. The sleeves of Mrs G's top falling over her hands.

'But he's gone now.' Ron expected the police would search for the lad in the woods. Why was she so distressed? Had the boy hurt her? Raped her?

'What? You said he was coming.'

'No. *Your dad's* coming. And the police.'

She just stared at him. Her mouth an open O shape. Something in her eyes, panic or disgust?

'He's been looking for you and your boyfriend. He's sick with worry.'

'Dylan's not my boyfriend!'

Dylan? Ron saw the man with the machete, screaming and red-faced, yelling for Dylan. Ron went dizzy. *Dylan? How did he fit—*

'I'm eleven.' Mouth twisted in a scowl.

'Exactly,' Ron said. 'That's what your dad said. Mike, he explained that you ran off with a lad you'd met online. It's called grooming. It might not feel like that but—'

'No! *My dad* is the one who kidnapped me! He's not even called Mike.' She bared her teeth. She was shaking head to toe. Even her halo of hair was trembling.

Ron felt foggy, clouds in his head. *What?* 'Come on,' he said, as if she was joking. Stalling to buy himself time.

'I can't stay here,' she said. 'You can't let him find me.'

'I don't understand. Just sit down, eh? Calm down a bit.'

She limped quickly to the door.

Ron moved to block her exit.

'Scarlett.'

'Let me go,' she said.

'I can't do that.'

'You believed him. You idiot,' she said fiercely. 'Look it up. On your phone. Jeanette Martin, Gregory Martin. 2014.' Her face avid with intensity.

Was it some sort of trick? To distract him so she could make a run for it. Not that she could run far with a sprained ankle like that.

'Go on,' she said. She was gasping, fast, shallow breaths.

Ron typed it in. Pages of links loaded. One word leapt out, over and over. *Murder.*

He clicked the first link. Photographs. Jeanette Martin, a pretty black woman smiling at the camera, a spray of flowers in her hair. Gregory Martin, paler and younger, dark-haired, clean-shaven, but recognisable as the man Ron had seen. Ron's eyes flew over the text, snagging on details: *wanted . . . strangled . . . suspicion of murder . . . daughter aged five who cannot be named . . . questioning . . . fled abroad.*

Fuck!

'Help me,' she begged.

'Jesus!' Ron said. 'I didn't know.'

'Don't let him take me again,' she said. 'Please. Please.'

Ron swallowed, ears buzzing, skin burning.

His mind darted around solutions – hide her upstairs, or back in the shed?

Too risky, too close. And with his van out of action there was no way to drive her out of danger. On foot she was crippled.

'Quick,' she pleaded.

He dialled 999. Asked for the police. Scarlett's eyes locked on him as he spoke. Tension bubbled through him as they made him provide all his own details before getting to the heart of the matter. 'Scarlett Martin, the girl who was abducted. She's here at Graybridge. And her father knows, he's coming for her. We need the police now.'

'Can you stay on the line and—'

'I can't.' Ron hung up. 'Have you ever ridden a horse?' he said. He didn't dare risk Gregory Martin finding her here, wasn't sure he'd be able to protect her from the man. She'd be safer down in the cave.

'Yes. I had lessons.'

'Good.'

He surveyed her. Grabbed the box of juice from the fridge. 'Here.' He thrust it at her. 'I'm going to give you a piggy-back, is that OK? It'll be quicker.'

She only hesitated for a moment. 'Yes.'

Ron turned and crouched and she climbed onto his back, arms round his neck, the carton in one hand. She hooked her legs around his waist.

A sense memory enveloped him, the children he'd carried from smoke-filled rooms, lifted from smashed cars, the ones he'd laid on body bags.

He left the dog in the house and, using his phone as a torch, jogged with her to the stable block.

His heart ached. How could he have been so stupid? So bloody stupid? He'd sensed something was off when Gregory Martin left. He'd dismissed it. Ignored his instincts. *Idiot.*

In the stables, Scarlett slid off his back.

Ron fetched Polly from her stall.

'This is Polly. She's very gentle, easy-going. She'll take you down along the path through the gorge. She knows the way. Even in the dark. Good night vision.'

While he was tacking up, putting on the saddle and bridle and adjusting the straps and stirrups, he told Scarlett where to go.

'You want to look out for a big stone on the left of the track, tall as you and pointed at the top. It's before you reach the waterfalls. If you see the waterfalls you've gone too far. You want to turn left just after the boulder. There aren't any signs but about fifty yards along there's a cave.'

She looked panicked. 'I won't be able to see.'

'I've a lamp for that. You can wait in the cave. You can shelter there. The police are on their way.'

'And so is my father.' Her voice cracked.

'I'll phone him, tell him you got away, that you and Dylan ran off down to the road and I couldn't catch you. I'll come and find you when it's safe.'

He led Polly outside and tightened the girth, fingers working as quickly as he could. It was hard with his thumb bound up.

'You hold her now. I'll get the lamp.'

In one of the storage lockers in the shed he found the headlamp he used for night rides, and for jobs about the place where he needed some light and to keep his hands free. He checked it was working and took it out to Scarlett. 'The on-off switch is at the top,' he said.

She pulled the elastic strap over her head, put the light on – it shone full in his eyes, dazzling him.

'OK. You need a hand up?'

'Other side,' she said. Her ankle. They moved round.

Ron laced his fingers together, biting down on the pain that flared from his thumb.

Scarlett put her foot into his hands, reached up to grasp the saddle, swung her other leg over and hauled herself onto the horse.

'If you need to stop, just a gentle tug on the reins. If you want to go faster, squeeze with both legs.'

Ron thought he heard the growl of an engine and sweat broke across his skin.

'Go now,' he said. 'I'll come and find you. Scarlett, I'm so sorry.'

She gave a terse little nod.

Ron patted the horse on the rump and said, 'Go on, Polly. Walk on.'

The horse and rider walked off towards the back of the property.

Ron ran home.

If Gregory Martin reached him before the police did, he needed to put him off the scent. Tell him the youngsters had run away. Conceal anything that might prove otherwise.

Ron scooped up Scarlett's wet clothes and, after a moment's indecision, stuffed them into the freezer. He threw back the living-room curtains, *nothing to hide here*, gathered up Mrs G's clothes and took them upstairs where he flung them into the wardrobe.

The plate of beans went down on the floor for the dog and Ron drank the glass of orange. Then he snapped on the radio and dialled the number that Gregory Martin, posing as Mike Carter, had left him.

Waiting for Martin to answer the call, Ron leant against the fridge, furious with himself.

It was guilt he tasted, bitter in his mouth. Guilt, a constant familiar.

Ron heard a car pull up outside the house. Prayed it was the police.

He went to the door. Saw Gregory Martin stepping from his car. The man who had strangled his wife to death. Ron felt his spine stiffen and his guts turn to water.

'I've just been trying to ring you,' Ron called. 'They got away. They made a run for it.'

Martin's eyes burnt bright with anger. He shook his head and walked towards Ron.

'How come? What happened? Where is she?'

*

Scarlett swayed from side to side as the horse walked along the broad path, the beam from the headlamp lighting up the dripping bushes and the rock walls of the canyon ahead.

She squeezed the horse with her legs, like Ron had told her, easing her into a trot. A motion that sent the light bouncing around.

Her heart was racing. It hurt like it was torn, a sharp pain.

If Mike found her, caught her . . . Maybe it was stupid still calling him Mike, but she would not call him her father. After what he did to her mum, to Nana? Now to her.

What did he want with her anyway? She daren't, she just—

The feeling swept through her again, the cold fear, the jumble of pictures. *Blue light. The humming. Getting milk from the fridge, spilling some as she poured. Taking it to Mummy. Curling up beside her. Stroking her hand. Blue light. Buttons. Running her fingers over the shiny metal buttons.*

Gusts of wind funnelled down the canyon, making a moaning sound that unnerved her.

Polly had slowed and Scarlett patted her neck, the heat of the horse welcome against her hand. 'Good girl,' Scarlett said, her voice breaking. 'Come on.' She squeezed her again and the horse resumed trotting over the stony ground.

Had Dylan come this way? She should look out for him, and his flashlight. What would he do if he saw her? *He's frightened of horses.* So he wouldn't want to get near, not while she was riding Polly. He'd probably run.

Scarlett heard an owl. A barn owl. They didn't twit-twoo but made a screech. She'd never seen one in the wild. They had big moon faces. They'd look scary, if you weren't expecting to see one. Like ghost birds.

Another squall of wind and the bushes that grew between the rocks and along the side of the path bent and shook with the force.

Sometimes she couldn't even remember what her mum had looked like. Only in photographs, not proper memories. Or what she'd sounded like when she'd read Scarlett a story or laughed. Or shouted, even. Scarlett tried to think of her as a real live person, the one who'd break-danced and made biscuits shaped like dinosaurs, but it was just pretending.

Mainly she was like a ghost, a gap, leaving an ache inside Scarlett that never really went away. An ache that made her angry, that made her want to shout at her mum for leaving her, for deserting her. For marrying *him*. Then for sending him away. If she hadn't—

And what had Scarlett done to help her?

Nothing.

You were five.

Nothing. You just let it happen.

'It's not your fault.' Nana had said that loads of times. But just saying something over and over and over again didn't make it true.

*

'Come in,' Ron said. Not because he wanted the man anywhere near him but because he needed to convince Gregory Martin that he was telling the truth.

In the kitchen Mungo had finished the beans and was wagging

his tail apologetically, as if unsure where things stood now regarding food.

'What happened?' Martin said, his eyes doing a quick sweep of the room. Face drawn and sharp.

Ron's scalp tightened. 'I'm sorry. I found them hiding in the outbuildings – well, the dog did.' He dipped his chin to Mungo. 'That's when I rang you. I had to come back here for my phone.' He tried to pick his way to a plausible account. Should he say he tried to befriend them or not? Admit that Scarlett had been in the house? Better to let Martin think the two of them were still together and that Ron believed he was a loving father.

'They didn't hear me, I'm sure.' Did he sound too defensive? Was he protesting too much? Ron pinched his nose, buying a moment to get his story straight.

'Have You Seen Her?' by the Chi-Lites was playing on the radio. Some sick irony.

'Anyway, I thought I'd leave them there and just wait for you. There's only one way in and out of here. Unless you go scrambling all over the hills. Place is walled in.' Would he check?

Gregory Martin hovered by the edge of the table, near the sink.

Ron moved to sit, hoping to appear defeated, submissive. He rested his wounded hand on the table, the bandage damp and smeared with dirt now. With the fingers of the other hand he traced the patterns on the table top, following the whorls and knots in the wood, looking up every now and again, but not sustaining eye contact. Tension drilling through his bones.

'The next thing I knew the dog was barking and I heard running outside. By the time I got to the top of the drive they were turning into the road.'

'You didn't think to go after them?' Gregory Martin said. 'A little girl?' His mouth worked.

'I'd never have caught them. Couldn't run for a bus. I'm too out of shape.' Ron caught the grate of self-pity and hoped it didn't irritate the man. 'I'm so sorry,' he said.

Martin compressed his mouth, leaching his lips of colour.

'Should we call the police?' Ron said, remembering the script. 'Or I can if you want to set off.'

'I will,' Gregory Martin said. 'You saw both of them in the outbuilding?'

'Yes,' Ron said. 'There's a gap in the wall. I could see through that.'

'What were they doing?'

Was it a trick question?

'Just sitting there. Resting, I think. She was all right – she looked all right.' Ron felt sweat prickle under his arms, trickle down his sides. 'I can't imagine what you must— Can I get you anything before you go? A drink or . . .'

The news came on the radio. *Derbyshire police have issued a child rescue alert . . .* Ron's fingers curled as he heard the words . . . *Be on the lookout . . .* He tried to talk over it, babbling. 'You should go in the car. They won't have got far. Not with this storm.' *Eleven-year-old Scarlett is described as . . .*

Gregory Martin's eyes locked on his, his expression morphing from suspicion to confirmation then rage. Ron saw that Martin knew he knew.

Martin moved swiftly, grabbed a knife from the magnetic block above the counter top. A boning knife.

Ron leapt up. He had height and weight on Gregory Martin but no weapon. The other man was fit and muscled. Still, Ron charged him. He would *not* let him go. He kept his eye on the knife. But it was a punch that Gregory Martin threw with his other hand, slamming into Ron's jaw with enough force to snap his head back and almost pitch him over.

Mungo barked loudly.

Ron fought to keep his balance, stepping back as Martin came for him brandishing the knife. Ron met the glass of the picture window, which juddered as he stumbled against it.

'Where is she?' Martin shouted.

'I told you – they left.'

Martin held the knife against Ron's chest. 'Where is she? Don't fuck with me.'

Ron didn't speak. He stared at the man, allowing all his loathing to show.

Mungo barked again, slunk closer, ears back.

Martin glanced at the dog, the knife twitched in his hand. Ron saw the hatred in his face. Would he hurt Mungo? He wouldn't hesitate, Ron was sure.

The dog growled and barked, bounced on his feet.

'Stay!' Ron instructed. 'Quiet.'

'Where is she?' Martin said.

Ron stayed silent. His heart pounded in his throat.

'Tell me.'

Ron said nothing. He clenched his teeth tight together.

Martin drew back the knife then lunged, stabbing Ron in the stomach.

No. Jesus. No.

It took a moment to feel the pain, but when it came, it forced Ron to gasp aloud. He tottered but Martin held the knife in place and any movement only increased the agony.

'Where is she?' Breath on his neck, the meaty smell of it.

Mungo was whimpering, pacing, claws tick-tacking on the hard floor.

Ron's vision blurred.

'Tell me.' Martin twisted the knife and Ron screamed, a high-pitched shriek of feral pain. His heart was thundering, agony clutching at his throat, his guts, tearing across his skin.

‘Where?’ Gregory Martin whispered.

Ron couldn’t talk. He wanted to say, ‘The road, they went on the road,’ but he couldn’t find the words.

He bowed his head.

He felt the tug as Martin drew out the knife, then another thrust. Into his leg this time. A spike of acid heat.

Warm liquid was spreading from his belly, to soak through his T-shirt and sweater.

Ron’s legs gave way. He folded, fell heavily, cracking his temple on the floor, the knife still sticking out of his thigh.

Ron couldn’t see, but he felt the floor vibrate as Gregory Martin walked away.

He could smell burning. No, that was wrong. That was before . . .

Chapter 18

'Lovers Leap,' PC Ali said, as they reached the end of the ridge. 'Beauty spot.'

'Not tonight it ain't,' Laura said. Any views were obscured by banks of cloud and the driving rain that drummed against the roof of the car, forcing them to raise their voices.

'Ooof!' PC Ali said, as a fierce blast of wind shoved the car, and he had to fight to right the steering.

'There's the house,' she said, her heart picking up pace. Down in the valley, lights were just visible, mazy in the veils of rain.

'Yes,' he said.

And there was the Discovery again. Easier to make out, as PC Ali navigated their descent.

And Scarlett? *Where is Scarlett?*

Laura's head hurt, a ringing pain in the back of her skull and a dull ache behind her eyes.

Lovers Leap, she thought. Some old story about a quarryman and a shepherdess. Star-crossed lovers and this their trysting place. The girl's father had forbidden the association and sworn to kill her if she disobeyed him. The shepherdess had lost one of her ewes in the spring snow and gone looking for it. The lamb had come too soon, stillborn. The shepherdess had used her shawl to stem the bleeding of the ewe then carried the animal to the sheepfold where it could rest.

The quarryman searched for his sweetheart at their rendezvous. Finding the bloodied shawl, he feared she'd been murdered and, deranged with grief, he threw himself off the ridge. Learning of his death, the shepherdess determined to follow him, and join him in the after-life. She hanged herself from the tree where his body had landed.

On a full moon it was said that their ghosts could be seen embracing at Lovers Leap.

Wouldn't he have seen her footprints in the snow, Laura thought, leading away from the bloodied shawl?

A plastic sack, the sort used to hold feed, building materials and chemicals, came flying through the air towards them. End over end, swooping and diving until it flattened itself against the windscreen.

Laura flinched.

PC Ali braked hard. 'Shit!'

He opened the door to reach out and tugged at the sack. The wind snatched it away. He had to use both hands to close the door against the gale.

Her radio squawked into life and her phone began to ring, then PC Ali's radio joined in. It took her a matter of seconds to absorb the news. Sighting of Scarlett Martin at Graybridge.

'She's here! Scarlett's here! Ronald Thorpe reported seeing her. Quickly!' She tried to swallow, her throat parched.

Near the bottom of the hill, stone gateposts marked the entrance to the Graybridge driveway. Maybe thirty yards further down the floodwaters spread, wind ruffling the surface and rocking the Discovery.

As they reached the top of the drive at Graybridge, Laura felt her stomach contract. *The Astra!* Parked beside a camper van.

'Oh, Christ, he's here, too,' she said. 'He's here already.'

'I'll block him in,' PC Ali said.

'Good idea.'

He manoeuvred the patrol car to park crosswise, close behind the Astra.

Would Gregory Martin have heard them arrive above the din of the storm? There were lights on in the house, curtains open. Trees around the grounds thrashed and flailed in the winds.

'See if anyone's home,' Laura said.

They crossed the few yards quickly to reach the house, but already Laura could see the living room was empty. It looked like something from one of those homes-and-gardens mags.

They edged along to the front door. Inside the house a dog barked.

Laura hesitated a moment and signalled that they should cross to the other side of the door and look through that window.

She braced herself, knowing what Gregory Martin was capable of, what the man had done to his wife.

'Jesus!' She saw a man lying on his side on the floor, back to them. Bushy red hair. He wasn't moving. A dog standing over him. No sign of anyone else.

'That's Ronald Thorpe,' PC Ali said.

'Call an ambulance and see if we can get any back-up.'

While PC Ali made the call, Laura tried the door. It was closed, latched. She banged the brass knocker, hands stinging. There was no response.

Putting her mouth to the letterbox, she called, 'Scarlett? Scarlett? This is the police.' Listened but heard nothing.

'We need to get in there,' Laura said.

PC Ali tested the door. 'It's solid.'

'The windows, then.'

She moved back to the kitchen window and peered in. Noticed how the edge of the rug, the line of the table, carried echoes of their reflection, not just one but two. Triple glazing. Unless that was the concussion talking.

'You don't happen to have a lump hammer, on you, do you?' she said.

PC Ali gave a quick smile. 'No, Sarge.'

'You can call me Laura.'

'Right.'

She waited. Bobbed her head at him, a nudge.

'Oh, Ahmed,' he said.

'Come on then, Ahmed. We have to get in there.' Determined. Focused. Blood thudding in her ears.

He turned and looked about. Laura tugged at her hood, holding it against the snatch of the wind.

'What about this?' he said. A birdbath, stone, a bowl on a pedestal.

'Can you lift it?'

Ahmed bent his knees, put his arms under the bowl and strained. Grunting, he managed to raise it and stagger with it a few feet, then lowered it, propping it on its side so he could roll it like a wheel.

He shoved it and let it go and it trundled forward and hit the glass which cracked, a zigzag line across the centre.

'Yes!' Laura said.

The dog barked and ran to the window.

'Again,' Laura said.

She left him panting with the effort, and went to look in the patrol car for anything she might be able to use. Black dots filled her head as she bent over the boot. She thought of bees. Hector and the bees. She tasted fear and swallowed it. No time for that.

A jack, and a tyre iron. Her side shrieked in protest as she tested them. The jack was heavier.

She took it over to the window and she and Ahmed took turns attacking the glass with their different implements. Laura gritted her teeth against the stabbing in her rib. The blisters on her hands were oozing and itching, the taste in her mouth brassy and bitter.

The panes crazed but held in place. 'What's it made of? Bloody graphene?' she panted.

Ahmed launched the birdbath dish again and, with a deafening crash, the fractured glass collapsed into thousands of crystals, glistening under the lights. She thought of the chandeliers in the buildings in Spain. And the one Hector's parents had bought them for a wedding present.

The dog was whimpering, making advances and retreats.

'Good dog,' Laura said, stepping inside. Glass crunching under her feet.

'Mr Thorpe? Ronald?' She moved round so she could see him properly and spotted the knife embedded in his leg, the dark stain across his stomach, the bandage on his thumb vivid red with blood where he held his belly. Blood pooling on the floor from the stomach wound. His eyes were closed, his face ashen.

Christ!

'Can you hear me?' Her pulse galloping, she shook his shoulder. 'Mr Thorpe, Ronald. Ronald?' His chest moved, he gave a sigh.

'He's breathing,' she said. 'Get me some cloths, towels.'

Ahmed flung open drawers, brought her a pile of tea-towels and table mats.

Glancing back, she saw the knife rack, the set that matched the blade in Thorpe's leg. Two empty spaces. Had Martin taken the other?

'Check upstairs,' she said to Ahmed. 'And be careful.' The floor shook as he bolted.

Laura folded a towel, pressed it against Ronald's stomach. He moaned.

'Ronald. I'm Laura, I'm with the police. There's an ambulance coming. Help is on the way. Where's Scarlett? I'm looking for a girl called Scarlett. You said she was here.'

Ahmed came back in. 'No one,' he said.

'Ronald, I'm a police officer. Is Scarlett here?'

Ronald Thorpe blinked, his eyes seemed to fade in and out of focus. Or was that hers?

Was he conscious?

'Woods . . . back,' Ronald Thorpe said.

'Scarlett? Scarlett's in the woods?' Laura said.

'Yes. Gave.'

'Gave? Gave what?' Laura asked.

'Cave,' Ahmed corrected her. 'He said cave.'

'Cave?' She looked up at Ahmed.

'Think so.'

The cloth she held was crimson, soaked through. She lifted it away and folded a fresh pad. 'OK. Her father, Scarlett's father, did he do this to you?' Did he understand?

'Yes.'

'A boy called Dylan?' Ahmed said. But Ronald Thorpe's eyes slid shut.

'He's out,' Laura said. 'Still breathing.'

'I'll go,' Ahmed said.

'I'll wait for the ambulance. Get Scarlett. That's the priority. Anything else is a bonus. Just get Scarlett.'

'OK.'

He moved to go.

'Ahmed, you've got a Taser?' Laura said.

'Yes.' He patted his belt.

'Right. Well, listen. If you do find Gregory Martin, do me a favour, will you? And fry the fucker.'

*

Dylan thought he was imagining it at first. A chinking noise in the distance, like someone hitting a shovel over and over. Or banging a hammer. He stopped, crouching in some bushes to listen, flashlight off.

The wind blew hard, all the trees and bushes whipping about in a roaring sound that swallowed everything else.

Then the wind died away and it came again. Faint but definitely there. *Tap. Tap. Tap.*

Or was it his heart? *Fuck!* Dylan pressed a palm to his chest but he couldn't really tell. He ached everywhere after the crash. He felt as if he'd been given a good kicking.

There was another noise, further away in the other direction. Like rushing water, not just rain falling. A stream?

But the banging kept on, a steady beat, and when he put his hand on the ground he thought he could feel vibrations.

Whatever it was, it was getting closer.

He didn't want to wait and find out.

He wiped the wet and grit off his hand and rose, unable to see much of anything but shadows on shadows. Black shapes silhouetted on dark grey.

Before he turned to move on, a star of light appeared, swaying high above the path.

Dylan swallowed. Watched the beam glance off dripping trees and spiky branches bent crooked by the wind.

The chinking coming from the same place as the light.

He thought of Transformers with their great hulking feet. Arnie in *Terminator. Jurassic Park.*

Get a fucking grip.

If he got up and ran now it might see. He shuffled deeper into the bushes, felt thorns ripping up the sides of his legs.

The light kept coming, high up. Why was it so high?

Then he made it out. *Scarlett.* Scarlett on a fucking horse.

His mind zigzagged like a pinball. Why was Scarlett not with the Ron bloke? How come she'd left the house? Why was she on a horse? Had she nicked it? Why the fuck would she nick a horse? Was she after him, Dylan? Or his money?

Cold fingers of water crept down the back of his neck.

None of it made sense.

Some horses, thoroughbreds, racehorses, they were worth a fortune. People nicked them. But not usually little kids like Scarlett, who had enough going on trying to ditch her crazy father.

Should he wait or leg it? She'd see him in the bushes if she looked down that way. And the horse, what would the horse do? *A kick in the head from an animal like that can kill you.* Shatter the skull.

They came on towards him and he buried the bottom of his face in the holdall, just leaving enough space to peer out.

The horse got closer, then slowed down, the tapping rhythm lost. They were almost level with Dylan. His scalp itched. He held his breath.

The beam swung around in an arc, Scarlett looking left and right, her face sharp with panic. Then she turned the horse about and walked back a few yards. She stopped again, leaning over to one side. The light played over a tall grey slab of rock. What was so interesting about a rock?

Dylan watched as the horse circled and Scarlett guided it past the rock and went left, walking away from the path.

Why? Why leave the path? Was that a way out of here?

Dylan couldn't see her now. He waited a while, then climbed out of the thorn bush.

He slung his holdall over one shoulder and grabbed the flashlight. He crept along to where she'd left the main drag but there was no sign of her or the horse. No glimmer of light from her head torch.

He sneaked up to the tall rock, which he could just make out, paler than the dark around it and with a faint glimmer to it.

He turned on his flashlight, keeping it angled close and low, ready to snap it off again if needed.

It was just a rock. Nothing special about it, no markings or anything.

He didn't know what she was up to but he'd leave her to it. He'd only just got rid of her anyway. This was clearly the main path, not where she'd gone, so he'd stick with it.

He turned his back on the standing stone and walked on.

Fierce wind buffeted him and thunder rumbled overhead. Storm Dennis: there'd been warnings on the news. Risk to life.

Yeah, tell me about it.

The path wound left and right, the stone walls of the canyon towering over him. The sound of running water, which he'd noticed before, grew louder, and as he turned a sharp bend his torch illuminated a vast waterfall plunging down to a pool below. Wide, rippling streams poured over the rim of the cliff, thundering down in sheets, spray forming mist all around so it looked like something from the jungle. And the path ahead of him led straight into the pool of water.

'You have got to be shitting me,' Dylan breathed, staring open-mouthed at the impasse.

Chapter 19

The cave was enormous. A great mouth in the cliff wall. Silver beads of water dripping quickly from the edge. The opening was tall enough for Scarlett to ride into without getting off the horse. She edged Polly forwards, closer to the entrance. Her hands tightened on the reins, ready to turn back if there was something in there. Something horrible.

At the threshold she made the horse wait, scanned the cavern. The light moving over a silty floor and craggy walls that grew lower at the back. No litter, no drinks cans or old fires.

No monsters.

You could probably fit most of our house in here, she thought.

Scarlett made the horse walk in.

There was a musty smell, damp stone, but also a stink like wee, rank like the school toilets. Perhaps foxes had been here.

Scarlett looked directly up and saw a bunch of leaves stuck to the roof, moving a tiny bit. Leathery, all the same colour brown.

Bats! She smiled. Bats. *Awesome!* They must be hibernating.

She had seen bats fly at night – some passed outside the back of their house on summer evenings. They ate up the midges and moths and other insects.

Scarlett didn't want to disturb them. They wouldn't like the light. She thought about turning it off but she couldn't face the dark. She dipped her head down and murmured to the horse. 'Good girl.'

The rain had soaked her, especially her thighs and knees and across her shoulders, which were sopping wet.

Scarlett breathed in the hot grassy smell of the horse. 'Good girl,' she said again, not sure who she was talking about any more.

'Good girl,' he'd said. 'Go to bed. Go back to bed.' And she had. Lain awake. Or had she slept?

Coming down in the dark.

Mummy sleeping on the floor.

Cold. Getting her a blanket.

And some milk.

The white puddle.

Mummy not drinking it.

Stroking her arm, her face. Patting her. 'Mummy?'

Scarlett cuddling her.

'Mummy?'

Running her fingers over the shiny studs on the base of the sofa. Milk sticky in her hair from the spill on the floor.

'Mummy?'

Scarlett shivering. So cold.

Little stripes of light coming through the kitchen blind.

Noises outside, cars and the dog barking next door.

Humming. Droning on and on.

Scarlett was scared. Lonely.

A bad feeling. Inside her full of bad things. A pain in there.

'Mummy? Mummy, please?'

Getting Mummy's phone.

Pressing the picture of Nana.

'Hello, Jeanette.' Nana's voice.

'Nana?'

'Scarlett?'

'Nana. Mummy won't wake up and—'

She fled from the memory, shaking her head, fighting to catch a breath.

'Wait in the cave. I'll come and find you when it's safe,' Ron had said. So she would.

Her mouth felt gluey, sour, and when she opened it she heard a smacking sound. *Drink something.* The carton of orange was zipped under her fleece. She got it out, unscrewed the lid and took a sip. Strong and sweet.

'Scarlett! Scarlett!' The shout was loud, close, angry.

He's here! How had he found her? Had Ron told him and betrayed her?

But Ron had called the police – she'd heard him. Or had he faked it?

Scarlett dropped the drink. Flinched. He might hear it, follow the sound and discover her.

'Scarlett. I'm not going without you. I know you're here. Stop messing about.'

The horse shifted its weight, the saddle creaked.

The wind outside was coming in bursts, spattering rain and making all the bushes shake and rattle.

If she just stayed here, stayed quiet, he wouldn't see her. The cave was hidden away. You had to leave the path and—

He'll see the light! Trembling, she fumbled with the switch, her fingers cold, sore, tired. She switched it off and the world was plunged into dark.

Scarlett closed her eyes, and leant along the horse, arms cradling its neck.

The darkness was inside her as well, another cavern, vast and deep. She didn't want to think, to feel, to remember.

'Scarlett!'

She hunched her shoulders, trying to shut out his voice. Squeezing her eyes tight shut, forcing patterns to burst behind her eyelids. Honeycombs of orange and white, discs of yellow.

A sheet of light, blue-white, electric, flooded through her.

She bolted upright, opening her eyes. Saw the after-image, the neon flare outlining the cave mouth.

The horse spooked, turned, restless, squealed loudly. The noise she made, echoed, amplified by the dome of the cave.

Thunder cracked and rumbled and Polly shrieked again, skittish. She spun round and Scarlett drew on the reins, trying to quieten her, stroking her, soothing her.

'There you are!' He was in the cave mouth, the torch on his phone a blinding blaze of light.

Scarlett was paralysed.

The horse paced, wheeled, huffing. She gave a whinny.

He stepped closer.

'Get down,' he said flatly. His eyes piercing.

Scarlett didn't move. Could she ride past him? Get the horse to canter and run him down? Race back to the house? But Polly was all freaked out by the thunder and lightning and she might refuse to leave the cave.

'Get off the horse. We're going.'

'No.' It came out so small and shaky. Had he even heard her?

Polly was snorting, ears flicking back and forth, waving her head from side to side.

He stepped forward and caught the bridle in the same hand as his phone so his torchlight dipped, leaving Scarlett in semi-darkness.

He raised his free hand. *A knife.* A big, sharp knife.

Her heart shrank. Clenched.

'Get down now,' he said quietly. 'Or I'll slit this animal's throat.'

I hate you. I hate you so much.

'Why?' Scarlett said, trying to keep the tears from her voice. 'Why have you come for me? So you can kill me too?'

He spat a laugh. Gave a shake of his head. 'You're my daughter,' he said.

'And she . . . my mother. . .' Scarlett's words were broken up, terror making it hard to talk. 'You left me to . . .'

'And now I'm back. All this dwelling on the past—'

Fury, bright as the lightning, electrified her. 'You killed her,' Scarlett shouted. 'You killed her.'

'She wouldn't listen,' he said tightly. 'If she'd just paid attention.'

Scarlett stared at him. Despising him. It felt like her skin was on fire.

'You killed her,' she said again, steadily. 'You left me there. You left me there and you ran away.'

'Get off the horse.' He lifted the knife towards Polly. Scarlett longed to rush the horse forward, trample him to the ground, but he would hurt Polly, she was sure of it. She couldn't let him do that.

She pulled her feet from the stirrups, a throb fierce in her ankle. She swung her leg over and slid down.

Would he kill her here? Now? Did he have another place in mind? Wherever he'd been going in the Discovery.

He moved towards her and she stepped quickly away.

'Why did you come back?' she said.

'Just walk.' He waved the knife.

Outside the rain fell heavier, drumming on the ground, bouncing off the rocks. Scarlett took a final look at Polly, still shifting and weaving, and stepped out into the storm.

*

Dylan had retraced his tracks from the waterfall and was crouching by the big slab of rock. It came up to his shoulders when he was standing and was pointed like a thin pyramid or a giant tooth.

He could hear Scarlett shouting, 'You killed her.'

Her dad must have found her. *Fuck.*

Dylan turned off his flashlight.

But when he looked round the edge of the stone there was no sign of Scarlett or the horse or Gregory Martin.

Sheet lightning swept over the gorge, illuminating everything, and Dylan saw the gaping hole in the rock. *A cave.* They were in a cave.

The rain came down like stones and he could just make out more shouting.

Dylan ducked back out of sight when a small beam of light reappeared. He inched to the edge of the stone, craning his neck, until he could see Scarlett, Gregory Martin behind her, shadowy except for the light cast by Martin's phone. No horse.

He should go. If he went now they wouldn't spot him. Double back to the house and stay out of sight. He couldn't be getting messed up in other people's business. Not with the trouble he was in.

'You going to kill me now?' she yelled to her father.

Was he?

Dylan risked another peek. Still she limped along in front. Gregory Martin wasn't holding her arm or dragging her. Then Dylan understood. He must have a knife on her. A knife or a gun.

Go. Get the fuck away. Leave them to it.

But she's just a kid. Her mother's dead—

I was just a kid, Dylan thought. No one ever looked out for me. No one had my back. *I can't be doin' with you, Dyl. You're a fuckin' nightmare.*

Walk away.

And let him kill her? After everything she'd done to escape?

It's not your mess.

Aw, fuck.

Even as he willed himself to run, Dylan was feeling about for something to use as a weapon. A stone, perhaps. His fingers ran over lumps of rock but they were embedded in the grass. He shuffled back and grasped about, finding only more wet grass and mud and stone.

A fork of lightning stabbed down in the direction of the waterfall, and across the path from him, he glimpsed a fallen tree. A tangle of black branches.

Dylan scurried over there, keeping close to the ground. Hands running over the wood, searching for a decent piece. He tugged at one branch but it snapped, thin and brittle. He froze. Had he been heard? He listened, but there was only the hiss and drum of the rain.

His fingers found a bigger branch. He dragged at it and it came away. As wide as his upper arm and about the same length as a baseball bat. Solid. Slippery. A few small twigs sticking out but no time to trim it. He carried it back to the standing stone and huddled down.

What's your plan, then? Scarlett was in his head like an earworm.

His thighs ached from the crouch. Now he could hear their footsteps behind the beating of the rain. He saw another glow of light break the darkness. She had her head lamp back on, looking down so the cone of light picked out the ground in front of her.

Dylan tightened his grip on the wood, poised to spring when Gregory Martin was close enough. Scarlett in front might see him, start and give the game away. He hoped she'd have more sense.

Dylan's throat ached, his jaw was gritted, back rigid.

This was mad. *Fucking mental. Leg it now, you dickhead.*

Then they came, turning onto the main path, approaching the rock.

Dylan held his nerve, waited until Scarlett drew level with him, waited another second for her to take a step, two steps, then he sprang up and lunged, smacking the end of the branch as hard as he could into Martin's head.

Scarlett screamed.

The blow hit Martin on the jaw and sent him tipping back. Dylan raised the branch again, ready for a second strike, but Martin, almost sprawling, bearing his weight on one hand, bounced up, and kicked out hard, driving his heel into Dylan's knee.

A snapping sensation and Dylan collapsed, dropping the branch. Then Gregory Martin was over him and Dylan saw the steel, felt the jarring in his shoulder and his arm and his chest. One. Two. Three.

Three strikes and you're out.

*

The paramedics, a grey-haired woman and a fresh-faced lad with a quiff, were working on Ronald Thorpe and had succeeded in stemming the loss of blood from his stomach. Now they were preparing to transfer him to the ambulance.

Laura knew better than to ask for predictions about how he would be. Paramedics didn't like making guesses. Ronald Thorpe still hadn't regained consciousness but that could be the shock.

She washed her hands at the kitchen sink as quickly as she could, the burns on her palms shrieking with the friction. The water ran clear but the coppery smell of blood still lingered.

Ahmed had left her the keys to the patrol car and she ran out to move it, leaving a space beside the Astra, so the ambulance could get in closer to the house.

'Where will you take him?' she checked, coming back into the kitchen.

'Chesterfield,' the woman said.

'OK. Can I leave you to it? My colleague . . .' Laura gestured outside, impatient to go after Ahmed.

'Yeah, sure,' the woman said.

'What about the dog?' the lad said.

'We won't leave without arranging for some welfare,' Laura said. 'I'll shut it in the living room then it can't go wandering. And if other officers arrive before you leave, please direct them to the woods at the back.' She'd given them a bare-bones account of events. Told them that the fugitive was believed to be carrying a bladed weapon and was hunting his daughter.

'Will do.' The woman was strapping buckles across Ronald Thorpe. He was motionless on the stretcher.

Laura took the dog by the collar and walked it out of the kitchen and across to the hall to the room opposite. She hurried to fetch its bowl of water, spilling some as she bent to put it down, and the shaft of pain tore through her side.

She took the tyre iron with her, easier to wield than the jack if it came to that, and used her phone to light the way. The rain was teeming down, and she had to narrow her eyes against the blasts of ferocious wind.

The path led past some outbuildings and through woods down into a gully.

By torchlight she could see that the muddy ground was churned up, marked by footprints. If Gregory Martin had come this way after leaving the house he'd soon have seen that other people had used the path recently.

It was hard to run but she walked as swiftly as she could, sometimes losing her balance. Her knees felt unsteady, rubbery, as if she might faint.

Breathe. She closed her eyes for a second and the world spun.

Maybe she *should* get checked at the hospital. And she needed someone to recover her car.

She wanted to crawl into bed, wrap herself around Hector and pray that Mateo would sleep for a few hours. But right now the priority was Scarlett.

Somewhere out here there was a cave, Scarlett hiding in it. And her father rampaging after her. No word from Ahmed yet. That niggled at her: he was so young, inexperienced. Perhaps she should have insisted he wait with the injured man and she go after Martin – even if she would have been slower.

Too late now.

Oh, just get on with it, she scolded herself. *And look sharp.*

*

Scarlett stood shivering by the big stone. Every nerve in her body shrieking at her to run.

Dylan was on the ground, panting, his shoulders curved as if he was trying to curl up. The sight of Mike stabbing him kept repeating in her head. Fast. Cold. Mike hadn't shouted and screamed or anything. Just knifed him, like a robot would.

Go! Run!

Scarlett turned, began to sprint.

Mike's shout stopped her in her tracks. 'Get back here or I'll give him some more and finish the job.'

He wouldn't, would he?

Mike was kneeling over Dylan and held his knife at Dylan's neck. Dylan was staring at Scarlett. His face white as milk. Eyes drilling into her.

'You go, he dies,' Mike said.

Scarlett saw Dylan swallow, his Adam's apple bobbing up and down. Dylan who'd tried to help her. Who'd hit Mike.

'It'd be your fault then,' Mike said.

And she'd be just like him. Running away.

But perhaps she was anyway. Inside. She had his blood, his DNA. A murderer's daughter. That could never change. No matter what.

You did nothing. You didn't save her. You didn't stop him.

Dylan groaned.

Run!

'Scarlett,' Mike said, warning threaded through his voice.

The cold washed through her. She shuddered.

Cold skin. Milk. Spilt milk. Her lips dark.

Hot tears mixed with the raindrops on her face.

Scarlett walked over to him and stopped.

He straightened up.

She steeled herself, keeping her head high, waiting for him to stab her and hating him with every fibre of her being.

'Walk,' he said. He twirled the knife, showing her to turn round. 'Walk. And don't do anything stupid.'

'I wish you were dead,' she said. 'I wish you'd died instead. I hate you and I wish you were dead.'

Chapter 20

'Police! Let her go!' Ahmed shouted. He was out of breath from the run so he didn't sound as forceful as he wanted to.

Gregory Martin was about five metres away, his daughter just in front of him. And Dylan Ellis on the ground close by. Obviously hurt. Going nowhere soon, anyway. Which suited Ahmed just fine. He'd check him over as soon as he had a chance.

Scarlett looked smaller than he'd imagined, younger. Her hair, Afro style, sparkled with drops of rain. Her eyes lifted in hope when she heard Ahmed shout.

She wore big, baggy clothes, soaking wet from the rain. A jazzy patterned top. No purple coat.

Ahmed felt a surge of anger at how the man had played him at the service station. 'I'm meeting a friend,' Martin had said, nodding and smiling. And how easily Ahmed had let himself be fooled. Well, now he was going to make up for it.

And if you get it wrong?

He didn't need any negative thoughts undermining him. He was a police officer. He was a professional. He could do this. And he'd see both of them – Gregory Martin and Dylan Ellis – in court. See them pay for their crimes.

'Walk,' he heard Martin say to his daughter, ignoring Ahmed.

She looked terrified.

Negotiation, not confrontation. Defuse the situation. Flash cards in Ahmed's head.

'It'll be better all round if you let Scarlett go. Then we can sort this out.' Even Ahmed wasn't sure about that. How on earth did this get sorted out? And he didn't expect Martin to be convinced. 'No one else needs to get hurt,' Ahmed added.

'Move,' Martin said. Scarlett startled and took a step forward. Ahmed thought he'd poked her from the back. Had he cut her?

Ahmed's hand tightened on his Taser.

'An armed response unit are on their way,' he said. 'And a hostage negotiator. And I need to caution you that I have a Taser and I'm authorised to use it. But let's just try to sort this out now. This isn't doing anybody any good, is it?'

Ahmed had talked people down before, twice. Three times in fact, counting the woman at the Monument in Leek. The first had been a man on an aqueduct over the canal one night. A man who'd been about to jump. Two hours Ahmed had talked with him, tried to shift him off his insistence that 'They'd all be better off without me'.

Ahmed had gone home afterwards. And cried in the shower. Not sure who for, if he was honest. Just that life was hard for so many people, and the man's fragility had got to him. Even though Ahmed thought suicide was selfish and that you should just keep going because you owed it to other people not to hurt them like that.

A few weeks later an envelope had come for Ahmed at work. Inside was a postcard with a photograph of the old viaduct and, on the back, *Thank you. You saved my life and I will always be grateful. Tony.*

The other time was a lad robbing a minimarket. He had a baseball bat. Ahmed had been on patrol. He recognised the lad from previous encounters, knew enough about him to lay his options out and get him to see that things would be ten times worse if he didn't come quietly.

The lad had been buzzing, balancing on his toes, swearing and cursing and close to exploding. But Ahmed had persisted, calling him 'mate' and talking about his mum and how she'd feel if he got sent down for a long sentence. Eventually, after smashing his bat into the cold drinks fridge (which was really not necessary and pissed Ahmed off, though he hid it at the time), the lad let Ahmed arrest him.

But this? A stone-cold killer. Ahmed didn't think he stood much chance.

And while Gregory Martin had the knife on Scarlett, Ahmed couldn't do anything to risk him using it.

Scarlett was rolling her eyes. Was she ill? Fitting?

No – not rolling. Signalling. Signalling to him. Staring straight at Ahmed, intently, so he had to narrow his eyes against the glare of her headlamp, and then casting her gaze down to her right in a swooping motion without moving her head. She did it again and again. Ahmed took a swift glance, let his torch play slowly over the ground. Was there something on the grass? He didn't know what she was trying to show him. Then she moved her hand, small movements in front of her belly that only Ahmed could see. Pointing to herself then rolling her fingers and flicking them down to the side that she'd been looking at.

Ahmed reminded himself to talk as he watched, covering his interest. 'You let her go, you come with me, and we can sort it all out without anyone else getting hurt.'

Scarlett repeated the whirling motion with her fingers, then made a walking sign, scissoring them in the same direction off to her right.

He got it! She would rush to the right, exposing her dad to Ahmed. Was it too risky?

Before he could hesitate she held up five fingers and was counting down. *Five. Four. Three.*

'Walk, now!' Martin said aggressively.

Two. One.

Scarlett dropped, rolling forward, crashing through the underbrush, then flipping over on to her hands and springing into a back flip.

'Taser! Taser!' Ahmed fired, hitting Martin in the right thigh. Martin staggered, body spasming with the charge. But he fell forward, knife extended, and the blade slid across Ahmed's cheek. Ahmed dropped his phone and clutched his face, the burn across his cheekbone. Blood hot and wet. He sank to his knees with Scarlett's scream ringing round the canyon.

*

Laura paused for a moment, taking in the scene. No one had reacted to her approach. No one was moving. She moved her light over the tableau. Was she too late?

Oh, Christ.

Ahmed, sitting, had his back to her. His torch threw a stripe of light across the rough terrain to two figures on the ground. Gregory Martin, lying on his side. *Yes, we've got him!* A tangle of Taser wire glinting, the barbs in his thigh. Next to him Dylan Ellis. She recognised him from the CCTV. Ellis lay still but then she saw him blink. Alive, then.

'Ahmed?'

He turned.

Oh, God. His face was cut, a wound going from his temple across his cheekbone, almost to his nose.

'Are you OK?' Laura said.

'Yes.' He raised his hand and pressed it to the cut.

But Scarlett? *Where's Scarlett?*

She swung her phone about, heart hammering, made out a pair of feet beyond a pillar of rock.

Laura hurried over.

Scarlett was slumped against the stone. She wore a headlamp, the beam angled down, a pool of light in her lap.

Laura swallowed. Took a breath. 'Scarlett?'

Slowly Scarlett raised her face. A thousand-yard stare in her eyes.

'Scarlett, I'm Laura. I'm a police officer. I've been looking for you. Are you hurt?'

'They are,' Scarlett said. 'They all are.'

Laura looked back at Ahmed, who was following their conversation. She got onto her knees. 'I've been looking for you for hours,' she said to Scarlett.

'Have you?' A glimmer of disbelief. Scarlett's face was bruised. And she looked shaken, frightened, but otherwise seemed unhurt.

'Yes. In fact I ran into you earlier,' Laura said.

'What?'

'In my car. We crashed.'

'I'm sorry, it was . . . I didn't know he was going—'

'Hey, it's fine.' Laura touched Scarlett's shoulder. 'Nothing's broken.' *Well – maybe a rib.*

'Weren't you chasing Dylan?' Scarlett said.

'Only because he was driving you. How come you were with Dylan?'

Scarlett hesitated, a frown on her face. 'I just was. We gave him a lift.'

Laura sensed she was protecting the boy. 'We know he took the Discovery.'

'I went with him. To get away,' Scarlett said. She looked down at her lap.

Something had changed. Everything was quieter. Laura could hear Ahmed panting in shaky gasps and the patter of drops of rain from the trees, the sound of rushing water, but there was a break in the rain and the wind had fallen. Was the storm moving on?

'Are you all right, Scarlett?' Laura said.

A nod.

'Leaving the note, that was really clever.'

'I want to go home.' Her eyes filled with tears.

'I know,' Laura said.

'But Nana?'

'Yes?'

'Is she . . .? He said she was dead.'

A flash of hatred for the man's cruelty lanced through Laura. 'Your nana's fine. She's waiting for you.'

Scarlett's mouth trembled. Tears spilt.

'Really?' she said, sniffing.

'Really.' Laura drew out her phone and dialled the number. The wet had saturated the knees of her trousers.

'Laura?' Urgency tearing her voice.

'Beatrice. I've someone here wants to say hello.'

'Nana? Oh, Nana!' Scarlett was sobbing and wiping her eyes. 'Yes, I'm fine. The police are here. It was just . . . Oh, Nana . . . I don't know, somewhere out in the countryside.'

A few more sentences, then Scarlett passed back Laura's phone.

'Beatrice, we'll take her to A and E at Chesterfield General, just to make sure everything is all right. I'm not sure how long we'll be. We need to sort out transport. I'll let you know when we get there. OK?'

'Thank you. I can't— Thank you so much, Laura.'

Laura's throat tightened. 'I had some help.' She glanced over at Ahmed. Fingers pressed at the bridge of his nose, eyes shut, shoulders slumped. Harrowed, shocked. A world away from the uptight young man she'd dealt with earlier in the day.

Laura lifted the tyre iron and walked over to him, picking her way over the rough ground, sodden grass, lumps of rock and hidden tree roots.

He'd put down his torch and started to reload his Taser, she saw the shake in his hands.

'That cut needs stitches,' she said. 'But you'll be OK. Good work.'

His mouth quivered, tightened. He was losing it. She needed to pull him back, give him focus, some purpose.

'Ahmed?'

He looked up slowly, blinking.

'Radio in. We want three ambulances. OK?' she said.

'Yes, Sarge.'

'Call Control and tell them you're arresting Gregory Martin.' She glanced over to the figure in the gloom, barely visible in the dark.

'Me, Sarge?'

She turned back to him, 'It looks like you caught him,' Laura said.

Ahmed nodded, eyes glistening. He gave a wobbly smile.

A blur in the dark behind them, a rustle of movement, the slap of footsteps on wet grass and the grunt of effort. Gregory Martin was up, knife in hand, lunging towards Scarlett.

Laura flew at him, swinging the tyre iron up and onto his arm with all her strength, gasping aloud at the piercing pain in her side. Martin's knife went flying, flashing in and out of sight as the light from their torches glanced off it.

Martin snarled but he kept going.

*

He was coming!

Scarlett was on her feet and running. A branch hit her face, knocked her off balance. She stumbled and fell.

Her heart beating too fast, too hard.

Someone shouted, 'Leave her, leave her alone!'

She scrambled up.

Dylan had the knife. He reached Mike.

Dylan was moving in a funny way, lopsided, bent over, but he kept shouting, 'Get away from her, you mad bastard.'

He was between Mike and Scarlett, waving the knife, slashing it from side to side. Mike darted back as if he'd dodge round him – he was faster on his feet because Dylan was hurt.

'Come here, you little bitch,' Mike said.

Scarlett moved backwards. 'No!' she shouted. 'I'm not going with you. I'm not. I hate you!' She could feel the heat in her face and a terrible twisting in her belly. 'You are not my father.'

Mike was still dodging, Dylan trying to block him. Laura was closing in on them, the tyre iron in her hand.

Terror sang in Scarlett's blood, in her marrow. Terror and anger.

There was a word, like divorce but not that. Discard. Displ– *dis– disown!* 'I disown you,' she yelled. 'You're not my father. I won't go with you. I wish you were dead.'

Then a shout from Ahmed: 'Taser! Taser! Stand clear!' And Mike was jerking and falling. He landed hard on his back on the ground. Scarlett stared at him, waiting to see if he'd jump up again. Her breath coming in little snatches.

Dylan was bent over, hands on his knees, gasping.

'Dylan?' Scarlett wanted to say thank you but it was really hard to talk without crying and he just gave a nod. A really tiny nod, then moved to wipe his nose on the back of his hand.

'You're bleeding,' she said.

Blood was trickling from under his sleeve over the back of his hand in little streams. He dropped the knife.

'Sit down,' Laura said to Dylan. 'Or, better still, lie down. I'll see if I can find something to use as a dressing. Is it a knife wound?'

'I'm all right,' Dylan said. But he lay down anyway. Not far from Mike.

'He stabbed him three times,' Scarlett said.

Laura looked at Dylan again. 'Nine lives, eh?' she said.

Scarlett retched. Bile filled her mouth. She bent to spit. She was shuddering – she couldn't stop. Like someone had hold of her and was shaking her as hard as they could. Like she was a puppet. A stupid, frightened puppet.

Chapter 21

Dylan lay on his good side on the muddy grass in the dark. He reckoned if Gregory Martin had hit anything important when he'd stabbed him, an organ or an artery, he'd have been well dead by now. It was starting to hurt but nothing as bad as he'd expected.

Ahmed, the fed in uniform, who'd been poking round at the service station, was on the phone.

The woman with the red car, who'd smashed into the Discovery, seemed to be in charge. Small and dark-haired, he'd seen her flinch as she picked up the knife. Something paining her. She was squatting, talking to Scarlett. Scarlett's lamp casting a beam like a spotlight over the pair of them.

He couldn't let them take him to hospital. They'd arrest him as soon as he was patched up. Confiscate his money. So he needed to get out of here while he could still think straight. He could feel the weird buzz from the fight messing with him. Blunting the pain. Like a high. Shock, probably. *You have to get your shit together and soon.*

He hit the same brick wall. No phone. No wheels. And he didn't rate his chances of walking far with three holes in him.

God, he wanted a smoke.

How had Gregory Martin got here? Sick bastard. Had he found some wheels? Had he?

Oh, please?

Dylan edged a little closer to the man. Keeping his movements slow and smooth, he reached out and slid his hand into Martin's coat pocket. Found metal and the smooth bulk of a plastic fob. Car keys! *Get in!*

Dylan retrieved the keys and put them into his own pocket without looking at them.

Ahmed had finished his phone call. Now he shone his torch at Dylan. 'Dylan Ellis,' he said.

Dylan's mouth went dry. He said nothing.

'You drive a Vauxhall Astra.'

'Not me,' Dylan said.

'Yes, you,' Ahmed said. 'You were seen leaving a house in Coopers Close earlier today.'

'Where?' Dylan said. *Fucking hell.*

'In Leek. A man in the house was taken to hospital. He was pronounced dead on arrival.'

Ah, shit. He felt something fall inside him.

But that had nothing to do with Dylan. No way that was his fault, he wanted to tell the bloke: I called the ambulance for him.

'Don't know what you're on about, mate,' Dylan said. 'You're mixing me up with someone else.'

Ahmed began to argue but the other one, the woman, interrupted him. 'Ahmed, can you cuff Mr Martin? We could do without any more surprises.' The man was still out for the count.

As Ahmed came over, pulling handcuffs from his belt, Dylan shuffled away a bit, keeping the holdall and flashlight with him.

Dylan watched Ahmed lift one of Martin's arms and place it on his stomach. Then Ahmed froze – Dylan saw his back stiffen.

Ahmed reached out and put his fingers on the side of Martin's neck, feeling for a pulse. Then he leant in close, ear next to Martin's face.

Ahmed whispered, 'Shit.'

He placed his hand on Martin's chest, then sat back on his heels and called, 'Sarge.'

The woman turned, frowning, like she'd heard the alarm in Ahmed's voice.

'He's not— Can I have a word?' Ahmed said.

She left Scarlett and walked over. 'He's not breathing,' Ahmed told her quietly.

'Shit,' she said. 'You sure?'

They both had their backs to Dylan.

Now or never.

Dylan moved onto his knees, then climbed to his feet, trying not to grunt.

Scarlett must have seen him move – she was watching him, her face full of questions, but then her attention was drawn back to the drama surrounding her father and he was shielded by the dark again.

He slipped away, careful steps, sensing his path in the blackness.

Dylan felt light-headed, like he'd been on the laughing gas. That burst of hysteria from sucking on the balloon. The wheeling, fizzing spin of it.

He staggered. *Steady!* A twinge in his knee from the kick Gregory Martin had landed.

But he was upright and walking so he'd be OK.

You need a chemist.

A Tesco would have stuff. Get some bandages, clean himself up. Phone, food, fags. Then a train. Depending on what car Martin had got his hands on.

He switched his flashlight on once he was out of sight of the others, sick of trying to find his way in the dark. Held it in his bad arm, the holdall on his other shoulder.

Finally he saw the lights of the house. A squad car and beyond that the Astra. *The fucking Astra!* He laughed. *Random or what?*

The dog was barking as he got closer. He saw one set of windows had been completely trashed. There was blood on the floor inside. That bloke Ron's blood? Who else's could it have been?

Like all of a sudden he could taste it, metal in his mouth.

Fuck, he'd seen enough blood to last a lifetime.

He wiped his hands on his trackie bottoms and pressed the key fob. Rewarded with an answering chirp, a flash of lights.

Dylan put his bag into the car.

There was a thudding ache now in his arm. That hurt more than his shoulder or chest. But he'd have to use it to shift the gears.

She'd been right: nine lives.

The car started first time. He reversed back, then turned and drove out onto the road, the Discovery floating in the flood below.

He climbed the hill in second gear, his teeth set against the throbbing of his arm, and had just reached the summit when he saw the flashing blue lights of an ambulance heading his way.

Dylan pulled in to give them plenty of room to get past. The driver waved his thanks and Dylan waved back.

He looked out across the black hills, made out the lights of a plane winking through the clouds.

It's stopped raining, he thought.

He gave a long breath out, lips pursed, then shook his head, smiled and drove on.

*

I've killed him.

He'd Tasered the man. And now Martin was dead. Unresponsive. The enormity of that was crushing him.

For the second time that day Ahmed was faced with administering CPR. But this time he didn't need to overcome any reluctance at the thought.

Fists clenched, fingers interlaced, one hand on top of the other, pressing down on Gregory Martin's chest. One hundred beats per minute. The lyrics to the Bee Gees song 'Staying Alive' helped him keep time.

Wake up. Please wake up.

A drop of blood fell from the cut on Ahmed's face onto Gregory Martin's coat.

Ahmed's knees were soaked from the damp ground, his sweat turning cold so he felt chilled everywhere, his skin raw.

Behind him he was dimly aware of Laura comforting Scarlett.

Ahmed cupped his hands and blew air into the man's nose and mouth. Arms aching, he resumed compressions.

Then there were torches and voices. Paramedics with packs of kit.

'Got this now, mate. How long's he been down?'

Ahmed told them, moved out of the way and knelt. So tired.

He wanted to walk into his home, be fussed over and looked after. He wanted to be clean and dry and warm and safe.

Laura touched his shoulder. He looked up. 'You did everything you could,' she said. 'You did everything right. You know that?'

He nodded, unable to speak.

'And what you did saved that little girl.' Then she scowled, swung her torch round over the surrounding ground and back. 'Where the hell is Dylan Ellis?'

Ahmed put his hands to his head. *Aw, man.*

*

'Scarlett,' Laura said. 'We're going back to the house now. Are you all right to walk?'

Scarlett gave a nod, then remembered with a jolt. 'Polly!'

'What?' Laura said.

'The horse. She's . . . I left her in the cave.'

'Horse?'

Scarlett set off for the cave. Not looking at the paramedics. At the stretcher.

A sick feeling. A terrible dread was sweeping through her, like the tide coming in. A tide of cold, dirty water.

Laura followed her.

What if Polly's gone? What if Scarlett had lost her?

But as soon as she got close to the cave, Scarlett heard the sound of snuffling breath, of hoofs scuffing the ground.

Scarlett approached her slowly, unsure if Polly would still be on edge from the storm, but the horse dipped her head and nickered in greeting. Scarlett rested her head against Polly's, and the horse nuzzled her. Scarlett smelt dusty hair and the tang in the air. Remembered the bats.

She was so tired.

And so sad. Tears leaked from her eyes and she stayed nestling against the animal, until Laura said, 'Scarlett? OK?'

Scarlett led Polly out of the cave.

'How come you had the horse?' Laura asked.

'Ron, he lives at the house. He found us in the shed and he thought—' *It was all such a mess.* 'Well, he told him that we were here.'

'Ron told your father?'

'Yes, because he'd told Ron that Dylan was a paedophile. And he was grooming me. And then when I told him it wasn't true he put me on the horse so I could get away more quickly before my father came back.'

'I see.'

A memory came out of nowhere. Her father piggy-backing her, like Ron had done. Scarlett would pull his ears to turn his head. And sometimes blindfold him with her hands. How could that be the same person?

'Where is Ron?' Scarlett said.

'He's gone to hospital,' Laura said.

No! Scarlett's stomach flipped over. 'What happened?'

Laura hesitated a moment and then she said, 'Gregory attacked him.'

He was hurt. They were all hurt. Because of him. And because of her.

'Do you want to ride it back?' Laura said. 'Would that be easier?'

'Yes,' Scarlett said.

Laura helped her up, and they walked back to Ahmed near the rock. The paramedics were still there. *He* was still there. So that must mean they might be able to save him. Scarlett couldn't tell what she felt about that.

I wish you were dead. That's what she'd said. And she'd meant it. But . . .

He'd killed her mum and he'd hurt Ron and Ahmed and Dylan. He'd hurt everyone.

Ahmed walked at one side of the horse and Laura at the other and together they made their way through the limestone gorge.

Scarlett heard the owl again and then the howl of sirens, like wolves almost, a whooping noise bouncing round and round.

The blue lights.

Mummy won't wake up.

Scarlett closed her eyes and felt the horse moving beneath her, rocking her. To and fro, to and fro. Slow and steady.

Chapter 22

They reached the stables and Laura helped Scarlett down.

'Ron got the saddle from there.' Scarlett pointed to the shed. 'That's where we were hiding.'

'You and Dylan Ellis?' Ahmed said.

'Yes.'

Ahmed went to the shed. Did he think Dylan might be hiding in there again? Scarlett knew Dylan was cleverer than that. But he was hurt. How could he even walk after what—

'Scarlett? Scarlett?' Laura was calling her name. 'How does this undo?' She was peering at the saddle.

Scarlett showed her, sliding the stirrups up before unbuckling the girth.

'It's a bit heavy,' Scarlett said. Laura helped her lift it off. Scarlett heard her breathe in sharply as she took the weight. Perhaps because her hands were sore.

Laura called to Ahmed, 'Can you put this away?'

'I think we're supposed to rub her down.' Scarlett remembered that happening at the end of their lessons.

'She'll be all right,' Laura said. 'She's not been out for long, or gone very far.'

Scarlett could hear the siren growing louder, closer.

'But who'll look after them if Ron's in hospital?' Scarlett said, a sudden panic squashing her breath. 'And there's a dog, too.'

Ahmed came back out of the shed. 'I've got details of the house-sitting service.' He held up his phone. 'I'll contact them.'

'But what if no one's there?'

'Then we can use the RSPCA,' Laura said. 'The animals will be OK. We'll make sure.' She spoke slowly, holding eye contact. The wild feeling inside Scarlett settled a bit but didn't go away.

Scarlett led Polly into the stables. Patti, the chestnut mare, greeted her stablemate and Scarlett watched the way they swung their heads close together, nickering to each other.

Laura waited in the doorway.

Scarlett put Polly into her stall, slipped off her bridle and hung it on the wall. She closed the half-door, then stroked her and said a silent goodbye. Maybe she could just stay there, sleep on the hay by the horses.

'Scarlett, we should go,' Laura called.

As Scarlett stepped out of the stables the siren stopped. A flash of blue light swept the sky in circles.

Blue light.

She understood then. That must have been when the police came or the ambulance. The blue light was *after* she'd rung Nana.

They'd called to her through the letterbox, telling her to open the door. And she'd fetched the step and climbed up and turned the latch.

People had come inside. Lots of people. Talking quietly, asking questions. Some went through to Mummy.

Then Nana was there. She'd come in and knelt down and opened her arms and Scarlett had flown to her. Burrowed into her embrace. Stealing her warmth. Soaking up her love.

Nana's chin on Scarlett's head, Nana sniffing hard, shudders in her chest.

'Don't cry, Nana,' Scarlett had said.

But that had only made her cry harder.

They walked round the corner and the house was lit up like before, but now there was an ambulance outside and another was coming up the drive.

'The Astra's gone,' Laura said to Ahmed.

'I don't believe it!' he said.

'Crafty little bastard,' Laura said.

Scarlett realised they were talking about Dylan. She wondered where he was.

Mike stabbing him again and again.

The knife flashing, one, two, three.

She didn't want to think about that. About anything.

Laura and Ahmed arranged that he'd drive to the hospital and see them there.

Laura and Scarlett went to meet the second ambulance.

'We rang for transport for three casualties but we've only two now,' Laura told the paramedic. 'One of the injured parties has gone walkabout.'

'We'll cancel that one, then. We're stretched to the limit tonight. Road accidents, trees down, flooding, the lot.'

'If you can take Scarlett, I'll come in with her,' Laura said.

Scarlett couldn't bear waiting any longer. She just wanted to get away. 'I'm OK,' she said. 'We can go in the police car with Ahmed.'

Laura hesitated. Then she said, 'If they say that's all right.'

The paramedic called to his colleague to cancel the third rig, then asked Scarlett to step into the ambulance. He went through lots of questions, looked at her cheek, her ankle and in her eyes with a flashlight. He checked her blood pressure and listened to her breath and her heartbeat and he counted her pulse. Then he said everything looked fine and she could go in the car but he made her put a blanket on because she was wet through.

As she stepped down, the other ambulance, the one that must have Mike in it, drove past them, its lights flashing. *Wish you were dead.* Scarlett's stomach knotted and she felt goosebumps prickle across her skin. She wanted to hide.

'Can we go?' she said to Laura.

'Here he is,' Laura said, pointing to the patrol car.

Ahmed stopped to collect them and Scarlett got into the back. She had to unwrap the blanket to fix the seatbelt.

She leant her head against the window and closed her eyes.

Now and then bursts of chatter came over Ahmed's radio. And Laura was talking on the phone, talking about Scarlett and her father. Scarlett didn't want to hear. She kept seeing the knife, and Mike's face. She tried to distract herself. Thought of her and Faye dancing.

It seemed like a million years since they'd done the hand jive outside Faye's house. Not just this afternoon.

She started the sequence of moves in her head, drowsy, draped in the blanket, the heat creeping back despite her wet clothes. She kept losing track.

The drone of the engine and the shushing of the tyres on the road filled her head.

Then Laura was waking her up, saying, 'Here we are, Scarlett. Out you get.'

*

The waiting area was crammed and the air felt steamy from people in damp clothes. Laura was glad they were sitting near the entrance: each time the automatic doors opened to admit new patients a welcome draught of cooler air came in.

Ahmed had spoken to the triage nurse at Reception while Laura sat with Scarlett. Now he was waiting for his number to be called.

'Aren't you going up?' Ahmed said to her, jerking a thumb at the reception booth.

'I'll be all right,' Laura said.

'Is it your hands?' Scarlett must have noticed the burns.

'And concussion,' Ahmed said.

Laura shot him a look. *Shut up!* She didn't want Scarlett to feel any worse about the crash.

She keyed her phone. 'See?' she said to Ahmed, flashing the screen his way. 'NHS recommendations for dealing with concussion at home.' She didn't mention her broken rib but she knew there was no treatment for that, only rest and painkillers.

Scarlett was swathed in the red blanket, her face grubby and the oversized boots filthy. Laura's own clothes were smeared with streaks of mud and speckled with bits of vegetation and grit, Ahmed's uniform the same.

Another siren split the air, an ambulance driving into the bay. Someone seriously hurt, Laura realised, when they went straight through into critical admissions instead of coming into Reception. Someone needing resuscitation or emergency surgery.

'I'll get us some water,' Laura said, pointing to the cooler in the corner. She thought they were probably all at risk of dehydration. 'Ahmed?' He shook his head.

She drank a cup herself and brought one for Scarlett. Scarlett gulped hers down.

'When did you last eat?' Laura asked her.

'Packed lunch at school,' Scarlett said.

'You must be famished.'

'A bit.'

Ahmed's number was called and he followed a nurse through double doors at one end of the room.

Laura glanced at Scarlett. Her head was lowered, eyes half closed. Her lips were chapped. The bruise on her cheek was darker and tear tracks streaked through the grime on her face.

Laura couldn't begin to imagine the terror she had experienced. What must she be thinking and feeling now? Numb, perhaps, in the aftermath of the day's events, but that wouldn't last for ever.

'Scarlett,' Laura said. 'I'm going to come and see you in the next couple of days so I can find out everything that happened today. I need to write a report, you see.'

'OK,' Scarlett said.

'We'll do it when your nana can be there and we'll take it nice and slowly.'

'Will I have to go to court?' Scarlett looked anxious.

'I don't know yet,' Laura said. *It depends on whether your father survives.*

Dribs and drabs of information had reached her as officers pulled together a picture of Gregory a.k.a. Alan Martin.

He ran a fitness centre and kick-boxing gym in Bilbao, north-west Spain. He'd cleaned out his bank account and left the country without a word to anyone since he'd got wind of the domestic-violence complaint against him. CCTV from him boarding the ferry in Santander showed him carrying only a small rucksack. Presumably that was now in the back of the Discovery.

Laura's phone pinged. A message from Ahmed. *Can you come and see me ASAP. Treatment Rm 12.*

Still waiting for Beatrice. BRT, she replied, trusting that at his age he'd understand the shorthand.

What did it mean, Gregory Martin travelling with so little luggage? That he planned to end it all? Kill himself and Scarlett? Or was it simply pragmatic? It would have been too risky for him to go to the apartment and pack, take too long. Leaving immediately bought him time.

How long had the car been hired for? Laura checked. A week. That didn't exactly fit with the action of someone intent on suicide. So had he come to kill Scarlett? The more Laura thought about that, the more it didn't add up. There had been several opportunities when he could have done just that. He had shown no compunction about using a knife on Ronald Thorpe and Dylan Ellis. Even attacking Ahmed, a serving police officer.

She opened the file that summarised the investigation into Jeanette Martin's murder six years ago. First checking that Scarlett couldn't see her screen, she searched through the documents. She found a psychological profile on Gregory Martin. Laura opened it and began to read. After the breakdown of his marriage Martin had vowed to initiate custody proceedings for Scarlett, claiming that Jeanette was an unfit mother. That she was depressed and unable to cope.

Martin fits the profile of a malignant narcissist. Like most narcissists he is charming, controlling and unable to accept any other view than his own. While most narcissists would never go so far as to use violence, as it damages their image of themselves as perfect and above reproach, this is not the case with malignant narcissists. Martin will still believe he is unique and perfect and will blame Jeanette for his actions, blame her for driving him to murder. He will have no guilt or shame.

A rush of cool air and an amplification of sounds from outside. Laura looked up and there was Beatrice Foster, just inside the entrance doors, her face working with emotion. She wore a green-and-white patterned headscarf and a long green mac. Laura saw her eyes fix on Scarlett. Witnessed the strength it took for her to compose herself before she walked towards them.

Scarlett jolted upright in the seat beside Laura. 'Nana!'

Laura moved so Beatrice could take her place.

'Here she is. My lovely girl,' Beatrice said.

'Everything's fine,' Laura said to Beatrice. 'I'll be back in a bit. Can you wait here till then?'

Beatrice gave a quick nod, eyes fastened on her granddaughter. Sitting, pulling Scarlett onto her lap.

*

Ahmed was waiting for someone to come and stitch his face when there was a knock on the door to the treatment room.

It was Laura.

'Listen,' he said, 'there was this guy—'

'You OK?' she interrupted.

'Yes. Need stitches.' The wound had been cleaned and steri-strips held the edges of it together. 'But, look, they brought this bloke in on a trolley. He had orange trainers on, bright orange.' Ahmed couldn't believe it when he'd first noticed, his stomach had dropped and a rush of adrenalin had bumped up his heart rate.

Laura looked blank. She leant back against the examination table, arms folded.

'The man who attacked Ronald Thorpe with a machete, the one who cut his thumb and his neck. The one who was looking for Dylan Ellis, *he* wore bright orange trainers.'

'Got it,' Laura said, her eyes lighting up.

'Right. So we need to know who he is,' Ahmed said.

'Where is he now?' Laura said.

'They've taken him down to X-ray.'

'OK. I'll go and see what I can find out.'

'There's something else,' Ahmed said. He felt the heat rise up his neck, his shoulders tighten, tongue thicken in his mouth. Another thing he'd done wrong.

'Go on.'

'He was in an accident. He came off the road where that mudslide is.' He waited for her disapproval, her censure.

'Ah, Jesus,' she said. But there was a mischievous glint in her eyes. She was trying not to laugh!

He felt a surge of irritation. 'It's not funny,' he said.

'Oh, I don't know.'

'If I'd have closed the road—' It had crossed his mind at the time: he'd *known* someone might get hurt.

'We might have lost Scarlett,' Laura said.

She was right but . . .

'Left her at the mercy of that maniac,' she added. 'It was the right call.'

Was it? He could barely sort out up from down at the moment.

'Any word on Martin?' Laura said.

'Not yet,' Ahmed told her.

'Right. I'll see what I can find out about your man in the orange trainers.' She pushed herself away from the bench and left him there.

He closed his eyes, blew out a long breath. What if the man with the machete died? What if Gregory Martin did too? Both down to Ahmed. He felt heartsick.

And he needed to pee.

He didn't want to miss getting his stitches done but he'd no idea how long he'd have to wait. They were obviously rammed. He couldn't hold it much longer.

He left his jacket on the chair and went out into the corridor, shutting the door so the room would look occupied, then followed the signs for the Gents.

He'd glimpsed the wound on his face in his car mirror but seeing it under the harsh light in the mirror in the toilets was a shock. It was so vivid, a crimson arc held together with steri-strips. Another inch and his eye would have gone.

Oh, my God, Ahmed! Your beautiful face! His mum would go bananas. She'd be harping on about what a dangerous job it was.

Scarred for life.

He thought of Heath Ledger playing the Joker.

Is that how people would talk about him now? The Asian copper with the scar? And every time he met someone, that would always be the first thing they noticed. The mark of violence.

He wanted to cry for a moment, but he closed his eyes really tight and gripped the washbasin until it passed.

On his way back to the treatment room he heard someone call his name. He turned to see Sameena. From college. *Sameena!* In her nurse's uniform.

'God! What happened to you?' she said.

'Kitchen knife,' Ahmed said.

'That's one way to get my attention.' She locked eyes with him. Eyes even darker than he remembered. Deepest brown and glimmering. Outlined in sweeps of black. Gold on her eyelids.

'I didn't—'

'Joke.'

Ha-ha.

'Did you get the guy?' she said.

Can't discuss police business. 'Yes,' Ahmed said. 'I thought you'd gone to London.' She'd broken up with her boyfriend and Ahmed had thought he might be in with a chance, told her maybe they could go out to eat sometime, but she'd left before he'd summoned up the courage to ask her properly.

'Didn't work out,' she said. 'I was paying nearly all my wages for a shoebox full of cockroaches. Commuting three hours a day. So here I am.' She held up her hands, palms to the ceiling. 'Ta-da! Are they going to stitch that?'

'Yes.'

'It'll be all right, you know.' She nodded at the cut. That made him feel a bit better. 'Give it a few years,' she added, mouth twitching into a smile. 'So, you'll have a bit of time off, then?'

'Maybe.' Ahmed had no idea. He wasn't planning to go on the sick. But he had regular days off between his shifts anyway.

'Phone?' She held out a hand.

'Eh?'

She just beckoned with her fingers.

Ahmed passed her his handset and her fingers flew over the screen as she transferred her number to his contacts.

This was good, right? She wasn't just messing with him?

'Here.' She handed it back. 'You can take me for that meal sometime. Once you can chew properly.'

'A date?' He didn't mean to say it out loud.

'Or are you with someone?' she said sharply, a shadow clouding her expression.

'No. No, I'm not.' He rushed to reassure her.

He felt like there was more to say, questions he should ask or things he should tell her, but he didn't know what they were.

He gave a smile, though he wasn't sure it worked because, with being numb and covered in plasters, he couldn't really tell if his face moved properly.

'Laters,' she said, giving him a cheeky look. And then she was gone.

*

Ron was falling, backwards, head first. He tried to open his eyes and see where he was, what was happening, but there was only a void. Him falling back into the darkness.

Ideas, notions, images were beyond his grasp. There like ghosts on the edge of the abyss. Wavering like fog, like smoke. On he fell, down and down and down.

A flash of meaning. A girl, a horse.

He reached for more but it spun away, blown on the wind.

Someone talking, calling his name. Words he couldn't follow.

Chapter 23

Nana!

She was there, pulling Scarlett onto her knees, like Scarlett was still a little kid. Arms wrapping round her. Scarlett breathed in the orange and coconut smell of her hair oil, and the sweet woody scent of the perfume she used.

She felt the familiar contours of Nana's body, the slope of her chest, the heft of her arms, the cushion of her thighs.

She was here.

Scarlett closed her eyes, counted the rise and fall of Nana's breaths.

They were quiet, both of them.

'Can we go home?' Scarlett said, after a while.

'Soon,' Nana said. 'We have to say goodbye to Laura first.'

The minutes ticked by as people came and went in the waiting area. Names were called out. One man came in shouting, but the guard went and told him to quieten down or he'd have to leave. The man sat down, muttering and shaking his head.

Then a nurse came up to them. 'Beatrice? I thought it was you! And this must be Scarlett.' She sounded excited.

This was Nana's hospital. They probably worked together. Lots of people here would know Nana.

'Back safe,' Nana said.

'Oh, thank God! Do you two need anything?'

'We're fine,' Nana said. 'Thanks, Tara. We're going home soon.'

'Take care, it's chaos out there. They've closed twenty roads just in Derbyshire and they reckon there's more rain to come.'

Scarlett found herself drifting close to sleep. The rhythm of Polly walking still echoed through her body. She thought of waves carrying a piece of driftwood to shore, bumping it against the sand. Almost landing, then sucked away again.

'Scarlett?' Nana shook her shoulder and Scarlett squeaked. That was where the seatbelt had hurt her.

Laura was back. She looked really tired and her hair had dried all flicked out.

'I won't keep you long,' Laura said. 'Let's just go through here.' She pointed and they followed her into a corridor where there was a bench to sit on.

Laura looked really serious. 'I've just had word that Gregory, your father, didn't make it. The doctors weren't able to revive him. He died. He was dead before he reached hospital.'

Scarlett felt like her heart was being crushed. She swallowed. *I wish you were dead.*

'How?' Nana said.

'We discharged a Taser when we apprehended him . . .' Laura told Nana about the knife and the woods and the Taser. Nana was sitting very still and quiet, but Scarlett saw how her hands were knitted tight together.

He was dead.

Should she be sorry?

If he was dead he couldn't come after her again.

You little bitch.

Just walk.

She wouldn't listen.

She'd wished him dead.

'Can we go now?' Scarlett said, standing up. Her throat hurt. A big lump there. She just wanted to go. *Now!*

Laura nodded. 'I'll be in touch to arrange a time to come and see you.'

'Thank you,' Nana said.

But Scarlett was too dazed to say anything.

Laura said, 'And, Scarlett, I'm sorry for all of this, for everything that happened today. Taking you like that, hurting people, that was a terrible thing to do. I'm sorry you had to go through all that.'

Scarlett's chest ached. She nodded. Nana took her hand and they went to the doors and Scarlett remembered in a rush.

'Is Ron dead too?' she said, turning back to Laura.

She could feel Nana looking at her. Nana wouldn't know who Ron was, what he'd done, but she didn't ask any question. Perhaps she could tell that Scarlett wasn't ready to explain it all. So much had happened.

'He's in theatre.' Laura looked sad. 'They say he's lost a lot of blood.'

'OK?' Nana pressed Scarlett's hand but Scarlett hesitated.

'I'll let you know as soon as I hear anything,' Laura said.

'OK,' Scarlett said. And she squeezed Nana's hand back.

I wish you were dead. I wish you'd died instead. I hate you. She'd got her wish. She'd wished him dead and now he was. Her mother was dead and her father was dead. They were both dead. Everything was a mess. Everything.

*

Laura met Ahmed outside the main entrance. In the sodium glare the stitches on his face were savage black spiky notches across the wound.

'How many?' she asked.

'Twelve.'

He looked wretched. She was pretty sure it wasn't the injury that was bothering him but the news of Martin's death.

'It'll be OK,' Laura said, as she zipped her coat against the chill.

'If I'd just aimed better—'

'There was no time. Listen, there'll be an inquest and a post-mortem. The death will be referred to Professional Standards but you used proportionate force, given the situation. You gave a warning. He'd already been Tasered once. There's no way you could know—'

'That I'd kill him?' Ahmed said flatly. He met her gaze, then broke it.

'Anyone would have done the same,' Laura said. 'At least, anyone with any sense. God knows what he'd have done if you hadn't put him down again. He's been on our most wanted list for six years. Today he violently assaulted three people, as well as abducting his daughter. You'd have been failing in your duty *not* to try to disable him.'

'Death in police custody.' He shook his head, an expression of sadness in the cast of his eyes and the set of his mouth.

'I know what you're saying, what that sounds like, but this wasn't neglect or brutality. He wasn't unarmed or fleeing the scene. There was no mistreatment by you. He was armed and dangerous. There were four of us there at risk of harm. We needed you to stop him.'

He flexed his mouth, the nearest she reckoned she'd get to an acknowledgement that what she said was valid.

They watched as an ambulance pulled in, sirens dying mid-whoop.

She didn't want to rubberneck while the paramedics retrieved their patient so she turned away and signalled for Ahmed to follow her, walking past the trio of smokers who were ignoring all the No Smoking signs, block capitals stating there was no smoking anywhere on hospital trust grounds.

Around the corner, by some disabled parking bays, Laura stopped.

'So I found your orange-trainers guy. . .' she said.

Ahmed's expression shifted, shedding the misery, his face alert now.

'Colin Hardcastle. A Leeds address,' Laura said.

'That fits,' Ahmed said. 'Dylan Ellis, Lloyd Campion – they're all from Leeds. The house in Leek – I think they were using it for dealing – county lines. Maybe I should go and see this Hardcastle now and talk to him.'

'Hold on.' Laura put up a hand. *Ow!* The sting as the skin stretched. When would she learn? 'He's going nowhere. Fractured pelvis and two broken legs.'

Ahmed sucked air through his teeth.

'You can talk to Admissions tomorrow. You won't be able to arrest him until he's discharged anyway.'

'OK. And I'll need to get Ronald Thorpe to identify him as his assailant.'

Ah, shit.

Laura toed the floor.

'He's not—?' Ahmed said.

'No. But it could go either way. The stomach wound, there's a risk of sepsis and he lost a lot of blood. We'll have to see.'

'Big bloke, though,' Ahmed said.

'Not sure it helps, actually,' Laura said.

A taxi pulled up and a young woman got out, weeping and wiping at her face. She hurried into the building.

'Can you hang on a minute?' Laura said to Ahmed.

She walked over and asked the cabbie if he could take her back to Matlock. Praying the roads would be passable. 'I know it's advance bookings only,' she said. She held up her phone. 'I can ring you, if you like. I'm a police officer.'

The driver smiled. 'I explain.' The guy radioed in, spoke to the dispatcher and gave Laura a thumbs-up.

'Two minutes,' Laura said.

She went back to Ahmed. 'You OK driving home?' she asked. She didn't know where he lived but hopefully it wasn't too far.

'Yes. I need to take the car back to the station first.'

'I think they'll let you off this once,' she said.

He gave a shake of his head. 'We're short of rides.' So conscientious. She considered arguing the toss but didn't think she could dissuade him.

'Drive safe, then. I'll be in touch. Oh, and, Ahmed . . .'

He cocked his head, waiting to see what she had to say.

'I'm going to nominate you for a commendation.'

'Sarge?' he said, the surprise turning him formal.

'Today was a horror show. Without you— Well, let's just say I'm glad I ran into you. Even if you did try to arrest me.'

Before he could respond, Laura walked away and climbed into the cab.

She sat back, her bones soft with fatigue.

'Shocking weather,' the driver said.

Tell me about it.

*

It was late when they got home. Everyone inside, curtains drawn. The wind blowing fiercely, twigs scattered all over the pavement.

As Scarlett got out of the car she caught a flash of herself standing there earlier, thinking for a moment that Grandpa was there.

Wetting herself.

Frozen to the spot.

Him lifting her in.

She didn't want to remember that, none of it, but the moments kept popping into her head, like adverts on websites.

'How about something to eat?' Nana said, when they were inside.

It all looked the same. Nana's material and sewing-machine, the clothes on the ceiling rack. The new paints Scarlett had bought on the window-seat. The big yucca plant. Scarlett thought of it all being here without her. What if she'd never come back?

'Scarlett?'

She couldn't talk. Her eyes burnt and tears leaked down her face.

'Come here.'

Nana took her to sit down. She stroked Scarlett's back. Now and again she said, 'It's OK. It's going to be all right.'

Scarlett cried until she couldn't breathe any more. She leant away from Nana, wiping her nose on the back of her hand. 'I need a tissue.' She laughed. How could she laugh?

'Go and get changed,' Nana said. 'Do you want some food?'

'I don't know.'

'Porridge?'

'OK.'

At the foot of the stairs she stopped. 'Have I got to have a shower?'

'Whatever you like,' Nana called. 'It might feel nicer.'

Scarlett did. Sitting down in the bath, because her ankle hurt. Letting the water pour over her.

She'd need to oil her hair tomorrow.

The pictures kept jumping into her head.

Dylan in the road.

Mike stabbing Dylan.

The bats.

Ron finding her and Dylan in the shed.

Writing the note.

Blood spilling through Ahmed's fingers as he held his cheek.

The red car crashing into them.

Mike threatening to cut Polly's throat.

Mike charging at her, that horrible look on his face.

She hit at her head with her hands. *Stop it. Stop it. Stop it.*

*

Downstairs she spooned Golden Syrup into her porridge and poured oat milk over it. And it was like she was watching herself do it. Like she wasn't properly there.

She was so tired. She was see-through, flat and hollow.

The server in the service station with her tattoos.

Mike calling Scarlett Victoria.

Bitch.

'I can't stop thinking about it,' Scarlett said to Nana. 'It's all going round and round.'

Nana nodded. She put down her drink. A big glass of wine. The glass was misty because the wine was so cold.

'You can't fight your thoughts,' Nana said. 'A lot happened today. Terrible things. You need to have a sleep, and tomorrow we can see how you feel. You maybe try writing some of it down or tell me about it.'

Why would she do that when she wanted to forget it all?

'I don't know,' Scarlett said.

'You can decide,' Nana said. She took a drink from her glass, put it down and drew a zigzag line in the condensation. 'It helped me some. When your mum died, I wrote it down like a diary.'

A jab in Scarlett's heart.

'But you will find your own way,' Nana said.

'What if I can't go to sleep?'

'You're coming in with me tonight,' Nana said. Not a question but like it was already agreed.

Scarlett yawned and Nana said, 'You go up. I'll be there soon. Brush your teeth and fetch your pillow.'

Scarlett climbed the stairs. In her room she looked round at the posters. Greta, *I want you to act as if the house is on fire, because it is.* The bear, the raccoons.

She couldn't look at the photographs: she couldn't face seeing her mum there.

Her heart hurt, like it was bruised.

In bed she listened to the familiar sounds of Nana clearing up downstairs. She was home. And Nana was here. Nana was all right.

Scarlett wondered if Dylan had been caught and whether someone was looking after Ron's dog. Then she remembered the sensation of riding the horse and the dusty grass smell of Polly. She heard the rain start again, tapping against the windows, and the waterfall rushing and gushing and the waves crashing onto the shore, but by then she was already dreaming.

Chapter 24

Laura crept into bed and lay back gingerly.

Hector was snoring, slow, light breaths that made her think of the waves on the shingle where they went swimming on holiday. The cove close to his family's home.

We should book flights, go before the school holidays, she thought, sleep already unravelling her thoughts. June. Mateo will be old enough to enjoy the water.

*

The pinnacle of rock toppled and slammed into her side with a crushing pain. Laura screamed and reared awake as Hector scrambled upright. '*¡Dios mío!* Laura. You OK? What? What is it?'

'You grabbed me.' She panted.

'I put my arm around you. I didn't grab you.' He sounded pissed off.

Mateo cranked into life, a wail rising in pitch and volume.

'I've hurt my rib,' she said.

'How?'

She couldn't handle this now. 'I bumped into something.' Mateo was roaring. 'I'll tell you in the morning.'

Carefully she climbed out of bed. 'Has he had any Calpol?'

'At nine o'clock,' Hector answered.

It was five now. So she could give him another dose, a drink of water, sing some songs, but odds were Mateo would decide the new day had already begun.

She was right.

Hector joined them at eight. Laura was half asleep at the table, mind trying to gather together all the things she needed to do at work. Mateo was playing with his wooden cars, crashing them into each other.

'We got her back,' she said to Hector.

'That's great.' His eyes lit up.

'Yes, it is.'

She needed to tell Hector the rest but hoped it would be better received once he'd had his coffee and toast. And she was clean and dressed. She'd only had the energy to wash her hands and face the night before.

'I'll grab a shower,' she said.

Her phone rang before she could leave the room. Work. She answered. 'I'll be there in an hour,' she said. 'Briefing at ten. Can you let people know?'

'Your hands?' Hector had noticed the burns. He was frowning.

'Yes,' she said. 'I'll explain in a minute.'

Her phone rang again. She left it, let it go to voicemail.

When she came back downstairs Hector poured her a cup of coffee and turned on the TV, switched the channel to CBeebies. Mateo trotted over and sat down on the floor to watch.

Laura looked at Hector: their screen-time rules didn't usually allow for this. He tilted his head, *What?* and moved back to the table. He was being pragmatic. In order to have any sort of conversation they needed something to occupy their toddler.

Her phone rang and she reached for it.

'Laura?'

'Just seeing who it is.' And stalling. *Tell him.*

'So, we got Scarlett back but her father died in the process. He was Tasered.' Her voice sounded funny, brittle.

'Shit!'

'He was armed with a knife and he'd already hurt a police officer and two members of the public.'

Hector paled. She saw the muscles tighten around his jawline.

Mateo laughed and shouted at the TV.

Hector shook his head. 'And you?'

She didn't want him to dwell on the worst that might have happened. Ignored the quaking inside that still lingered. She needed to reassure him. 'I got there after most of that.'

'Where? Where was he?' Hector said, fingers stiff, tapping the table.

'In the Peaks, this little side valley south of Longnor.'

His hand stilled. He spoke slowly, quietly, 'You went in the wilds in a raging storm after a man with a knife. What were you thinking?'

'I was working,' she said steadily. 'I was thinking I'd rescue Scarlett Martin. And I did.'

'You didn't have a Taser?'

'No. You know I don't carry one. I'm fine, Hector. I'm home.'

His eyes darkened. 'Did you tackle him? This man?'

Laura hesitated. How to frame it? Lie? She couldn't. She wouldn't ever do that to him. There was no sugar-coating it. 'I hit him with a tyre iron.'

'*¡Madre de Dios!* Laura, you have Mateo, you have me.' Distressed.

'I know, and I have my job. What should I have done? Hung back and let him—'

Her phone rang. She glanced at it.

'Leave it,' he said. 'He could have killed you too.' Worry making him furious.

'He didn't *kill* anyone. Well, no one last night. Not the last I heard.'

Hector gave an exasperated roar, raised his hands and clamped them over the top of his head. Mateo scooted round and stared a moment, then turned back to the TV.

'If you . . .' Hector said. 'If you had . . .' She saw his anger and fear and the tears that sprang into his eyes. 'How could you?'

'I'm here. I'm fine.' She stepped closer. 'It's OK.'

He dropped his hands and sighed. 'I just—'

'I know. I did what I had to do. And I'd do the same again. In a heartbeat.' He knew this. It was who she was. And it was what he'd signed up to when they'd got married.

Laura waited until Hector's eyes met hers. Until his shoulders fell, resignation on his face.

She walked forward. Moved into his embrace. He squeezed her and she stifled a yelp.

'There's something else,' she murmured. 'I trashed the car.'

'What?' He let her go.

She held up her hands, palms showing. 'From the airbag. And that's when I hurt my rib. So I'll have to get a taxi. And I'll call the insurance.'

'Crashed into what?'

'A car carrying Scarlett. They engineered it so I'd hit them.'

Hector gave a shake of his head. 'Unbelievable,' he said softly.

'We got her back, though,' Laura said. 'She's eleven years old, Hector. She was five when he killed her mother and she sat for hours with the body before she called her grandma for help.'

He twisted his head as though he didn't want to hear her.

She thought of Scarlett by the standing stone, that look in her eyes. And later how she had railed against her father. Her courage.

'I'm OK, yes?' Laura said.

He looked at her for long enough before closing his eyelids in acceptance. 'It drives me loco—' He exhaled noisily, tilted his face up towards the ceiling.

'I know,' she said. 'But I'm OK. Something like this – it's once in a blue moon. Most days the biggest risk I take is the drive to work. You know that. I'm OK. We're OK.' Her heart swelled, tenderness for him. She reached up to kiss his cheek but he turned his head to meet her lips. Kissed her. A hard, fierce kiss. A kiss that she returned in kind.

*

Knocking at the door startled Scarlett. She wanted to race upstairs and hide. *Don't be stupid.*

Nana noticed. 'Wait there,' she said.

Scarlett heard the door open, and Nana talking to someone, quietly so Scarlett couldn't catch the words. Then Nana came back through. 'It's Faye and Jason. They want to know if they can come and see you. Play for a bit.'

Scarlett shrugged.

'I can tell them another day?' Nana said.

Scarlett gave a nod, but as Nana walked away she changed her mind. 'Wait. Say yes.'

'Just an hour,' Nana suggested. 'Unless you get tired sooner.'

'Yes.'

Scarlett felt awkward when they came in and shucked off their coats and shoes. But Faye didn't seem to notice. She came over and hugged Scarlett.

Jason nodded and said hello. He was blushing and that made Scarlett blush too.

'You go upstairs,' Nana told them.

'I sprained my ankle,' Scarlett said, leading the way. 'I've got to hop.'

'You can't hop upstairs,' Faye said.

'No. I just go slowly.'

In Scarlett's room, Jason murmured, 'Cool,' as he nodded to the gym rings. He'd not been in there before. 'Can I have a go?'

'Yes,' Scarlett said.

He put one foot through each ring and pulled himself up until he could hang upside down from his knees. He had a bandage on his hand.

'I bet you can't stay like that for five minutes,' Faye said.

'Time me,' Jason said.

Faye opened the timer on her phone. 'All the blood goes to your head,' she said.

'I'm a bat,' Jason said.

'I saw some bats,' Scarlett said. 'In a cave.'

Faye looked interested, like she was about to ask something, but then she stopped. Scarlett wondered if she'd been told not to be nosy. Then she decided that she didn't really want to talk about any of that so she sat back on her bed and said, 'What happened with the talent show?'

'It's cancelled,' Jason said. His hair all hung down, almost brushing the carpet.

'Postponed,' Faye said. 'Till you . . . till you're better.'

It was Jason who'd seen the car stop outside Scarlett's house, Nana had told Scarlett. That was how Laura had been able to find him, by tracing the Discovery.

Scarlett wanted to thank him.

'You're going red,' Scarlett said.

'How long now?' he said.

Faye looked at her phone. 'Oh, no. I forgot to start it.'

Jason swung his legs free and slithered to the floor. Then he put his hands through the rings and twizzled over.

There was another gap where no one said anything and Scarlett thought maybe she shouldn't have agreed to see them because it felt all weird, then Faye said, 'Oh, my God, you have got to see this Tik-Tok with rabbits. It's so funny.'

And Jason came over and sat next to Scarlett with Faye on the other side and they watched loads of Tik-Toks and laughed so hard that Scarlett got a stitch.

*

When they'd gone she helped Nana cut out squares for the quilt she was making and soon it was dark.

They didn't put the telly on, like they usually did. Nana explained there might be some news on about it and Scarlett didn't want that. But then Nana found a movie they both liked on Netflix, *The Little Prince.*

It was OK mostly until teatime when Scarlett felt sick looking at her plate. The beans and rice steaming and all the pictures in her head. Pictures from when her mum died. The milk and the sound of humming.

She put down her fork.

'Scarlett?'

'I can't eat it,' she said.

'OK. We can always warm it up later. You want anything else?'

Was that humming sound her breathing? Was she moaning?

'When . . . you know when—' Scarlett bit her cheek. A tightness in her chest.

Nana waited, patted at her food with the back of her fork.

'When my mum was—' Scarlett's voice broke but she forced herself on, the words tumbling out in a rush. 'I think she was alive. There was this noise like a humming. I think she was making the noise.'

Nana pressed her lips together. She was frowning. Was she cross?

'Humming?'

'Yes.'

Nana put down her fork. 'Did it stop and start?'

'I don't think so.'

'Did it change at all?' Nana said.

'No. But if she was moaning and I didn't—'

Nana's face cleared. She looked sad but not worried. 'It was the fridge, Scarlett.'

'What?'

'You got her some milk to drink.'

'And she couldn't,' Scarlett said.

'That's right. But you left the fridge door open. That noise, that was the fan trying to keep the temperature low. It was like that when we came.'

'Really?' Scarlett's heart missed a beat.

'Yes. And from the police reports, what they said, it looked like your mum was . . . she was dead when you found her. She was dead when he left.' Nana's voice wobbled and she reached out a hand and took Scarlett's. 'And even if that *hadn't* been the case, you did everything in your power to help her. You tried to keep her warm, you tried to give her a drink. You did everything you could. You were just five. A baby. None of it was your fault. Not then, not now. None of it.' Nana squeezed Scarlett's hand so hard it hurt.

'None of it,' Nana said again. 'You hear me? None of it.'

*

All the roads were closed. Dylan had tried rejigging routes on the phone he'd bought but it was all diversions and severe weather warnings. Half of Wales underwater.

In the end, so knackered he reckoned he might spark out at the wheel, he had searched for somewhere to spend the night and checked into a Premier Inn just over the border.

He'd already changed into his spare clothes in the bogs at the Tesco he'd found so he had something to wear that wouldn't draw attention while he bought supplies. His top had stuck to his shoulder, the blood there dried, and he'd had to peel it off, cursing as he did.

He stocked up on fags and bought some lagers. A bottle of rum, too, and a big bottle of Coke. He piled it all on the checkout. Clothes and a new jacket. Pair of crap trainers cos his were a mess. He'd found dressings and painkillers and antiseptic cream. Chosen a suitcase to put it all in. Hard shell type on wheels.

'Flooded out?' The checkout girl looked sorry for him.

Dylan nodded.

'It's a nightmare, isn't it?'

'Everything gone,' he agreed.

Then he used the disabled toilet so he could strip off and wash his wounds without anyone walking in on him. He spread some Germolene around each cut and covered them with adhesive dressings. Downed some ibuprofen. Put on the brand-new clothes, ripping the plastic price-tag ties with his teeth. He took the money out of the holdall and ditched the bag along with the old gear.

The café in Tesco had been shut, but there was a Subway in the same complex and he ordered a meatball marinara and ate it in the car.

At the Premier Inn he chucked the cushions off the bed and watched some telly, had some rum and Cokes mixed in a mug from the tea tray. There was no smoking in the hotel so he had to trek downstairs and outside for one before he turned in.

He slept like a dog. Slept through his alarm. Woke up with a start the next morning, moving too suddenly, and his arm hurt like fuck.

He'd looked up the news before he set out and saw that Gregory Martin had died and Scarlett had been safely returned to her family. He felt a punch of victory at that. She was OK. And part of that was down to him. That was a good feeling. He couldn't ever tell anyone about it but he knew. And so did she. And the feds who had been there. He'd stepped up and she was alive. That was something. The world wasn't totally gone to shit.

*

The Astra coughed, bucked and died on him in the back of beyond. A two-lane road and nothing but fields on either side, occasional signs in English and Welsh.

Rage rolled up his spine. He shut his eyes, waited for the heat to leave him.

He should take the plates off the car and get rid. But he wasn't sure he had the strength to roll it into the ditch and he didn't want to start bleeding again.

Best find out where the nearest taxi service was and ring for a ride. Smoke first.

He was lighting up when he heard the blare of a horn and his heart flip-flopped. He looked up, expecting to see the feds, poised to run, but it was a breakdown truck, pulling over in front of him. It was battered, the bodywork scratched. The name on the side of the door, *Thomas Recovery*, splattered with mud.

He saw a teenage girl in the passenger seat.

The driver jumped out and called, 'You needing a tow? You want a garage?' Short bloke, thickset, with a red face, black overalls.

'It wants scrapping,' Dylan said.

The girl opened her door and stepped down. She had overalls on too. Her hair was dark, thick and wavy, down to her waist.

'Do that for you an' all,' the bloke said. 'Give you forty quid for it.'

'Fifty,' Dylan said, having a punt.

'Got your documents?'

Dylan shook his head.

'You need to send them in when you get home. Else they'll be after you for the road tax.'

Dylan nodded. They'd be after Lloyd, if anyone. He was the registered owner.

'Where you heading?'

Dylan went blank.

'Give you a lift with us? We're just up the road.'

'That'd be great. Thanks.'

'Bryn, and this is Megan.'

She looked at him, twirling a lock of hair round her fingers.

'Dylan.'

'Welsh, that is,' Bryn said. Dylan shrugged, His shoulder stung and he gritted his teeth. He'd no idea why his mam had called him Dylan. She'd never talked about it. But he was pretty sure there was no Welsh connection.

Dylan went to get his case out.

'Best leave your gear in there,' Bryn said. 'No room up front.' He had a strong Welsh accent and Dylan had to concentrate really hard to follow him.

'Holiday?' Megan nodded at his case.

'Flooded out,' Dylan said. 'Up in Sheffield.' First place he thought of. Would they check? Why would they? Anyway, he'd be long gone.

'You're not! Oh, Da, he's flooded,' she said.

He felt a flush of pleasure at her sympathy.

'Where you going to stay?'

'There a hotel?' Dylan said.

'There's the Lamb,' she said. Her father nodded. He counted out five tenners for Dylan from a scruffy old wallet.

Dylan watched while Bryn lowered the ramp and he and Megan hooked up the Astra and winched it onto the back of the truck. Then they secured it with straps.

It wasn't far to the town and for that Dylan was glad. The truck was noisy, too, which reduced the need for chatter. It had started raining again.

They pulled up outside the scrapyard. Megan opened the big gates and Bryn drove through.

Towers of metal, crushed cars, fridges and washing-machines, iron bars and corrugated sheets were stacked all round.

Once they'd rolled the Astra off the truck and onto solid ground, Dylan got his suitcase out.

'I'll show you the way to the Lamb,' Megan said.

'OK, ta,' Dylan said.

The houses here looked different, kind of plain, grey or white, but now and then one was painted bright blue or pink. They reminded him of the seaside. And the walls along the road were made from big stone boulders.

'You lost much?' Megan said, as they walked along the narrow street. She had her hands tucked under her arms, probably because of the rain. Dylan set the pace: he had to take it slowly but she'd think that was because he was lugging the case.

'Everything.' And for a moment it felt like he had. His whole life gone, and his blood chilled, but then he reminded himself he had the money. And he was still breathing.

'Well, that fifty should pay for the night,' Megan said.

'No, I'm sorted for cash. Just everything else is gone. House is a wreck,' he said.

'You been living on your own?'

He hesitated.

'Sorry. I'm being nosy, isn't it?' She smiled. Teeth a bit crooked but a nice smile.

'Nah, you're OK. I'm on my tod. No ties.'

'Well, look, if you fancy tonight, we meet up, a bunch of us, of a Saturday. Pig and Garter. Just if you likes the company.'

'Ta,' Dylan said. 'I'll be fine but, yeah, thanks.'

'So where will you go?'

'Dunno. Just get away for a bit. Need to start over,' Dylan said.

'I wouldn't pick here, mate,' Megan said. 'Not unless you want the quiet life, working on a farm or packing veg or in a scrapyard. Die of boredom.'

Would it be so bad? Something like that. Take it easy, tread water. Some sort of normality for a change.

'Here we are,' Megan announced, stopping outside a pub. The ancient building all crooked-looking. Signs in the windows. *Home Cooked Food* and *Real Ales*.

'And the Pig's at the end by the square.' She pointed down the street. 'We'll be there from half seven.'

Dylan stood his case up, lit a fag, cupping his hand over it to try to keep it dry.

'You should try vaping. Better for you, isn't it? To be honest, those things they'll kill you,' Megan said.

'Live fast, die young,' Dylan said.

'Be a real awful waste, though, wouldn't it? Crying shame,' she said. And for a moment he thought she was coming on to him. She rolled the *r*s and her voice slowed and swooped up at the end. Or was that just her accent?

He watched her walk away while he finished his smoke.

Maybe he would check out the get-together later. Couldn't hurt. Find out if Megan was hooked up with anyone, see if she knew any casual work going.

Boring sounded good. For a bit at least. *You could just forget about Lloyd and Col and the dealing and all the pressure for a while, stop looking over your shoulder all the time waiting for stuff to kick off. Though you'll need a few days before you can do any lifting and shifting. Plenty of money to last you meanwhile. And here's probably as good a place as any to hide.*

He thought of Scarlett, hands on hips, small and defiant. *What's your plan, then?*

That's my plan, he thought. And it'll do just grand for now.

Chapter 25

The photographer from the local paper wanted to meet them at the police station in Chesterfield so Ahmed got the all-clear from his sergeant and drove over there first thing on the Monday morning.

They posed this way and that, *Chin up a bit, try turning slightly to one side, straighten your shoulders, look at me.*

'So how's it going?' Laura said after. 'You OK?'

'Fine,' Ahmed said.

She stared at him for a moment, as if she was giving him a chance to say more. When he didn't, she gave a sort of shrug with her eyes. 'And Dylan Ellis?'

'No sign,' Ahmed said. 'And the guy in Leek, Peter King, it was a natural death. A seizure. He'd bitten through his tongue. That was why there was so much blood.'

'He was the one you thought Dylan Ellis had killed?'

'Yes.'

'How old was he?'

'Peter King?'

'Dylan Ellis,' Laura said.

'Seventeen.'

'You could make a strong argument for him being treated as a victim, then. Exploited, groomed into dealing drugs. Policy is we try to give them a way out, an alternative.'

'If we can find them,' Ahmed said. 'What about Scarlett?'

Laura screwed up her mouth. 'Early days. She's resilient. But she's in the best place she can be. Beatrice – she's amazing.'

Ahmed wondered if Scarlett could sleep at night. And Laura?

He had dreams, always the same dream. Running, running and his pursuer getting closer. Ahmed's feet slowing, legs heavier and heavier, sinking into the mud, barely able to move forward. The shadow at his back. The mud setting like concrete round his ankles. Looking down to see his hands full of blood. Waking drenched in sweat, sick and shaky.

His parents knew. They'd heard him, and asked him about it. His mother saying it wasn't surprising, given what he'd been through.

*

Ahmed's mum bought five copies of the paper from the corner shop.

'Page five,' she said. 'And there's a headline on the front page.' She was grinning at him, puffed with pride in spite of her worries. 'I wish they'd waited till you'd had your stitches out,' she added.

'It'd be old news then,' his father said. 'You look fine, son. Good.'

'It'll be online too,' Ahmed said.

He leafed through, the rest of the news all related to the storm. Rescues and floating cars, flooded retail parks and livestock in danger.

There was the photo, him and Laura, staring ahead, looking serious. The text was short and missed out most of what Ahmed had said in answer to the reporter's questions.

The paper had been given a statement by the police press office at headquarters. And Ahmed had received a call briefing him on what to say if he was asked anything relating to Gregory Martin's death. He'd learnt it by heart because he didn't want to make a mistake. *Any death is extremely regrettable but I can't say any more at present as the incident is under investigation.*

But he'd not be able to relax until Professional Standards had cleared him. It was a shadow over everything. The fact that he'd killed a man, that he, Ahmed Ali, had killed someone, ended someone's life – even a murderer like Gregory Martin – made him feel compromised. Dirty or ashamed. He couldn't explain it to anyone else. Even Laura just kept telling him that he'd had no choice, that he'd saved Scarlett. But he wished it could have happened differently.

He could feel his mood start to darken.

'You ought to celebrate,' his mum said. 'We could invite people over, have a meal.'

Ahmed groaned inside. She meant well but he felt stifled. Like he'd be stuck here for ever. No life of his own. 'I might have plans,' he said.

'Plans?' His dad looked up from the paper. He'd turned to the puzzles section.

'Yes, plans.'

Ahmed texted Sameena then and there. Easier than calling, when she could trip him up with her teasing and backchat.

How's tomorrow night? 7? Meet you by the Memorial? There were a few places to eat around there. She could pick.

Ahmed's thumb hovered over emojis. He could never decide whether to use them. They were so . . . babyish. But everyone else went mad for them. Or a kiss? Was it too soon for a kiss? When he hadn't kissed her in real life. But if he didn't put anything it read pretty cold really. He quickly jabbed *x A* and sent it.

If he hadn't heard anything by tomorrow lunchtime he'd have to ring. See if she'd been fooling with him all along. Or was busy or—

His phone pinged. A string of emojis: a wine glass, a rose, a face blowing a kiss.

A yes, then. Something lightened inside him, brought a curl of pleasure.

'I'm going out for tea tomorrow,' he announced.

'Ooh.' His mother's eyes danced, his dad waggled his eyebrows. And Ahmed felt his cheeks grow warm.

*

Ron's mother was visiting, had come bringing grapes and chocolate, orange juice, a newspaper and a phone charger, a full set of clothes, pyjamas and three lots of underwear from Marks & Spencer, when there was a knock on the door to his room.

Ron expected it to be a nurse. They were still monitoring him. The surgery had been successful and the main concern now was to ensure there was no lingering infection.

But the woman who came in wore a trouser suit. She was short and curvy with dark hair. *A doctor?*

'Hello, I'm Detective Sergeant Laura O'Neil,' she said. 'Laura.'

'Right.' He'd had a message that a Sergeant O'Neil would be coming to talk to him. But he hadn't realised it would be today. Apparently this was one of the officers who had found Scarlett and rescued her from her father.

'I can wait,' she offered. 'I'll come back.'

'No, it's fine.' His mum got to her feet. 'I could do with a sandwich.'

'Thank you,' Laura said.

His mum picked up her shoulder bag. 'You want me to fetch you anything?'

Ron shook his head.

'How are you feeling?' Laura asked, once they were alone.

'OK,' he said. 'You were at Graybridge?'

'Yes. I'd like to ask you about it, if you feel all right to talk now.'

'Yes,' Ron agreed. He felt awkward, still in a hospital gown, tucked up in bed. But he couldn't do anything about that.

She sat in the chair.

'It was a crazy day,' he said. 'One thing after another.'

He told her all he could, from finding the phone on the way to the vet's up to the point where Gregory Martin heard the radio news headlines and saw that Ron was lying to him.

'I don't remember anything after that. I know he must have

stabbed me but it's . . . There's just a blank. Nothing till I woke up after the operation.' He thought for a moment, trying to summon something more, but the memories stalled at the same point.

'I was in the kitchen?' he asked.

'Yes,' Laura said. 'We had to break through the windows at the front.'

'Christ!' he said, imagining the hassle that would cause. He was insured for house-sitting but he had no idea if it would stretch to something as bizarre as this. He knew that the agency had arranged emergency cover so presumably whoever was there would have to sort out repairs.

Laura paused as if she wasn't sure how much he wanted to hear.

'He used a knife?' Ron said.

'One from the kitchen set.' She met his gaze and he nodded, eager for her to continue. He wanted to know everything. It was part of trying to figure out what he'd actually been through.

'You had a stomach wound, and the knife was lodged in your leg, near your thigh.'

'You saved my life.'

She gave a quick smile, her brown eyes warm. 'I think the doctors did that. You'd lost a lot of blood but you did manage to respond and tell us where Scarlett was hiding.'

'Really?' Relief swept through him. After placing Scarlett in jeopardy he had been able to do something to redeem himself. Help them find her, save her.

'Yes. She'd reached the cave and she was in there with the horse when Gregory Martin tracked her down.'

'I'd told him they left, went down to the road, but once he realised I knew who he really was, he wouldn't have believed that,' Ron said.

'That's right. He went looking. He'd followed the path leading out the back and through the gorge. Scarlett says the horse got spooked by the storm and made so much noise it gave them away. Dylan Ellis tried to intervene and Martin stabbed him several times.'

Christ!

'He'd taken another of the kitchen knives. My colleague Ahmed Ali, whom I think you'd met earlier . . .'

'Yes,' Ron said, remembering the young officer. Gripping his pen tightly as he made his notes.

'Ahmed Tasered Martin, but Martin managed to cut him.'

'Oh, God,' Ron said.

'When I reached them, Martin attacked again. Between us we were able to keep him away from Scarlett, and Ahmed Tasered him a second time.'

'And he died?' Ron had learnt that much from the news.

'Yes. Dylan Ellis left the scene in spite of his injuries. And Ahmed wants to see you about doing a video identification for the man who'd attacked you earlier that day.'

'You found him?'

She nodded. 'Yes. He was in a road accident and is still recovering. He and Dylan Ellis were involved in drug-dealing in the area.'

Ron was glad to know that the man with the machete wasn't still rampaging around out there, angry and aggressive.

'And Scarlett?' His last glimpse was of her on a horse in baggy borrowed clothes. He recalled her anguish when she realised he'd tipped off her father. *How could you do that? How could you? You believed him. You idiot.*

'OK,' Laura said, with a guarded tone, implying it wasn't all plain sailing. 'Witnessing all that. It's traumatic. Not just physically but mentally too.'

'I know. I was in the Fire Brigade.'

'Ah.' She gave a nod. 'That's hard. You'll have seen some stuff.'

'Yes,' he said.

'That why you left?'

'Sort of. And I was gay. I am gay.' The words were out before he realised he was going to say them.

'That was a problem?' Laura said.

He blew out a breath. 'It was then. In that station.' He *never* talked about this. He'd never told anyone. 'There was this one guy, leader of the pack, he was on my case.'

It unspooled in his head. How outside the bike shop in town, Josh had stopped to put his sunglasses on while Ron held the bicycle for him. Josh touched his forearm, a thank-you squeeze.

'Ronnie boy! Fancy seeing you here.' *Lance!* Ron's throat had closed. He'd whipped round, moving away from Josh.

'What you up to, then?' Lance said, his eyes flicking between Ron and Josh behind him. 'Off for a *ride*, are you?' Lance's eyebrows underscoring the innuendo.

'No,' Ron said. Stepping further away from Josh. Not looking back, not acknowledging him. 'On the way to the train.' Ron made a show of glancing at his watch. 'Have to go.'

'Leaving your friend?' Lance said, a cold smile, eyes glittering like diamonds.

Ron didn't look back. Didn't look to where Josh stood. He frowned at Lance, shook his head, as though Lance was deluded.

'Have to rush,' Ron said, forcing a smile. 'See you Wednesday.'

He'd walked away without turning round, leaving Josh there. Abandoning him. Betraying him. Denying him.

Back at his flat. He texted Josh. *I'm so sorry. R.* But there was no way ever to make it right.

Now Ron smoothed the hospital sheet and said to Laura. 'He outed me. Made things . . . very difficult. And the next shout we got, a house fire—' He broke off. Emotion blocked his throat, made him ball his fists.

Two in the morning and into the fire tenders. A semi-detached in Balsall Heath.

'Got your passports, lads?' Lance's tired old 'joke' trotted out whenever they were called to a neighbourhood where lots of Asian families lived.

The house ablaze, lighting the summer night. Neighbours calling, weeping. 'Kids in there, mate, three kids and their parents.'

Lance ahead of him, full kit, breathing apparatus. Going in. Ron pausing on the threshold, hearing the roar of the fire, Lance's barbed comments in his head.

Ron so tired. Hesitating a moment, less than a second. Surely less than a second. Hate molten in his veins. Heart black with hatred. Burning cinders. Ash in his mouth. Thinking of Lance, of Josh, of himself.

Not concentrating on the job at hand, the actions that had been drilled into him. But waiting a heartbeat. A heartbeat too late, as the first floor collapsed. Killing everyone inside. A couple in their forties, a twelve-year-old girl, nine-year-old boy, eighteen-month-old baby. And Lance, who was trying to save them.

'He went in ahead of me and I hesitated,' he said to Laura. 'And the guy died. The guy and all the family in there.'

'And if you'd gone straight in?' Laura said.

Ron gave a shake of his head. *I'd have died too.*

'Survivor's guilt,' she said.

'I know. I'm sorry.' He waved a hand. What the hell was he laying all this on her for?

'You talk to anyone?' she said.

He shook his head.

'I've a mate,' she said. 'She was at the Arena bombing in Manchester. Just happened to be there with her daughter.'

Ron nodded.

Laura stared at the floor. 'She was in a really bad way. She told me later that the only thing that helped was EMDR therapy.' Laura flicked her hand over her eyes. 'You heard of it?'

'No.'

'Eye movement desensitization and reprocessing. Doesn't exactly trip off the tongue. But it's a way of reprogramming the brain after trauma. Works really well for post-traumatic stress. They use eye movements – somehow they help people to process trauma, change the script. Google it, you'll see.'

Maybe he would.

'OK.' She took a breath, exhaled. Patted her knees as though coming to a decision and got to her feet. 'Well, Ahmed will be in touch and we may be requesting a written statement from you for the Martin inquest.' She paused at the door. 'We have your home address?'

'Yes. I'll be at my mum's for now.'

'Great. Thanks.' She closed the door after her.

His mum had made it pretty clear that she expected Ron to recuperate at her house in Brum. But after that?

Did he want to pick up the pieces, carry on house-sitting?

He liked the peace he found looking after animals, the sense of freedom in getting into the camper van and heading somewhere new. But did he really like his own company or was solitude just a hiding place? Somewhere he couldn't get hurt again. Did he want another fifteen, twenty years like this?

Those days with Josh, he'd never been happier. The beauty of him, tracing the knots of his spine, watching him on the dance-floor, the sheer life of him. The food they shared. Waking up and hearing Josh singing in the shower. Stories, swapping stories and gossip. Cycling on a Sunday morning. Watching the Tour de France.

For years what came after had tainted all of that. Now Ron was so tired, so sick and tired of feeling inadequate and worthless. He was tired of hiding, lying, of the suffocating guilt.

He'd almost died at Graybridge. But he *hadn't*. He thought of Scarlett and all she had to overcome.

He saw an image. Scaling a hill, a couple of dogs at his heels, and someone alongside him. Sharing. Sharing what he loved, what he cherished, with another person.

The thought was shocking, exhilarating, forbidden almost.

He rubbed his finger along the scar at the base of his thumb, the rough red scab itching as it healed, and he promised himself that once he was back on his feet he'd open the door. He'd make himself available and see where it led. Because he could have died, bled to death locked in with that poor dog. And Scarlett could have died too.

It might mean starting online. That was where people found each other these days, wasn't it?

Who'd have him? Fat and pushing fifty. He was probably kidding himself, but if he never tried he'd never know.

Chapter 26

It had been weird going back to school with everyone staring at her even though they were trying to hide it.

At first she'd felt angry. She'd wanted to go up to them and shake them and shout, 'What? What? I'm still me, you know. Not some freak.' Or scare them: 'Look at me like that and I'll kill you.' *You know I'm a murderer's child.* But she just ignored it. She could tell some of them were buzzing with questions and curiosity, eyes all hungry. Busy with whispers when her back was turned. She caught snippets: *She killed her dad . . . he tied her up . . . a massive fight . . . hid her in the woods . . . ransom demand . . . stabbed loads of people.*

But after a few days things felt more like normal, and one thing about school was that when she was busy, doing the work and practising for her SATs, she could just forget about it. About everything that had happened.

Faye and Jason walked her home. If Nana's car wasn't there they'd come in and play for a bit until Nana got back. She never asked them to. But that first day when they reached Faye's house she felt her stomach turn over and her knees go weak and Faye said, 'We'll come up the hill, good exercise.' Even though Scarlett hadn't said she was frightened. Maybe Faye just sensed it. Or perhaps the grown-ups had talked about it and told Faye to offer.

It was stupid really because it wasn't like it could happen again.

He wasn't going to magically come back to life and grab her. Her brain knew that but the rest of her – her body, her heart, her guts – didn't.

She told Faye and Jason a few things about it all. Little bits just slipped out when they were together. She'd say something like 'We went in this flood and the car was sinking.' And Faye, usually Faye, would ask a question or two and Scarlett would answer. 'We climbed out the back and went through the water. It was freezing.' Then Scarlett would change the subject.

She'd not talked about the worst bits yet. Not to them. Maybe she never would. She'd had to say it all out loud to Laura and that had been horrible, even though they'd let her stop whenever she wanted to.

At the end Laura had asked if Scarlett had any questions.

'What about court?'

'There won't be any trial. There'll be an inquest into your father's death. That's in a different sort of court, what we call a coroner's court. But I'm pretty sure you'll be able to just send in a written statement.'

'Why did he come back?' Scarlett said.

Nana was sitting next to her and Scarlett saw her fingers pinch together.

'He was cornered,' Laura said. 'He'd been violent to the woman he was living with in Spain.'

Scarlett felt a swirl of unease at the thought of him with someone who wasn't her mum. Then she felt stupid for thinking like that. 'Did he kill her too?'

'No. But it was serious assault. So he had to leave everything and go on the run, and you, you were the only thing he thought he had left.'

Scarlett frowned. What did she mean?

'We can't be one hundred per cent sure but everything points to him intending to take you back into his life. Not to hurt you.'

'What then?'

'To be a parent. To assert his rights. Bolster his view of himself as a wronged parent.'

'That's stupid,' Scarlett said.

'Like you were his property, control you, own you,' Nana said, steel in her voice.

Scarlett glanced at her.

'It *was* stupid,' Laura agreed. 'He'd never have got away with it. And then when you challenged him, when other people got in the way, he was very, very angry. That enraged him and he lost all control.'

Nana flexed her fingers and moved in her chair.

'What he did was wrong,' Laura said. 'It was cruel and it was abusive.'

Scarlett felt sad inside, a melting sensation. Because she could remember him when he was just her dad and he loved her, and why couldn't he have just stayed like that? Then none of it would ever have happened.

*

Today after school Nana's car was there, and when Scarlett went in, Nana was sewing the quilt, the machine trundling away.

'There's something for you there,' Nana said, pins clamped in the corner of her mouth. She nodded to a box on the table.

Scarlett picked it up, saw the picture. *A phone!* 'A phone! But you said not till high school.'

Scarlett took it out. *Brilliant!* It looked like the one Faye had.

'I changed my mind.' Nana took out the pins and dropped them into the wooden dish with the magnet. 'Maybe if you'd had one . . .'

'He'd have taken it off me,' Scarlett said, guessing what Nana was thinking. 'He'd have thrown it away. It wasn't your fault, Nana.'

'You hear yourself?' Nana gave a smile.

It wasn't your fault.

'Yes.'

'Good. It wasn't yours either, none of it.'

'I know.' She did, but it was like being scared of him coming back – she knew, but she didn't actually believe it. Not deep down.

'You need a screen protector. And a cover if you want. They should have them in that shop near the school crossing.'

'Yes.' She'd get one with a pattern, bright colours. 'This is so cool.' She went and hugged Nana.

'Homework?'

'Maths. Can I get a crumpet?'

'Just one. It won't be long till tea.'

Scarlett took her snack upstairs and raced through her geometry so she could explore her phone. She wanted to ring Faye but she didn't know her number.

Back downstairs she entered Nana's number into her contacts. Then she rang her. And they had a silly conversation with each other where they could hear everything in real life and over the phone a fraction of a moment later, a tinnier version.

Tea was courgette fritters and fries and spicy carrots, and afterwards Scarlett played with her phone, working out how to do stuff while Nana sewed some more and listened to music on the radio.

Someone knocked at the door. Nana answered it and came back in with Faye's dad, who was carrying a wide black box and wires.

'We've lost the remote,' he said. 'But you can use the buttons on the front.'

'What is it?' Scarlett asked.

'DVD player,' Nana said.

'You want me to hook it up?' Faye's dad offered.

'No, we'll manage, thank you,' Nana said.

He left them to it.

'What's it for?' Scarlett said.

'Playing DVDs,' Nana said, on her knees.

Did they have any DVDs?

Nana huffed and puffed, reaching for the cables at the back of the telly, and swore a bit until she managed to connect them and a display came on the screen. The front of the DVD player lit up and read *NO DISC*.

'Now,' Nana said, getting onto the sofa. 'Sit here.' She patted the place beside her. 'You've been telling me you can't remember your mum any more.'

Scarlett felt a shaft of misery. Saw her mum's lips dark, the pool of milk.

'And I can't find any other photos of her with you as a baby, not apart from the ones you've already seen.'

She held up a DVD in a plastic case. 'This is from before you were born. But I thought you might like to see it.'

'Where did you get it?' Scarlett said.

'I put the word out at the hospital. Social media. They're all connected on Facebook and Twitter and Instagram and whatnot. Anyway I thought someone might have something saved. And a man got in touch. His daughter was in the same crew. He had it on video and he got it copied to DVD for us.'

'What crew?' Scarlett said.

Nana opened the case and handed her the disk. 'Put it in the slot at the front.'

Scarlett did.

'Now press play.'

Scarlett pressed and went to sit back on the sofa.

And there she was! Scarlett's heart leapt. Her mum in the middle of the stage, a semi-circle of others behind her. Scarlett knew her straight away. She looked like Scarlett but darker and her hair was in cornrows.

The picture was grainy and the colours a bit weird, but it was amazing to see her. The music started and she body-popped and break-danced, like her arms and legs were made of rubber. A smile on her face. A smile that warmed Scarlett all the way through. She was lovely. So pretty, just brilliant at dancing. She looked so happy.

Splits, then a head spin at the end, and wild applause as she took this massive bow, then pressed her palms together in thanks. Still beaming.

This was how Scarlett would remember her. Happy and beautiful and talented.

And every time that Scarlett danced she would dance with her.

Side by side.

Dancing for her life.

Acknowledgements

Thanks again to my writers' group – Livi Michael, Sophie Claire, Anjum Malik and Jennifer Nansubuga Makumbi – whose feedback always makes my work better. Our meetings are a real pleasure (even on Zoom!). Thank you to all the team at Constable, especially Krystyna Green, Jess Gulliver, Christopher Sturtivant, Rebecca Sheppard, Bekki Guyatt, Brionee Fenlon, Lucie Howkins and Anna Boatman. Thanks to Hazel Orme for excellent and thoughtful copy-editing. *Gracias a* Jim Hirsch for checking my Spanish. And thanks to my brilliant agent, Sara Menguc.

CRIME AND THRILLER FAN?

CHECK OUT THECRIMEVAULT.COM

The online home of exceptional crime fiction

KEEP YOURSELF IN SUSPENSE

Sign up to our newsletter for regular recommendations, competitions and exclusives at **www.thecrimevault.com/connect**

Follow us

@TheCrimeVault

/TheCrimeVault

for all the latest news